# Praise for
## *The Road to Woop Woop*
## *and Other Stories*

"Bacon delivers a commanding and visionary collection of speculative shorts, encompassing surrealism, fantasy, science fiction, and gorgeous, painterly literary fiction. It would be a disservice to call any of these 24 stories the stand-out, as each is impressive and beautifully rendered in Bacon's distinct, poetic voice. The stunning title story follows a pair of lovers on a tense road trip that grows increasingly surreal, told in rhythmic, abstract prose. In the moving "Swimming with Daddy," a little girl reflects on how her father taught her to swim. The humorous "Beatitudes" tells of the first meeting of a young siren and a salesman who has been turned into a toad. Science fictional offerings include "Ace Zone," about a young woman traveling from planet to planet to draft soldiers into her battalion, and "Playback, Jury of the Heart," a tale of love that transcends time and space. Complex, earnest, and striking, Bacon's impeccable work is sure to blow readers away."
—PUBLISHERS WEEKLY (Starred Review)

"The 24 stories that make up Eugen Bacon's new collection *The Road to Woop Woop and Other Stories* run the gamut in terms of tone, genre, and structure. There are experimental, modernist pieces reminiscent of the New Wave, namely "A Good Ball," "The Enduring," or "A Man Full of Shadows"; playful, self-aware tales such as "The Animal I Am" and "Wolfmother"; and reflective, melancholy stories like "Swimming With Daddy" and "The One Who Sees." As Seb Doubinsky rightly points out in his Foreword, what ties the collection together is Bacon's distinctive voice (which Doubinsky compares to free jazz) that nimbly shifts between the lush, the opaque, and the colloquial (Bacon, like myself, is fond of Aussie slang) . . . Bacon's passion for language and her willingness to play with the short-story form, to never settle on one type of narrative or genre, make this an exciting collection that's well worth picking up."
—Ian Mond, LOCUS MAGAZINE

"An exciting and transcendent literary experience with an air of magic anybody should be able to appreciate."
—Maddison Stoff, AUREALIS MAGAZINE

"Eugen Bacon writes assured, lyrical prose wherein timeless tales bordering multiple genres are hunkered. At the conflux of myth and memory, where cultures meet and twine, her stories devour the past whilst illuminating the future. Reading Bacon is an immersement, a journey. The stories she tells are those to relish."
—Andrew Hook, award-winning editor and author of
*Frequencies of Existence.*

"Delightful, depressing, delicious, desirable, fulfilling. The stories gathered here are airy and prismatic, and the gravitas of Bacon's worldview does not preclude intimacy or mischief. Many cultures converge and challenge each other in this collection and these prove to be at odds with the equally pressing need to be an individual in the world. The answer is often to weave myths and fables from different traditions imbued with the politics of gender and race, perhaps best illustrated in the persona of the Phoenix which recurs in different guises and with different attributions throughout the book."
—Dominique Hecq, award-winning poet,
novelist, short story writer

"Eugen Bacon writes with cheekiness and a fierce intelligence that shines through every page of her work. Right from the first sentence, the voices of each of her narrators grab the reader with their lucidity, their panache, and their uncompromising observational rigor. This rigor manifests itself in the freshness of Bacon's prose, making the reader reconsider all expectations related to genre, identity, and gender stereotypes, and opening up new possibilities with every turn of phrase. Her work may be rooted in the conventions of sci-fi, yet its speculative nature is grounded in the most surprising, realistic details that serve to blur the boundaries between literary genres and suggest a more fecund apprehension of what literature might be. Bacon's narration sometimes borders on the erotic, sometimes on the raw truth of human frailty, but is always delightfully subversive and unapologetically transgressive. When Ursula K. le Guin said that fiction, poetry, drama 'cleanse the doors of perception,' perhaps she was talking about this invigorating quality present in the work of Eugen Bacon. If Bacon's shorter works are any indication of her handling of longer narrative arcs, then readers of her forthcoming novel are in for a delicious and satisfying treat."
—Roanna Gonsalves, award-winning author of
*The Permanent Resident*

## Also by Eugen Bacon

### Fiction

*Claiming T-Mo*
*Her Bitch Dress*
*It's Folking Political*
*Hadithi & The State of Black Speculative Fiction*
*(with Milton Davis)*
*Black Moon: Graphic Speculative Flash Fiction*
*Ivory's Story*

### Non-Fiction

*Writing Speculative Fiction*

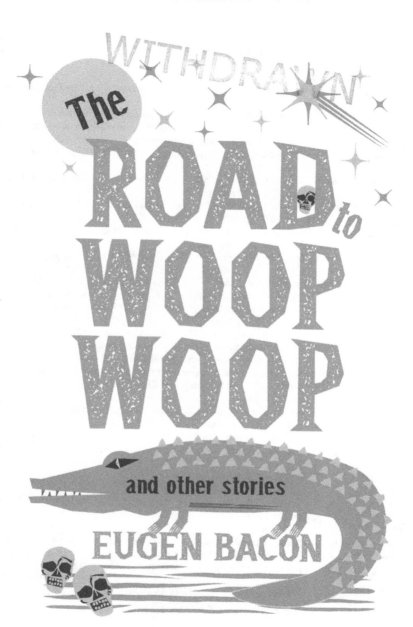

# The ROAD to WOOP WOOP

and other stories

EUGEN BACON

Meerkat Press
Atlanta

"Swimming with Daddy," originally published in *Meniscus*, Australasian Association of Writing Programs, 2016

"A Nursery Rhyme," originally published in *Dying & Other Stories*, Fiction4All, 2018

"Snow Metal," originally published in *Bards and Sage Quarterly*, 2018

"A Maji Maji Chronicle," originally published in *Bukker Tillibul*, Swinburne University of Technology, 2015

"A Good Ball," originally published in *Other Terrain Journal*, Swinburne University of Technology, 2019

"A Case of Seeing," originally published in *Dying & Other Stories*, Fiction4All, 2018

"Five-Second Button," originally published in *Antipodean SF*, Issue 243, 2018

"Diminy: Conception, Articulation & Subsequent Development," *TEXT* Special Issue No. 32, *TEXT Journal*, 2015

"Mahuika," originally published in *Every Day Fiction*, 2017

"Being Marcus," originally published in *New Writing*, Routledge, 2015

"Scars of Grief," originally published in *Bukker Tillibul*, Swinburne University of Technology, 2014

"Ace Zone," originally published in *A Hand of Knaves*, the Canberrra Speculative Fiction Guild (CSFG), edited by Leife Shallcross and Chris Large, 2018

"A Pining," originally published in *Stylus Lit*, 2019

"Dying," originally published in *Bringing It Back*, Horrified Press Anthologies, 2018

"Wolfmother," originally published in *Antipodean SF*, Issue 231, 2017

"A Man Full of Shadows," originally published in *Dying & Other Stories*, Fiction4All, 2018

"Playback, Jury of the Heart," originally published in *Playback, Jury of the Heart*, Fiction4All, 2017

ISBN-13 978-1-946154-31-6 (Paperback)
ISBN-13 978-1-946154-32-3 (eBook)

Library of Congress Control Number: 2020948950

Cover and book design by Tricia Reeks
Interior art by Tricia Reeks

Printed in the United States of America

Published in the United States of America by
Meerkat Press, LLC, Atlanta, Georgia
www.meerkatpress.com

*For the stories we yearn to tell, the diversity of our voices. I am many, betwixt, a sum of cultures.*

# CONTENTS

# FOREWORD

## SEB DOUBINSKY

To write a foreword for a collection such as Eugen Bacon's *The Road to Woop Woop* is actually quite the impossible task. Impossible not because of the collection itself, which is perfect and masterly sewn together, but rather because of the sheer impossibility of describing, albeit introducing, such a beautiful writing craft. Eugen Bacon doesn't only write stories, she assembles them like strange, out-of-worldly objects, that both feel familiar and yet radically uncanny.

Many reviewers have noted the natural ties to Octavia Butler—another masterful storyteller—but Eugen Bacon is, in my eyes, idiosyncratic. Her Blackness does not come through style, reference or identities, but through a vision, a peculiar way of looking at the world from another supernatural perspective, which encompasses all traditional narratives. Her magic is her own, family-inherited, homegrown and yet universal. We have all encountered her ghosts, murderers, creatures and witches, but only notice them now.

To write a foreword to this collection is only, in my eyes, adding superfluous words to stories that do not contain any. Everything is narrated sparsely, in an economy of vocabulary and descriptions that only someone like Shirley Jackson could achieve—in a completely different universe, of course. The only fitting intro of Eugen Bacon's collection can solely be done through music.

I read *The Road to Woop Woop* listening to a fabulous free-jazz album by a much unknown musician, Sam Rivers. No music could have been better: the mix of melodies and deconstructed improvisations, the broken-up dialogue between instruments, the ever-flowing textures mingling or moving away from each other, everything seemed to accompany perfectly the patchwork of styles, stories and narratives contained in the book.

Like a free-jazz musician, Eugen Bacon will capture the reader's mind by mutually associating and dissociating narratives and characters, but launching on short, relevant flashbacks or digressions, by adding the right amount of unsaid to what is being told.

In my eyes, *The Road to Woop Woop* is both a modern classic and a fabulous and unforgettable free-jazz album of magical dimensions.

—Seb Doubinsky, author of the City-State Cycle series

she lives out woop woop    a noplace filled with ghosts
random within her grasp slipping in a language of desert
a mirage of memory in the middle of nowhere    the back
of beyond unloved by the camera    who stands a chance

# THE ROAD TO WOOP WOOP

Tumbling down the stretch, a confident glide, the 4WD is a beaut, over nineteen years old.

The argument is brand-new. Maps are convolutions, complicated like relationships. You scrunch the sheet, push it in the glovebox. You feel River's displeasure, but you hate navigating, and right now you don't care.

The wiper swishes to and fro, braves unseasonal rain. You and River maintain your silence.

Rain. More rain.

"When's the next stop?" River tries. Sidewise glance, cautious smile. He is muscled, dark. Dreadlocks fall down high cheekbones to square shoulders. Eyes like black gold give him the rugged look of a mechanic.

"Does it matter?" you say.

"Should it?"

You don't respond. Turn your head, stare at a thin scratch on your window. The crack runs level with rolling landscape racing away with rain. Up in the sky, a billow of cloud like a white ghoul, dark-eyed and yawning into a scream.

A shoot of spray through River's window brushes your cheek.

A glide of eye. "Hell's the matter?" you say.

"You ask *me-e*. Something bothering you?"

"The window."

He gives you a look.

*Classic*, you think. But you know that if you listen long enough, every argument is an empty road that attracts unfinished business. It's an iceberg full of whimsy about fumaroles and geysers. It's a corpse that spends eternity reliving apparitions of itself in the throes of death. Your fights are puffed-up trivia, championed to crusades. You fill up teabags with animus that pours into kettles of disarray, scalding as missiles. They leave you ashy and scattered—that's what's left of your lovemaking, or the paranoia of it, you wonder about that.

More silence, the cloud of your argument hangs above it. He shrugs. Rolls up his window. Still air swells in the car.

"Air con working?" you say.

He flexes long corduroyed legs that end in moccasins. Flicks on the air button—and the radio. The bars of a soulful number, a remix by some new artist, give way to an even darker track titled 'Nameless.' It's about a high priest who wears skinny black jeans and thrums heavy metal to bring space demons into a church that's dressed as a concert. And the torments join in evensong, chanting psalms and canticles until daybreak when the demons wisp back into thin air, fading with them thirteen souls of the faithful, an annual pact with the priest.

Rain pelts the roof and windows like a drum.

He hums. Your face is distant. You might well be strangers, tossed into a tight drive from Broome to Kununurra.

The lilt of his voice merges with the somber melody.

You turn your face upward. A drift of darkness, even with full day, is approaching from the skies. Now it's half-light. You flip the sun visor down. Not for compulsion or vanity, nothing like an urge to peer at yourself in the mirror. Perhaps it's to busy your hands, to distract yourself, keep from bedevilment—the kind that pulls out a quarrel. You steal a glimpse of yourself in the mirror. Deep, deep eyes. They gleam like a cat's. The soft curtain of your fringe is softening, despite thickset brows like a man's. You feel disconnected with yourself, with the trip, with River. You flip the sun visor up.

Now the world is all grim. River turns on the headlights, but visibility is still bad. A bolt of lightning. You both see the arms of a reaching tree that has appeared on the road, right there in your path. You squeal, throw your arms out. River swerves. A slam of brakes. A screech of tires. *Boom!*

The world stops in a swallowing blackness. Inside the hollow, your ears are ringing. The car, fully intact, is shooting out of the dark cloud in slow motion, picking up speed. It's soaring along the road washed in a new aurora of lavender, turquoise and silver, then it's all clear. A gentle sun breaks through fluffs of cloud no more engulfed in blackness. You level yourself with a hand on the dashboard, uncertain what exactly happened.

You look at River. His hands . . . wrist up . . . he has no hands. Nothing bloody as you'd expect from a man with severed wrists. Just empty space where the arms end.

But River's unperturbed, his arms positioned as if he's driving, even while nothing is touching the steering that's moving itself, turning and leveling.

"Brought my shades?" he asks.

"Your hands," you say.

"What about them?"

"Can't you see?"

His glance is full of impatience.

You sink back to your seat, unable to understand it, unclear to tell him, as the driverless car races along in silence down the lone road.

+ + +

If it hadn't been such a dreary morning, perhaps the mood might be right. But a bleak dawn lifted to cobalt, to brown, slid to gray. One recipe for disaster that simmers you and River in separate pots.

This spring is of a different breed. It traps you, brings with it . . . fights. You gripe like siblings, the inner push to argue too persuasive. Smiles diminish to awkward; words sharpen to icicles.

Kununurra was a break long overdue. A planned trip. Your idea. A dumb-arsed one at that for a romance on the line. As though different soil would mend it.

+ + +

"*Drive?*" River had asked.

"Best within the price bracket," you said.

"Do I look half-convinced?"

"People drive," you said. "It's normal."

"Seems normal to take the plane."

"If we drive, River, what do you think the concern is? What?"

"If we drive my road rover? I hope for your sake to never ask myself that question."

"That's called pessimism."

"Who's pessimistic here, Miss Price Bracket?"

You flipped.

Despite his harassed face, he stunned you by agreeing to the trip.

Everything was organized to the last detail. Everything but the climate. A few hours into the day, the weather window opened, torrential rain that left a curtain behind. Despite the planning, you got lost. Twice. Ended up doing a long leg to Kununurra. Gave shoes for another fight.

+ + +

Irish Clover in "The Road to No Place" chants her soulful lyrics:

*You say you'll climb no mountain with me*
*I'll go with you anyway*
*Darling I'll follow you*
*Somewhere we've never been.*

*I'll go with you to the sun and to the night*
*I'll go with you where the water is wide*
*I'll go with you anyway*
*No Place is where we'll be.*

*You say I'm not your rain, your rainbow*
*But you're my earth, my blanket*
*You're my canopy, my tree*
*I'll go with you anywhere we've never been.*

Not saying a word about River's uncanny state, one he doesn't appear to notice, makes you feel complicit with the devil. Like you've already sold your soul, and there's nothing you can do about it.

Your dread melts to curiosity. You glance at River and his lost hands and let out a cry. His belly downward is gone. Just an athletic chest and a head, cropped arms driving a car without touching.

"River?"

He doesn't immediately respond, emotions barricaded within himself. When he looks at you, it's with a darkened mood. "Have to listen to that stupid song?"

You want to tell him that it's his car, his radio. That he has no hands and no legs, and what the goddamn fuck is happening? But all you say is, "No," a whisper in your throat.

"Will you turn it off?"

"No."

"Be like that."

No reason has its name, its talent, written on this new grumble. Its seeds sink deeper, water themselves richer, flower more malignant blues.

Though he maintains the same proximity in his hacked body, so close you can almost hear his heart talk, he is drawn away from you, accepting without question the space, its margin creeping further out.

You grip the seatbelt where he can't see it.

*River is . . . my big red lobster. Beautiful, until the fiend.*

Two springs ago, you were working at a garden restaurant. He stepped into your life with a guitar across his waist, a rucksack on his back. *An avid traveler,* you thought. He caught your eye. *Rapture,* you thought. And then he smiled. *Hey presto.* Reminded you of the heartthrob muso who won the Boy-up Brook Country Music Awards years back. Your thoughts turned unholy.

*We fell in love swatting sandflies . . . in Broome.*

Longing swells, you feel empty next to a stranger.

Before the trip, before he became this . . . this . . . your body was willing, the mathematics of your need. But everything around it failed. Night after night, you turned to your pillow, swallowed in thought. One day, you feared, the pillow would mean more than River.

Sometimes you never kissed.

Just a melt of bodies, a tumble of knees, flesh against flesh, almost cruel. Thrusts that summoned a climax that spread from your toes.

$+++$

"Jesus!"

"Goddamn!"

Your responses are simultaneous as an overtaking truck judders, sways dangerously close, pushes you nearly off the highway.

Silence for a startling second stretches miles out.

$+++$

You switch driving at dusk. River lightly snores. Just his dreadlocked head and broad shoulders—his chest is gone. The road rover is a power train. You glide with your foreboding. River takes the wheel at dawn. You sleep. Wake on instinct. It's a strange world in the middle of nowhere. A blue-green carpet with fluid waves. Ears of grass stir, tease, declare interest in everything about you.

Sandy gold stretches a quarter mile deep, some dapples of green with burnt yellows. Beautifully rugged in parts, it reminds you of River's morning face. You glance at him, what's left of him: black gold eyes and an ivory-white jaw—skeletal. Clouds dissolve to shimmering threads across the ocean-blue firmament.

The road rover halts at a divide.

"Left or right?" says River.

"Right."

A whiff of aftershave touches your nostrils. You can almost feel him on your skin.

"Dying for a piddle," he says.

"Me too. Where do people go in this wilderness?"

"The bush?"

You wipe your forehead with the back of your hands. "River?"

"Yes?" Just eyes—the jaw is gone.

You hug your knees. "I wonder about us—do you?"

"I wonder about it plenty."

Your stomach folds. You rock on your knees.

"Maybe we should, you know . . .take time off," you say.

"We *are* taking time off."

You pull at your hair, worrying it. Tighten a long strand in a little finger.

"Let's not fight. Please, River."

"Okay. What now?"

"Don't know."

The road rover rolls into a deserted station.

"Well," the engine dies, "I'm going for a piddle."

"Me too."

You slip on canvas trainers, hug a turquoise sweater.

+ + +

You depart, perhaps as equals, not as partners.

You step minutes behind into the station, seek the toilet. River is nowhere to ask. You see it, a metal shack, labeled.

You push the door. It swings with ease.

You climb down a stone step, jump sodden paper on the ground. The walls are dripping, the floor swirling with water.

But the need to go is great.

You move tippie-toe toward one of the cubicles, take care not to touch the wetness.

Later, as you wash your hands, a cubicle door opens. River—nothing visible, but you know it's him—comes out.

"Dripping mess," you say. "You could have warned me."

"What—spoil the surprise?" Your heart tugs at the lilt in his voice.

"Can't find the dryer. What's this?" You move toward a contraption on the wall.

"Don't touch—" begins River.

You've already pressed it.

"—the green button," he finishes lamely.

A moan on the roof, roar, and a glorious waterfall of soapy water spits from the ceiling. The deluge plummets, splashes and bounces off walls, floods you.

You screech, try to run. Slip.

Drowning in water, you lift your head and see a silhouette like a shimmering light forming of River. It is bolts of lightning shaping out a man. His translucent body is standing in the waterfall. Now he's there, now he's not. He's shaking clumps of drippy hair, roped, from his face. "Washed itself, did it?"

He's still wavering in and out like a breaking circuit.

You rise, coughing.

You guide yourself with palms along the wall. Squishy shoes make obscene sounds. Your nipple-struck T-shirt draws your sweater tighter. You stare, horrified. Sobbing denim clings to your legs.

"I just touched it," you gasp.

*Drip! Drip!* says the wall.

"Oh, you beaut," laughs River. Now he's a silhouette, no longer twinkling in and out. There's his smoky self, his smoky smile.

The ceiling sighs. The flood gurgles and narrows its cascade to a dribble. Dripping walls, clomps of soggy tissue float in a puddle.

He comes toward you, not the drift of a ghost, but walking, misty leg after misty leg. The blackest, most golden eyes hold your gaze, until you're enveloped in his steamy form, in the waft of his aftershave: an earthy scent of cedar and orange flower.

"We'd best get these clothes off," he speaks to your hair. You clutch him, nothing solid, just the emanating heat of his fog. It leaves you with a pining for the touch of him—a longing for his finger tracing the outline of your nose. His mouth teasing the nape of your neck.

You don't know about tomorrow, whether River will ever be as he was, different from the torment he is now. Present, yet lacking. But he's your rain, your rainbow. Your earth, your blanket. You'll go anywhere with him.

Suddenly, you feel more. You feel more deeply.

# SWIMMING WITH DADDY

I get it right in the second tumble-turn. I approach the wall with speed, push my nose to my knees, heels to my hips, big kick off the wall.

I have been practicing the dolphin kick.

You take in the perfection of my glide. There's warm pride in your eyes, soft eyes that look at someone in a personal way. You don't wear glasses with big metal rims these days. Eyes couldn't see better, you say when I ask.

Little flutter kicks lead to the hand stroke and away, away I go. I like it when the weather is good like today, when sundown rays through the natural light ceiling put golden shimmers in the pale blue chlorinated water. The floor is tiled, tiny insets the size and shape of sticky notes. I imagine each tile has a message I listen for when you are silent. I track ebony lines at the bottom to keep my swim straight.

"Learn the feel of water," you say.

You never swam a day in your life, yet you have wisdom to know. You speak clearly, concisely, with ease—easy words, easy eyes of a friend. Your voice is different than before, perhaps then it was alive. Not that now it's dead, just calming. You calm me.

I smile.

You're my daddy tortoise, my Moses, my Mandela—his spirit lives, my Brer Terrapin like in Uncle Remus stories.

"Remember how Terrapin deceived Brer Buzzard?" I say.

"I told you that story."

"Same way you told me those why and how stories. Why the crocodile lives in the water. How the zebra got his stripes. When the hyena found his laugh."

You weave your hands together. Big hands. Strong handshake. Best way to know a person's self is by how they shake your hands, you like to say.

You are well traveled. It is no wonder you have come to visit. Melbourne.

I bought CDs of music you adore: the soulful sound of *Mama Africa*. I used to call you the black Irishman, perhaps for your love of the Irish: their humor, their coffee—stirred and topped with cream. The whiff of whiskey on your breath after breakfast was never disagreeable growing up. It was for me simply a daddy smell, a happy daddy smell.

One couldn't tell how well traveled you were, how well educated, when you visited Grandma in the village. You wore tire soles and a sheet around your waist. Handwoven batik in colors of the rainbow. You didn't like a shirt or trousers in tropical heat that dizzied mosquitos. You drank *toggo*, pure banana brew cool from a calabash, washed it down with the soup of goat entrails slowly simmered over a three-stone-hearth fire.

I liked how you did the voices, tawkin' Suthern like when you did Uncle Remus. You first told his stories straight after your conference in Atlanta, Georgia, USA—your work paid for it. I sat on your lap, rested my head on your solid chest and you told me the Terrapin story.

You said:

Dey social, shake hands, ax each udder what happen ovah in de fambily. Den Brer Terrrapin he say to Brer Buzzard dat he tired o' eating grits, and dat's a fact. Dat he want to go into biddiness wid 'im, gittin' honey from de good ol' bumbly-bee. But Brer Terrapin crept alone into de hole, gobbled de last o' bumbly-bee honey, licked it off his footses, so ol' Brer Buzzard couldn't tell what he'd done.

You laughed telling that story, told me the moral was not about stealing or deception, like what Terrapin did, but about stupidity. You told me not to be stupid like Brer Buzzard else "de bumbly-bees gone come a-stinging you."

"Remember the story of the monkey's heart?" I say.

"You always loved water stories."

"Tell me the story."

"You're too old for it now."

"Tell me."

"What do you want to hear? How the little monkey who lived with his clan on the bank of the lake fell from the overhung branch of a baobab tree and the big croc lunged from the murky depths of the water and snatched him in his jaws? How the monkey didn't plead or cry, simply said he didn't have his heart, and the heart was the best part of a monkey for a croc to eat? How Croc believed the little monkey had left his heart on the topmost branch that fanned out leaves to the stars, so gods of land and water could spice it? How Croc opened his jaws and let Little Monkey leap across his back and tail, scramble to his tree to fetch the heart? And Little Monkey bellowed from the top for Croc to open wide for the god-loved heart, and instead hurled a big mango that cracked Croc's tooth?"

"*How hard is your heart, Little Monkey,* roared Croc," I say.

"Stupid does that to you."

You don't tolerate fools. Too much yam in the head, you call it. Sometimes you say too much onion, or cassava.

"You didn't tawk Suthern telling the monkey story," I say.

"It wasn't from the South."

"It wouldn't have made me forget our roots, the tongue of our forefathers, like how we prayed."

*Injina lyo tata* / In the name of the father

*No lyo mwana* / And of the son

*No lyo roho mtakatifu* / And of the holy spirit

*Amina* / Amen

Silent, you watch my backstroke.

"It isn't efficient," I say. "Feels like I'm moving blind. No eyes on the crown to see where I'm going."

"Follow the ceiling."

"It has no lines."

"Picture them."

"How?"

"A challenge then?"

You knew about raising the optimistic child without reading those books proliferating in the parenting section of bookstores. Labels on the shelves of the one around the corner on Flint Street near Twenty-Four Seven Pharmacy tell you where to go so you can grow a resilient child, one who is active and success prone. You taught me to stay hungry, to go the step when I was training for sprint team. You shook your head when my lips puckered because I'd lost a race. It's not about winning, you said.

Now you watch my swim, right there by the edge like a coach, even though I am the one who tells you about technique, about how I haven't refined mine because I taught myself.

"The stroke length isn't right. I don't get enough distance out of the stroke," I say.

"Lower your head." You surprise me with this observation. "Level your bottom with your back and head near the surface. Now increase your foot tempo."

Eddies of water cling to my skin.

I tell you I read about movement coming from hips down, body tipping on a seesaw for streamline, cheeks resting on water so I breathe cleanly every fourth stroke.

"Black folk's bottom is not made for streamline," you laugh. "But you're doing just fine."

I practice off the wall torpedoes.

"Head down," you say.

Suddenly you're there, in the water with me. You press my arms against the back of my ears. I dive, eyes downward. Kick, kick, kick. I finish with a breast-stroke, head tucked between outstretched hands, back and head aligned. I pitch and pull my body forward in the water.

You sit on the wooden bench along the wall as I rub down with a large beach towel.

"Too much cloth," you say. "Why not robe it?"

You like efficiency, neatness. You smacked me once with a stick when I let my nails grow. Long time, I was a child . . . I cried, not for pain. You weren't much for discipline. Mum was the flash temper. She gave it to you anywhere—church, school, playground—if you deserved it. Like when I ate fish, headfirst—slap! "You eat tail up!" Like when I spoke with a mouthful—slap! "Nothing wise comes from clog!"

My Melbourne apartment is not flash; it's not in Beach Boulevard. But it wears well a careless order: stacked paper neat on the table, arranged clothes on the four-poster bed rail, pressed sheets inside a blue doona . . .

I soak, listen to the soft sizzle of mango and coconut bodywash foam.

I remember how you took interest in the mouthwash when first you saw it. "Need all 945 milligrams of whitening? Can't chew sugar cane?"

"From where?"

We laughed.

You fingered my pore wash (200 milligrams), the soap free antibacterial hand wash (600 milligrams), the body scrub flannel shaped like a mitten, the black stone for my heels—you said it looked like the one your grandmother pressed on skin to take away poison from a snake bite. You liked the snow-white porcelain bowl for the toilet brush, its tiny blue flowers around the words "Eau de Cologne"; the spin toothbrush with its soft bristles; the squeegee window cleaning stick with its rubber lip to remove scrum off the glass . . .

The house is under my rule, but subconsciously I follow yours—the order, the cleanliness.

I ponder this in my immersion, knees up in the water.

Something in the air today, it's like someone has opened the cap off a bottle of nice booze . . . I feel heady. You're in the living room.

You used to massage my shoulders, best big hands ever. Far gone are those days, not since I peaked, arrived at an age when a father gets cautious with his woman-child.

The tub is wide as a coffin, more height from the bathroom's high ceiling, else I'd suffocate. I remember panic when I first learned to swim, face down in the water, it felt like a shroud over my head.

Clothed, I open the fridge, consider egg pasta veal tortellini.

You peer across my shoulder. There's something magnetic about you now, your physicality. You're a head and a half taller than me. Robust—not stocky, big bones. Look good in those wide shoulders.

What new thing have I brought from the supermarket off Queen Market?

I move aside so your eyes, those personal eyes that look at a soul, can take in the sparkling ice tea—four mini cans 250 milligrams each, the dairy-free yogurt—deliciously creamy, the tub says (1 liter), the horse radish cream (190 grams), the savory smoked tomato jam—made in Australia (300 milligrams), the apple cider vinegar in a bottle shaped like the neck of a giraffe (300 milligrams) . . .

"All this. How much?"

I estimate.

How so with ease we fall into our conversations!

"Don't throw your name," you say.

"What d'you mean?"

"The West is infectious."

"How?"

"Just saying. There's protein in rain termites, in green locusts . . . free and organic."

"Snatched from the air."

You prop yourself on the kitchen counter as I fill a saucepan with water to boil the tortellini. You smile at the splash of water into metal. You love sounds, like the distant clap of thunder when it rains, a symbol of transformation you say. After dinner you listen with a cocked head to the sound of the dishwasher on a cycle, *swirr, swirr, swirr,* then it gurgles.

*Gurgle. Gurgle.* Like how you did when you were sick.

Bitter, bitter cold in my marrow now. I remember Mother's ash-streaked face. She sat on red-brown earth surrounded by mourners. She looked ancient. Her going wasn't long after.

I cry sometimes, a little each year. Tendrils of grief, they bud and burrow.

"People die to continue the cycle of living," you say.

"No they don't."

"You're stronger than you think."

"I'm not. I keep myself busy. Haven't had time to scratch my bum since you . . . you—"

"I'm here now."

"Yes."

"Stop existing. *Live.*"

"Does grief take a holiday?"

"Your grief is the swim-on-it kind. It heals with water. Your animal spirit is the river shark. You have soul memory. In your swim you roam free."

"Will you? Swim with me?"

"Tomorrow I will," you say.

# A NURSERY RHYME

Venus and Magellan Thalassa sit on a patio of silvery sandstone overlooking derelict gardens in 17 Nautical Miles, East Tharsis. They are each enshrouded in a little world, buying time, catching up with time, toying with the notion of it.

To Venus it is safe being like this, not talking about things.

Unspeakable things have happened in their lives, clawing at normality. Now, the urge to speak is unmanageable. It hovers, it taunts.

Silently, they share a smoking pipe.

Her eyes are flat, his fretful.

A billow of smoke rises from her nostrils with her words. "It's been a long time since—"

"Sorry, my child," he says gruffly.

Time has dusted a bucket of ash into his hair, pulled at his face, added more wrinkles than before.

*Before what*? she wonders.

When he speaks, his chin dances.

"Should have come to Tharsis sooner," he says.

"Glad you made it at short notice." Something prickles her eyelid, invites her panic. No time for tears.

"Not every day one comes home to find a sitter floating head down in a bath," he says. "Lawmen ripping the residence. Shamen knee-deep beneath floorboards, all looking for clues."

Carrying no words for him, she broods.

His mobilis is slovenly parked at an angle, his haste to be here. Viking TJ Plates mark the new idea of him, her father. The years have added to his persona, easing the weight of ashy grays on his head, making them seem normal. Seeing him, she can almost be grateful he didn't go cranky with the loss of Maamy, chasing women half Venus's age.

That would suck, seeing him in such disarray.

Always an adrenaline junkie, going off like he did after Maamy died was no surprise. Settled somewhere in the hinterland, a place with fireflies so big they tapped you on the shoulder.

A meter out choked in weeds, lisianthus, cream chrysanthemums, adrasteas, Peruvian violets and rare cyclamens sway to a sluicing breeze. Further out, canopies of gnarled pines ghostly bend.

A patter of little feet, of a child racing on land solid as ice, lifts the silence. She leaps, humming softly. Words of her rhyme carry above outdoor filters of wind, leaf rustle and a swing of boughs.

"Maamy duck said *Quack! Quack! Quack! Quack!* but only four little ducks came back."

Venus and Mage fret, entrapped by silence despite Dee's song. Their lips fill with useless words that cannot undo the past or rouse the dead.

Each struggles to maintain it, the silence. Mage fails.

"Know what happened?" he asks.

She shrugs. "The lawman thought it was the phosphorous bleach. The cleaning agent. How the woman could have confused peach hair spa with toilet cleaner . . . She was practically cooked."

"How's Dee coping?" he asks, almost reluctantly.

Venus shakes her head, a gesture of near hopelessness.

"She liked Cora very much . . . But now look at her." She nods at her daughter. "Playing as though nothing happened." Venus had found Dee seated in the bathroom doorway humming, as skin fell off the sitter's bones.

Mage stares with near fascination at the child's strange eyes.

White arms of a late evening sun toss a backlight on her flaming hair as she glides a red-billed duckling across an invisible loch in the air. Opal eyes lift inside long lashes, past Mage to Venus. She gives a toothy grin, waves chubby hands.

Venus waves back.

The look on Mage's face perturbs her. She stares unseeingly at her hands.

"You don't like her," she says, matter-of-fact. "Dee." Pause. "But what about her? Playing now. She is your granddaughter! Do you think she is unmarked by seeing death?"

He lifts his head, taken aback.

"When Triton died," she says. "Guilt came, knowledge that I could not bring her daddy back. Maybe I spoil her some—"

"You've raised her in great vein," he says. "After Triton . . . I wanted you to come live with us. But your maamy, she was, she was—"

"It's fine, Mage."

She speaks consoling words, but her mind is set on night.

A strong, restless streak drives her to the brink of insanity, pressure of a different kind. Something happened years ago, something that forces imbalance into her life. Same something took Triton and now that thing, hell, whatever it is, brings a faceless male to her bed at dusk.

She looks at the sky, almost impatient. Night transports her to another world. Reluctantly, she waits out the sun.

"Better head off," he says, as if reading her skyward glance.

"Stay. Mage. Please."

He is already up. "I'll check out at the motel. Tomorrow. I promise." Rifles through his robe for his key.

Venus doesn't rise with him.

He ruffles her sandy hair. "All right, then, buster."

"May the goddess of Tharsis watch over you, Pappita," she repays his endearment.

He walks proud and upright, despite his age. Age. He wears it well. He points the key at the mobilis. The vessel hums.

Dee blinks unevenly, runs up to Venus and tucks a little hand into her maamy's larger one. Together, they eyeball the reverse of his vessel.

A whistle of combustibles on air, then a softer sigh.

"Well then, Dee," Venus says, cupping little fingers firmly in her palm. "Just you and me, skipper."

The child's glowing eyes nudge a smile.

Time chips away at Venus's fatigue.

As long as those carefree, ocean eyes hold.

✦ ✦ ✦

Dusk.

Venus's nipples are tender and frank, the rest of her maturity discreet.

He takes her masterfully, firmly.

Later, much later, she remembers the grain of his skin, the texture of callused hands on her breasts. The diffusion of her senses.

The clarity of pleasure.

And when the shadows on his face, the strength in his hands, the grace of his touch broker common ground, they seal mystery into her flesh.

She wafts in and out of sleep, as a giant ant crawls the length of her arm. Suddenly, she feels freedom. Clear, persuasive freedom.

Breakfast is an egg, a weeping yolk. A barbecue of stuffed innards and half a bowl of grain bubbles do for Dee.

Mage has checked out of the motel. Now, he dines with them. But forty minutes at the table with Dee gets him jittery and stupid; things he says, questions he asks. Like: Aren't her eyes sure green?

When Venus serves beet pie as a side, crisp and ripe with drippy juices, he pales as though he has seen blood. His gestures are wooden, the hold on his fork rigid. He holds cutlery as a weapon. Looking at her father silly like this, awkward and trying to be amiable around his grandchild, she wonders about his staying, whether it is a good idea.

Suddenly it seems ages since her husband died, since her *maamy* died, since the last time she saw Mage. It disturbs her that she recollects very thinly. Even circumstances surrounding Triton's suicide are hazy.

How did he manage to kill himself two ways?

He was dangling on a curtain, they said. Inward pulled pupils in his eyes bulging off the socket. A thin trail of blood edged along the whites, finding refuge down his cheek from burst vessels inside his head. And baby Dee, innocent soul, tickled pink at her father's death spasms and mouth froth, thinking it another game. Toddled freely at his feet, looked adorable.

The shaman broke Triton's fingers to ease the rigor mortis grip on a small brown cross dripping blood. Same cross that pierced his heart. Cause of death: strangulation. Or a sharp instrument through the heart.

+ + +

Only visible things in the family album linger Triton's memory. Curls, dimples, burgundy eyes. If pictures are worth more than a thousand words, why don't they reveal Triton to her? Venus can't understand it, especially when her dreams are filled with a male whose silhouette makes delicate shadows on a white wall, whose body is a salsa sensation, whose breath is warm as a rotisserie, whose hands are cool as a fresh spring, whose face is not Triton's.

She has a few days off, a power executive role in a publishing company inside a small settlement. The hours are insane. Basically, a graveyard shift. Tharsis is no metropolis, but the quarterly high gloss magazine builds a metropolis of Tharsis. A surreal world that gives meaning to people with mediocre lives.

And that sells.

But Dee, unlike the magazine world, is real. She needs a real nanny. The magazine doesn't sort that.

Venus hopes time gives enough cushion for the child to bond with another sitter. Yet she senses the Nanny Agency is wary. No one is available. Behind her back, the town talks—only to fall into hushed silence at Venus's approach.

She can almost understand it, their looks. It's as though they expect a pair of live bats to flutter out of her ears. Despite her wealth, a clouded air sits above the strange deaths of people around her.

Something happened.

Something leading up to Triton's death.

At the back of her mind is a quarrel or a shame. Perhaps a sadness. She doesn't know what or why.

All she knows is its significance in her life.

Sometimes, in her dreams, she sees a huge breaking sheet of water bursting on dark rock. Sometimes she makes out a sign and, on very candid nights, a name.

"The spare den has old smiteguns. Triton's," she says, lifting Mage's bags from his boot. "He was always into rifles, spearheads, deformers. Smiteguns were his best." She can almost smell the shine that gleams sun off the mobilis's new surface. She smiles. "Other than that, room's all yours."

She makes twice-cooked pheasant with berries for lunch in a granite kitchen of polished oak, straight from the land of Ananke, luminous bench tops and natural light.

Mage is at home with this effort.

Dinner.

Dee is upstairs in her den. She ran up two steps at a time, trailing fingers along the forged iron balustrade, this one from the land of Thebe. A wedding gift from Mage. Venus kissed her cool brow rested on a braided pillow as Ananke blinds lightly swayed.

"Mage?" Venus now says gently. "Who's Molten?"

He starts. "What?"

She has broken a silence of many years.

He swallows a great gulp of air. Shock in his eyes.

Though he sits straight on a high-back suede chair, she feels his knees knocking against hers under the table. He lowers his eyes before her gaze, perturbed by the vein of her talk.

In silence, she studies a spray of pimples on his age-furrowed face. Spots lift off his skin, unidentical yet evenly distributed. Two unobtrusive hooks on the lilac wall behind his head perfectly frame him.

Her gaze returns to the table where dancing light skips across and around their empty plates, spreading a warm glow. Layers of age on the teak wood form unique contours.

"Remember the night Maamy died?" she says slowly. "After she came from a walk in the forest?"

Gauze covers his eyes.

"Dee was kicking chubby legs inside a fleecy blanket sprigged with yellow daisies, waving pink arms," she says. "Going *Da da da*. Maamy looked ashen, clutching at her abdomen. Before she died, as she muttered incoherent things, in that sudden fever, she said something about Molten."

They sit in semidarkness. One barely breathing, the other making short, swift breaths.

Fire crackles in the hearth. Light catches the wood, trying but failing to warm the freeze of the chamber.

Palms lift to his face, as though flushing it with air. It needs no predicting. Mage is about to embark into the distressing terrain she has opened.

He begins lightly, as though it is of no consequence.

"What you ask me. About Molten. Something happened those many years ago. In Molten Rock."

She fondles olive and black lysithea paws in a vase on the table without turning her head. Their perfume spreads, it lingers.

"Molten Rock." She speaks softly, slowly savoring each syllable.

"Venus," he says. "Something horrid happened to you."

"What do you mean, Mage?"

"His name was Lawless."

No recognition flickers in her eye at mention of that name.

"See, you hitched with a *Ganymede*, Venus," her father says. "The worse of the worst."

"But no one has ever set eyes upon a Ganymede. They're invisible. And when they make themselves seen, they are hideous and red, they groan and gurgle and are terrible creatures to see. Their torsos are like snakes, fingers like tentacles. They are walking blood and pus and claws and brain. Wretched, how wicked . . ."

"He had a sect. Lawless was powerful, charismatic, evil. Three months. Three months he kept you—"

"Papa, don't!"

"Almost broke your maamy's heart. Finally, when it was too much and our lives began falling apart, I did the inconceivable. What can a father do?"

He throws his hands up helplessly.

"I paid a bounty hunter to abduct you. A shade whose body took all forms. Now she was a rock, a tree, darkness, an iguana. Morphed into the walls of the fortress, scuttled like a lizard along its white imposing walls overlooking a loch. She was a giant hawk when she carried you unconscious back to us. To your maamy."

His silence is more remarkable than his words.

"After the rescue, we moved you from state to state so the cult could never find you. A few months later, they were gone. The whole miserable lot of them. Doomsday. A suicide herb in the name of deliverance."

"No!" A nail of anguish cuts through her distress.

Suddenly, she understands the nights.

Her dreams, his caresses. The ghost of Lawless coming to reclaim her.

"Before he knew it," her father continues painfully, "despite his knowledge, the brother of the one who rescued you fell in love with you, Venus."

"No," she says again, hoarsely.

"Yes. His name was Triton."

"But how?" she cries. "Triton was not even a shade!"

"He lacked the gift. But he loved you very much, Venus."

"If what you say is true—how could I not remember? The Ganymedes? Lawless?"

"I used all within my power, money, to treat you, de-memorize you. It worked. And then the child was born. Not a child but a thing. It looked childlike and innocent but it was a monster nonetheless. Imagine Triton's grief, my fear, that you might have a relapse—remember the past."

"I didn't," her voice and eyes are flat.

Light from the fire warms the back of her pale hair. It lifts as she flicks her head, a defiance born of desperation.

"Venus—" he says with urgency, reaches across to her.

She pulls her hand away.

"Look at me, Venus. Look at me."

She keeps her face turned.

"There is no excuse for that sort of deception," he says. "The child is not Triton's. Now you know. You have to see we had to keep this secret—"

"I just wonder." She steps away from him, tipping her chair.

It crashes behind her.

She climbs over the fallen seat with outward calm. Inward she feels like death. She edges around the table.

"I'm sorry, Venus," he says.

"Is this how cheaply you dismiss your lies?"

"Your maamy died of a ruptured aorta and punctured spleen," he says quietly. That stalls her.

"How?" she says.

"Exactly."

"I don't understand—"

"Couldn't bring myself to tell you the shaman's verdict. Someone, something attacked her."

"Why now?"

"Telling you seemed inconceivable at the time."

"Why tell me now?"

She can't bear to see them, signs she has ignored.

Now they blur her vision. The hangman's necklace on Triton, the writhe of her maamy's agony, a sitter's body face down in the water . . .

"Why now!" she cries.

"It could be a point of life and death."

"Surely! Not!"

"I tell it as it is. That child is no child. Molten Rock created a demon."

Her face is blazing. She spits words rebounding from instant insult: "Bugger all, Mage. You may be my father. But you're crazy! And I thought I knew you."

Dampness collects and spreads in shiny driblets around his sun-whipped brow.

"Three years," Mage says. "Three years I've said to myself—*she's just a child.*"

"Don't make me choose!" yells Venus. "Dee is all I have between sanity and me. I won't choose between my daughter and your . . . your . . . warped logic!"

She cannot separate betrayal from her voice.

"A nanny's dead!" he cries. "Do you think Cora's death was an accident?"

"Yes, Mr. Slick," she retorts. "You know everything. Don't you!"

A tight expression shuts him from her world. She bounds to the door, footsteps angry and aloof.

Venus shifts her weight to a gentle purr of the bed, a soft sigh of sheets under her body. Far away, outside the sway of curtains, two dogs mourn pitifully.

Her eyes lift an inch. Sleep dust and dried tears clog her vision. Moonlight shifts with the blow of drapes, making clouds and droves of eerie paint patterns on the ceiling, inside a soft hum of the air conditioner.

Sleep brushes her eyelids.

A velvety song sprawls through closed doors down the hallway.

"Maamy duck said *Quack! Quack! Quack! Quack!* but no little duck came back."

Venus feels herself going down, down.

Water shimmers across glistening rock in this haze. Lawless steps through a glass pivot door spilling white light from an open terrace. He is transformed. Not smelling or spilling or oozing. Now, he is a god. He shrugs off his robe, touches her beneath the glow of a pendant brass, on a bed of solid timber, dovetail drawers and rustic charm.

More white light enters the den from a large open window. Giant ants pour in with the light, crawling toward them.

Shrouded inside a screen of trees . . . white walls . . . privacy, she strains against him, surrenders to his lips. Lips like glory parting hers. Gentle, probing. Soft, directional light in the manor balances the color of sex, wrapping around their naked hands and feet. Shimmers of rain out the window fall like specks of dust from the sky.

The taste of sleep in his mouth, his soft breath as he slips in and out of her, rouses her to the wetness of egg white. She tosses back her head and arches her back.

Surrender.

And the train of ants spills into the bed, blanketing their bodies.

+ + +

A big burst outside the den wakes her fully. Something falls with a thud. She understands the blink of disaster in seamless time. Shadows hang under the sleeve of her door.

Despite her speed of reaction, a smitegun goes off inside the night, above a dirge of sobbing wolves. The bang catches her hand on the doorjamb. She turns the handle down as a heavy smell of blood, guts and broken smoke rises in the air.

Night sings.

The smell, the horrid smell, fills her nostrils.

The door swings inward.

A flash of milk-white baby skin spattered with beads of fresh ruby trembling into the den. Straight into steady arms.

"Shush, my baby. I'll protect you through everything." Troubled, helpless, caring, Venus strokes the little flame head.

# THE ONE WHO SEES

"Solo! Solo!"

"What?"

"Will you look at the cookies in the oven?"

"Are you sure?"

"Don't mess with me, child."

Her warning from the bathroom is harmless. It's harmless from anywhere. But inside, she's a lion. That's her animal spirit. Assertive in her personal power, Mama is effective when she wants. As effective as Baba's square gaze, even from his photograph taken in Melbourne, now standing on the mantelpiece. He is graceful in a suit. Immaculate hands holding a conference paper on the impact of climate change. You stole his face—that much is clear from the portrait in its silver frame. Generous nose, lush lips. Tan skin like a kudu's. You have his antelope eyes, the specks of coffee inside the honey of his pupils. Eyes ever watchful.

Mama enters the kitchen. She's drying roped braids falling like a mane to her shoulders. The light of the fading sun enters the room from a large open window. It casts its softness on Mama's regal face.

You keep your eyes away from the gentle whiff of vanilla and sugar, from perfect golds in rotund circles, now cooling where you put them on a wire rack on the zebrawood table.

She directs her cat eyes at you. "How many have you gobbled?"

You smile. Looking at her is like seeing the heart of heaven pulsing on the savannah. She has laughter lines on her cheeks, skin smooth as the inside of a stone-hearth baked yam.

She presses her finger on a cookie. The texture is fine. "Should have known better, asking the jackal to mind the hen house."

"But I'm a leopard, Mama. That's my spirit animal."

"Leopard, jackal—what difference does it make? Both are hunters."

"But I'm the one who sees. That's the difference."

"Are you ready?"

"I'm always ready, Mama."

She looks at your collared shirt, short-sleeved; trousers, urban print; moccasins, ebony and shining like mirrors.

"The missionaries are teaching you well."

This you, the one you are now, stands apart from the children in Grandma's village with their polyester garments, ankle-grazer trousers and dirt-caked faces. Some urchins navigate the orange dust and savannah grass barefooted, if not bare bottomed. You miss their free loping, their sense of timelessness. You miss the khaki shorts and black sandals made of bicycle tires, the ones you wear when you go to visit Grandma. You take the ferry across the lake to get there. You miss Keledi: her warming eyes that weep, her laughter that tinkles, her special name for you—how she calls you City.

"I'm just from a little town over the lake," you tried to explain. "It's nowhere as big as the city where I go to boarding school."

"Boarding?"

"It has fences and gates. You sleep there."

"Closed inside?"

"A bell rings in the morning and you wake up—'

"A bell?" Her laugher tinkled. "Does the bell tell you to go to eat?"

"It rings to plan, so you know it's time to do something. Or stop."

"A bell." She rolled on the grass, wept with laughter. "Are you cows now?"

You did not tell her about the city's roads like a giant *koboko* snake with babies slithering near and far, how easy it is to get lost in the suburban heartbeat or the snatch of a stranger.

You are a child betwixt. The village and the town run in your blood. And now the city too.

"Is Baba coming to see me off?"

"You know he's busy." You avoid Mama's gaze, but she knows without seeing that tears are stuck in your eyes. "Come. Leopards do not cry." You feel the cotton of her yellow and black weaver bird dress, the heave and fall of her breast where your head rests.

Your father is your grandfather's son, and you do not mean it just in terms of bloodline. Your father and his father were men who took providing for the family seriously: your grandfather with his fishing nets, Baba with his new job—not-for-profit. Gone are the days when a twinkle danced in his eye, when he read you how and why stories: *How the hyena lost his tail; How the leopard got his spots; Why the snake lost his legs; When the tortoise got his shell* ... He still told some stories when he took a teaching job in the city college, but was weary when he came home. The stories—let alone the touching: a ruffle of hair, a grip of fingers on your chin, a press of palm on your shoulder—altogether stopped. Then you heard him arguing with Mama about putting bread on the table, about the new job and how it came with more money. He made a choice. As he more and more traveled and saw the world, his kudu eyes grew more and more distant and did not see you.

You often dream of your father. In one dream, the one that wakes you with soot in your heart, his body is an icebox. You are curled in a small space right there between his hooves. Despite ice flakes in your eyes, nose and ears, you are hot and cold all at once. You look up with questions: *Why did you, when did you ... How?* Baba's eyes are glass. In another dream, his antelope lips are frothed with blood. You take just a second and begin to cry with the knowledge of a span to one's time. The best dream is where you ride his strong back across a vast grassland. Time evaporates and the sky opens to infinity.

✛ ✛ ✛

You step out of the taxi. Mama pays, hands you the brown bag with cookies. The town station is not as big as the one in the city. Buses are arriving and leaving, spilling with passengers. People and animals everywhere, laughter, yells, horns, screeches. *Squ-a-ck!* A rooster escapes beneath the wheels of a parked truck. Mama guides you to your bus. A coolie helps her put your duffle bag in the luggage compartment of the overnight bus that runs across the country to take you from the small town to the big city.

You feel stupid, overdressed in the crowd. There is a woman carrying a basket of guavas on her head. *Are you well, my daughter?* she says to Mama. A man with muddy eyes is leaning against the bus, his back lined up against streaks of yellow, red and blue paint on the metallic body. He rolls tobacco into a cigarette, lights up. He catches your Mama's eye, nods in greeting.

"Looking forward to school?" Mama directs her question at you.

"I'm rapt," you say. "Rapt."

Her gaze reaches your soul. "Kids giving you stink?"

You don't tell her about the poking with a sharpened pencil, about the royal flush—your head in a toilet bowl. You vomited after that. You remember the heave sound. You always cry when you vomit. They outnumbered you. The missionaries know about the "freshie" inductions, but they do not interfere. *Nature runs its course*, says Brother Samuel. How was this nature? But you redefined yourself, intuited the wedgy. You saw them gang up, before they did. As they demanded that you strip to your undies, you untamed the leopard. You hissed, pulled out claws. Intuition guided your words. "Do you know who I am?"

They snickered but didn't come close. They looked at you, a strange animal.

"There's one of you, and many of us," some fool said.

"All I need is one."

"Who are you anyway?"

"Jungolo," calmly you said, and your feline spirit mushroomed with wilderness.

"Jungle what?"

"Touch me. And you'll see."

No one asked what the heck is Jungolo. You don't know why you said it. It was a choice perhaps, an identity, your own this time—unlike the choice or identity that Baba created for you with the town and the city and his not-for-profit work that took him to everywhere but you. You were not sure why, but you said it. It was creative and you were prepared to die with one person, and that was all that mattered. Perhaps that was your deeper understanding of life. Your passion and strength. None of the city kids, even the big ones, messed with you after that.

You don't tell Mama any of this. Instead you say, "Keledi talks to herself."

"Does she answer back?"

You both laugh.

You've never thought to ask who is Keledi, how you are related. She is there, Keledi is, at Grandma's. The daughter of a daughter of a cousin's daughter of a daughter . . . You cannot say for sure. She just is: Keledi. Tears shimmer on her lashes when she laughs. Her laughter turns out the pink in her lips, like the inside of a fish. She sleeps to the wink of starlight, wakes to the caress of sunlight. School has no bearing. Every day is the same . . . same different, and she approaches it with wide-eyed curiosity, no hesitation. She arrives to meet you from a point of equal, difference is unimportant. If you were a skyscraper and she was the jungle, she would treat you like you were both of the same river, moving downhill from one place to another, reaching and reaching uncontained.

You take swimming lessons at the boarding school. Keledi, who has never seen the inside of an instruction on water safety, breathing pattern or stroke technique, travels in the water like a fish. At the lake where women knead and beat clothes until they are clean, where men cast nets far out until they are swollen with a catch for the market, at this lake Keledi stands stark naked on a rock. She puts her hands together above her head, arches in a perfect curve, harpoons into the depths. You worry about typhoid, so you only toe the water's surface.

But Keledi glides back and forth in the black water, sometimes immersing her whole body for long minutes before spearing out at a place you didn't expect, laughing at your panic . . . She does not care about crocs or sickness. She is as healthy as the calf of a cow serviced by the village chief's strongest bull.

But there is a lot Keledi does not know. You haven't told her about the big plane that took Baba up in the sky all the way to Melbourne, into the middle of a faraway place and a changed time, where trains traveled under the ground and people in the same carriage did not look at each other, let alone say hello.

✦ ✦ ✦

The bus revs.

"This thing will push off in a minute," Mama says.

The tone in her voice is the same as the one she used when Baba one day came home after midnight. His body was gruel, careening into walls. Your first instinct was to laugh. But Baba, sensitive as a kudu, tugged at his belt and all your longing and fear folded into one. There was dread in your belly, and a cusp of craving. With a whipping comes a touch.

"I amuse you, k-kiddo?"

She-lion Mama stood between you.

"Leave. The child. Alone."

"The child I sired hasn't sired me. Even the lion protects himself from flies."

"But you're not a lion, are you?"

"T-teach some m-manners."

"Is your only tool a hammer? Then everything else becomes nails. You have never struck a child. Do you want to start today?"

He leaned his head against her shoulder, swaying as he stood, a giant antelope in her arms. You have seen his affection, of recent times to your mother only.

Later, much later, neither of them thought you were listening through thin walls of a two-bed in a cul-de-sac neighborhood where you hear everything.

"T-that's a bit absent, that nightie."

"Cost three hundred shillings and the rest. I catch you with another woman, she'll be the death of you. And drinking like that . . . It makes you angry at the boy, and anger and madness are brothers."

✦ ✦ ✦

Mama smells of vanilla and cinnamon, the scent of her perfume.

"But the bus isn't leaving yet," you speak against her breast.

Her push is gentle. "Traveling is learning. But you will return to the old watering hole. You will always return, my son."

You show the bus driver your ticket.

Mama has gone. She does not like goodbyes. A mozzie is buzzing around, digging into your arms. You remember the village, the vastness of landscape—space everywhere—and Grandma's fading light. You think of Keledi's tinkling laugh and her fluid, long limbs. Even though at eleven you were older, she ran faster. Together, you raced in a shower of dust under a scorching sun, shinned up trees to pluck papayas, rolled and wrestled over cow dung, returned ravenous to Grandma's clover leaf scent and her bubbling pot on a three-stone hearth.

You remember how, as you ate rice from a communal tray, dipped for bits of fish in a dense and inky broth, you talked and talked about this and that, even when Grandma squinted and said, "Children don't speak at the table, let alone with food in the mouth."

"There is no table," you said.

After the meal, you sat around the dying embers of fire, curled toes under your feet. Keledi rubbed her hands above the stone hearth, out of habit, not for cold. The night was awake with the buzz of creatures. The sky burnt red. There was rust in the air. In the town—even in the city—for all its floodlights, night closed like a fist. In the village the night bided its time.

You fingered Grandma's ash-dusted hair, and her half-blind eyes shone like silver.

"Is Keledi a peacock?" you asked.

"You would think it, with that beauty, her laughter at life," said Grandma. "But Keledi is a crow, a keeper of secrets. She brings healing and creation. She's insight, soaring over obstacles, searching for answers."

"How do you know all this?" you asked.

"Nobody is born wise. You learn, then you teach."

You often wondered if Grandma was a bat. She was nurturing, spreading her wings from the womb of Mother Earth.

Sometimes she talked about the late Babu, your grandpa. She told of how she never cast eyes on his strong jaw and smiling lips the color of rich berries until they were wed. How, as a young man, he moved without sound, no rustle of grass at his gentle tread. How, her big fisherman, his net caught the biggest tilapia in the village. Sometimes, when she paused from reminiscing, you and Keledi tossed up stories, the day's gossip gathered in your tripping and wrestling in dirt across the village: who was a night runner, who had sold his daughter to a suitor beyond the mouth of the lake, who was putting a witching spell on a neighbor through buried eggshells that induced barrenness, who had summoned the crocodile from the lake to take his child for wealth, who had found a *koboko* snake in the shed and that meant losing something precious . . .

✦ ✦ ✦

You have a window seat. You press your nose to the glass. A flood of nostalgia sweeps through you.

"What does your father do?" Keledi asked.

"He works in an office."

"It has walls?"

"Many people work in offices, they make money to buy food."

"Can't you grow cassava in your garden?"

"Mama's planted flowers. There are violets that go white and blue, daisies the color of the moon—"

The tinkle of Keledi's laughter halted you midsentence.

"Is your mother foolish?" She wiped tears from her eyes.

"She's got smarts!" you roared.

"She's got posh nosh. Are you going to eat flowers?"

And you understood about Keledi, her search for answers. But you also knew that you couldn't tell her, not then, of the dizzying height of Baba's multitiered office, how you pressed a button with a number to tell the lift where to stop and let you out.

✦ ✦ ✦

The bus coolie is announcing the bus is leaving. New passengers are running with buckets of tomatoes, bags of maize, cartons of cooking oil or bags of belongings that land squashed beside your luggage in the rib of the bus. The rest ends up on the roof, tied with rope—the coolie sees to it.

✦ ✦ ✦

The day you left the village, Keledi threw herself at you, knocked you to the ground. She kissed your ears and nose. Her eyes were shining, shining. Just as swiftly, she disengaged, flew off. You sat up, unfocused. As your eyes cleared, you saw Keledi soar with the wind, unquestioning that your school holidays had whipped by so fast, or of your return to the town or the city, or that you would come back to the village. When? It did not matter. Her world was timeless.

+ + +

You gaze out the window. Soon the bus will drive off. You are on the tip of entering a world altogether foreign to Keledi. How could she ever understand the city? Already the town with its offices and flower gardens is a strange animal.

Inside the flurry of activity outside the bus, your leopard spots the antelope from an impossible distance. He is a head above the rest, weaving his big shoulders across bodies and bags. You fling open the window.

"Baba!"

He follows your voice, locks his square gaze onto your window, in his graceful hands a bunch of yellow bananas.

Tires crunch, the bus rolls away from the station. That night, head on a stranger's shoulder, you surrender to the arms of a dream where your father evolves into his animal spirit. He's loping across grasslands, two-and-a-half meters long of him. He's a full-grown kudu, kilos and kilos in a bounce. The twist of his horns curls to the sky as he canters on the blonde grassland splashed with rays of the sun's yellow shimmer. You're a leopard, a seer. You gaze from the height of a baobab, sprawled on a furrowed branch. You study the antelope and his carefree jog. He is blind to a stir in the murmurless grass, the crouch and stalk of a lone lioness the color of the pale savannah. She's a wild cat, not your mother whose animal spirit is a lion. This one's hunger or that of her cubs is an unstoppable beast. She's flesh and bone, muscle and jaw. Her sudden tear closes the gap in a radical and committed leap. You hiss and puff out yonder from a tree, but can do naught. Nothing can deny the validity of your witness. Nothing delusional about your father's blood dripping like crimson tears along the untamed whiskers of a fat-pawed she-lion holding down his head.

You awaken to the whiff of vanilla cookies, crisp in their brown paper bag, the sweet aroma of soft and warm ripe bananas cradled on your lap, and a mausoleum in your soul.

# BEATITUDES

The young siren floated on the water reed . . . She remembered little of how she got there. Flashes came and went of an olive-colored field bathed in crimson, bones everywhere—fresh bones—some still evidencing sinews of torn flesh.

Other times she remembered a darkness that opened like a yawn, a terrible singing that was more of a war cry in a chase of ululation . . . Sea monsters. The creatures had climbed from the belly of the ocean and . . . and . . . her heart caught.

Her curiosity wasn't big enough to take her there. And she wasn't sure what to believe. But she could not disremember a little of her past, a time before the blackness. Her mind's eye saw green water and an emerald sky. The rest was blank.

Now here she was on an aquatic weed, forever floating to someplace or noplace, and the water was not green, and the burnt-orange sky not emerald.

Just then a poem shattered the core of her deepest misery:

*Blessed are they with a bearded arse,*
*for they shall receive no time for waxing*
*oh such levels of escapism.*

She looked at her tail where the horrid verse that held no rhyme came from. On her person, perched on her tail, was a toad. He was brown and warty and big black-eyed.

She looked at him. He looked at her. All was silent as the water quietly bucked. And then the toad renewed his croak:

*Blessed are they with a curious affection for a god of tithes,*
*for they shall inherit altar boys*
*whatever it takes.*

"Lay off!" cried the siren and flipped her tail.

"What the croak! I figured you'd eventually take heed." The suckers at the ends of his toes held fast to her tail.

"What are you!"

"A toad obviously. A better question is why am I."

"A traveling musician?"

"Streuth, no. I'm just a bloody toad."

"I can see that, living up to it with that godawful song or poem."

"Too right. But if you haven't noticed, this place is cursed." As if to prove the point, a sigh rose from the water. "And just so you know, it is not a song or a poem. It is a beatitude."

The reed quietly slipped along the eerie ocean.

## The Toad's Story

On reflection I didn't know if I was living my purpose on her king bed with its triple pillows, a perfect white. My mind struggled with the immeasurable space between putting down roots and making quests.

Kylie wanted stability. How do you plant roots in a traveling salesman who stumbled with his electrical wares—minishavers, saltshakers, tiny blenders and microwaves—into a Pentecostal church in Richmond, Melbourne, all the way from Perth?

Blue sky, the sun was out, there was this beautiful music coming from the church, it was like a spell. Maybe I needed saving: by this time people were buying online, not from traveling salesmen knocking door to door. I wandered in and there she was in the front pew with a fascinator hat.

It wasn't the pastor's hell and brimstone sermon that encouraged me to donate my wares to the faithful at the end of the service. I palmed out the last of the saltshakers and followed Kylie home like a puppy. I was a boy enchanted with finesse. And she was moneyed and lived in a honeycomb house spiraled with staircases. And she was bewitching.

But it didn't take long before I started feeling unwinged. But were my wings of feathers and wax like Icarus's, puffed up and ready to explode with regret forever and a day? Would I also fly too near the sun?

One morning I woke up and I was just the man in her bed. I stared from the past's frame and didn't recognize the identity that was me. I had been naïve, clasping in a fragile heart the ingredients that formed the essence of us. There was, oh, the pleasure of her kiss. And there was, oh, the wonderment of Kylie. As days passed, and months passed, and a year passed, then another, warm air and cold air encircled me and formed clouds that towered in an upward draft, and matured to a large and organized silhouette. And then it was rain, heavy rain whose energy dissipated and left me with bare facts and viewpoints, and bottomless knowledge that a thunderstorm was a cloud, a tall cloud that wasn't all thunder when it relaxed into a sedentary phase. She was bewitching.

Pushing thought into words was always clear to me. So when I half recognized destiny but the picture was crooked, and my mind fluttered to the hourglass woman who wore a fascinator hat in a Pentecostal church where tots spoke in tongues, and now I lay in her king bed, I wondered if the story offered itself to a twist.

When I got morose about it, she said, "Don't worry. Pull your head in."

Despite her enchantment, her persistence to get me baptized left me unconverted. This was the beginning of her turn. She became like a wicked stepmother, such a shrew, even to her own daughter. And she had this mirror she kept looking at. Mirror, mirror . . .

Most people let themselves go once they think they're all loved up, knowing they've harvested a mate. No need for effort. But not this one—she kept up the effort. No chance in hell that one day she'd wake up and look like she'd gobbled a few wombats.

Mirror, mirror . . .

Two years on, as I pondered more and more about my life with Kylie, I got into beatitudes. It was easy from the onset. I belted them out loud in the shower, piping out whatever came from my head:

*Blessed are they that lead with two chins*
*for they shall receive the canny one, but remain the hand model.*
*But good night spells in two ways, bloody oath, looks like I'm a donkey.*

Pissed her off real right. Like the night after footie finals, when the West Coast Eagles pipped Collingwood five points, less than a goal:

*Blessed are they that exercise the voice box at the stadium*
*for they shall receive guts and jumpers, scarves around their necks.*
*As for those two peanuts over there . . . fair dinkum, blessed, are they?*

You'd wonder what the heck's wrong with some shit about scarves and fair dinkum. Bloody nothing. It's just that Kylie barracked for Collingwood, and she was sore about her footie team losing to the Eagles and blamed the umpire and me and the rest of the world, even the good Lord, for she had prayed for victory. It didn't help that Kylie's teenage daughter, Narelle, was allergic to nuts. But the straw on Kylie's camel back was she thought the allusion to peanuts was to . . . It wasn't. It was bloody nothing.

I tried to make it up, took Kylie to this restaurant where they served fresh pink parcels of salmon dipped in sesame-coated rolls turned inside out . . . tender white strips of chicken soaked in enoki-infused broth speckled with crisp black seaweed . . . There we sat. Chatter as patrons wallowed in smorgasbords of complex and loved-up offerings, whispers as they drenched in sweet ancient wine that floated table to table in imperial striped jars. But the two of us . . . We sat in emphatic silence, navigating chopsticks, nibbles, tweets and texts, as we connected with all the world but us. Our eyes met over stone fruit brûlée, and she lifted the green dragonfly cast iron pot. "Tea?" she said, as though I were a stranger from someplace in history, and it was repeating itself.

Take it like this: Think of Kylie as the insomniac boss who surges up a plan, and it pitches clear in her goddamn head in all textural density in a color that sunburns everything, but it means nothing to everyone else in all imagination. I had no idea where to place her thinking. She would ask me to do something, task me to be the lead in delivering her vision, didn't care how I did it, so long as I did it her way. She wanted me to fix the roof, I fixed it. Hose the truck, I hosed it. Slave for her, I slaved, even as mischievous fae in the wind pressed against my ear and murmured that I'd never do it right, that in the end she'd flatten me with her heel, apologizing in full hush for any inconvenience my fuck up had cost her.

Mirror, mirror . . .

One day Kylie went mirror, mirror . . . and the mirror said Narelle was more beautiful.

The hate toward me and her daughter tripled. I'd steal at dawn to a place of memory, a beloved place I could sing out my beatitudes. The rush that swept through my body soared me to a play-filled wonderland enriched with blessedness and grace, the sermon right there on the mount.

But it was more than I bargained for—our outward declarations of inner hate. My beatitudes, her bossiness. It didn't matter how we ate or slept, and we slept together a lot when we felt the most spite. Our emotions dragged us to exhaustion in a trail of plummeting humanity jousting with thought. We were eaten up by our own monsters, and listened to the rain, burning, burning, and the ground around us sizzling like jazz.

So I took them to Lake's Entrance, Kylie and Narelle. Nothing like a change of scenery, right? Wrong. What her daughter did was speak to an altar boy with curls and big hands and the tattoo of a viper on his arm. We stayed in this motel, Union Club—Kylie and I in one room, Narelle in another. And when it was twilight, bang! bellowed the door.

"Jesus," I cried naked from the bed. A snap of wood at once with a tumble of door off the hinge. Ruby eyes, saber teeth and the yawn of a black-bellied snake dove into our room. A roar, and a she-beast that turned out to be her daughter cuffed me across the room . . . A blink of light and shade from the street outside the window. Me still scattered on the floor. In Kylie's trembling hands, the book of gods.

"I bind you. I command you," Kylie's ardor as she chanted to cast out the monster in Narelle. What was she, Kylie? But it worked. The ruby dimmed, and her daughter's eyes drew inward. The charcoal serpent recoiled into a tongue, the beast in the saber-tooth fled, Narelle . . . she turned into a mermaid with a big fat tail. And all that was left was Kylie and a choice to sit it out—shouldn't witches disappear before daylight?—or belly dance until dawn.

She danced.

She was dancing and making a sound that was howling or wailing. Then there was darkness like a great, big yawn, and it swallowed me. When I woke, I looked at myself in the mirror and I was a toad.

I started screaming, and Kylie pointed a finger. Suddenly I was floating on a water reed that turned out to bear you, dear you, my sad little mermaid.

Now tell me your story.

## The Siren's Story

I think I'm a siren, not a mermaid.

I was somewhere then something happened. I don't know where I'm going.

✦✦✦

They looked at each other on the floating reed.

The toad broke the silence. "Not much of a talker, are you?"

"It's all I've got. Can't remember much, sorry."

He hopped up her tail and took her hand. "Something about you . . . This toad thing, it's shifted my perspective . . . Sure you're not Narelle?"

"I don't think so, but we can try peanuts."

"The heck we will, an allergy is not something to treat with levity." He squeezed her hand.

Something in the water shifted. There was a giddiness in the air. A headiness that came and went.

She looked at him.

✦✦✦

She looks at him.

Her heart is a room full of blank photographs and cloud pillows wafting around rehearsing melancholy and reinstating torment. They drift threefold on the peripherals of kitchen walls and bathroom mirrors in a lost religion that came to beatitudes and spoke of destiny. To forsake the green water and emerald sky that is now burnt orange is like turning a blind eye to a topography of flames. But there is still no word, just somber silence in the floating photographs and neglected pillows cartwheeling unaligned past the blender and the microwave in a fairy tale of space that does not involve breathing.

✦✦✦

There was still no word, just somber silence in the floating photographs and neglected pillows cartwheeling unaligned past the blender and the microwave in a fairy tale of space that did not involve breathing.

"I think sea creatures climb out of the water every three hundred years," she said.

"Yes, oh, yes."

"Not me, stupid. Those mean-spirited ones that eat people."

"Sure thing, if you say."

"A great big finger put me on a water reed and pushed me afloat."

"That's right."

"You don't believe me."

The water was calm, everything was calm.

"You're so radiant," he said.

✛ ✛ ✛

The water is calm, everything is calm. "You're ever so radiant," he says.

She feels something curious and leans forward. She closes her eyes and presses her lips to his toad lips.

"Your tail . . ." he murmurs against her lips.

✛ ✛ ✛

"What happened to your tail?" he murmured against her lips.

"My tail," she whispered and opened her eyes. "I've lost my tail."

Her breathing was shallow. She gasped and leaned to the ocean as if it would breath for them both. The black ocean breathed, massive waves humping in silence. She felt his eyes in the hush and turned. But there was no toad all brown and warty with big black eyes.

✛ ✛ ✛

She feels his eyes in the hush and turns. But there is just a man, a beautiful man with a short crop and it is salt and pepper and he has the greenest emeralds in his eyes.

"The toad—"

"I'm here," he whispers. He is still holding her hand. "Do kisses break curses?"

She smiles.

✛ ✛ ✛

"I'd never leave you, I'm here," he whispered, still holding her hand. "Do kisses break curses?"

She smiled.

"I don't know if you'll give me a fair go, but we'll be right," he said. "Just know that I am not a man of virtue—I lived with a woman who was a shrew and she'll never welcome me home."

"I don't really care. Remember I asked you about traveling musicians?"

"Is this the most I've heard you speak?"

"I know a song," she said.

"Then sing it."

She began to hum a siren song:

*Blessed are they who speak and beg the garden of souls—too many of them now, such suffering and death—for they shall be rewarded with listening. Oh is our desire for more in sync with our poetic vision?*

"Amen," he said.

✝ ✝ ✝

"Amen," he says. "There's no rhyme, nothing. Your beatitude is as awful as mine."

"Blessed are we."

"Amen."

And together they float on the water reed to a place all their lives long.

# SNOW METAL

Torvill watches the girls. They outnumber the boys, aloof lads, most of them tradies at the weapons plant. Now the boys, hoods with a bit of income, play keystroke games on small electrode beamers, fiddle with music, act like they have a bit of class. The girls, similar in hip-huggers, in defiance of norm, are mostly signal sorters—these wear honey and black. Torvill understands their working rights, their privileges and independence, their resolve to build Goth hours in graveyard shifts for a lunar paycheck instead of settling as breeders like the rest of their lot.

He also understands the sorting process, what goes on in the pillared towers of the Enclave, an impregnable place, airtight security. In this messaging tower that "listens" to the galaxies, colossal pillars steeple into antennas that pick anion and plutonic noise, any wave leaking off space. It is here that intergalactic battles are lost or won, military or diplomatic secrets intercepted to much vantage. Intel-sensors snap signals into a looping continuum of capsules in a belt system, an intricate network that compresses the waves, sorts them on type, date, time and origin. Officers in encoding vectors decrypt the signals, assign weight quotient in terms of intelligence, emboss inferred threat into intel-chips for the senate.

Not all girls are graveyarders: scarlet and black indicates rank. These are the encoders: reserved. Unlike the sorters—who chat nonstop to each other, at each other, who gesture continually to demonstrate their talk—encoders hold a dignified air.

The Gate station vibrates. A distant drone grows loud, louder into the platform, until the vessel Shuttronix rolls to a halt. Shuffle, step. Shuffle, step. The crowd files forward. Each citizen takes turn, touches a magnetic pass to a flashing reader. Doors snap open, shut in an instant, boarding pass after pass.

Torvill is almost at the hatch when he notices her at the belly of the queue. Moot! She is a looker. Big hair. Her face is small, celestial. She is paired, he can tell. She wears rank, curvy in her officer's uniform. There is interest in the gold eyes that regard him. He returns her gaze. Burnt-orange lashes, wild and rich as her hair, flutter, then lower. A blush climbs to her cheek. She looks away.

+ + +

The Shuttronix rumbles, rocks. A blast of horn, then a wail. Momentum, a blast of speed, and the vessel spears into the sea. Torvill's stomach tightens. A sneeze gathers in his nostrils. He sees her again, two seats away, unmissable with that hair. Her head is turned. She is gazing at the sea's womb.

He flexes his knees, loosens the throb from his foot. He gazes again at the female. Her blazing head is upright, touching the minipod that holds her. Each pod is a capsule, luminous as magic, sturdy as titanium.

The chameleon sea shifts from a map of blue to streaks of silver. Then layers of white and gold vacillate between hues until little points of light fade, until the sea is deep, deep black, miles, miles out. As Torvill's breathing gets even, the vessel sighs, rocks, slogs its speed, judders to a halt and totality of sound.

"The Enclave," says an automat. "Termination point in seven seconds."

Torvill plows through the crowd. Ahead, so does she. He is two lengths behind her. She turns into the jaws of security, the Enclave. He waits at Zone 9 for a sensor shuttle to take him to Embassy Sanz.

+ + +

Three days. And though not a word is spoken, he sees it, understands it. He need not be told: the stagger of her heartbeat at the sight of him; lowered lashes when he meets her stare; a tilt of head; the quiet smile . . . The argue of emotion with her mind; she could well shout it. He hears it. He'd still hear it if she whispered it.

Hers is not a gradual melt—like the others. It comes instant. Magnetic.

Moot! It's a matter of Goth hours. But he is patient.

+ + +

He sees her outside the trapdoor; their shoulders almost brush. This time, he walks ahead. She tails.

"Sir," her voice raspberry.

He turns. The Enclave towers above them, a lime-tinted building, revolving, with spiked protrusions.

"Yes?"

"I *see* you."

"I see *you*."

"Work at the Enclave?"

"No."

"Snow." She stretches her hand. "Snow Metal."

"Torvill." Her grip is tight. "Gaulter."

"You new?"

"Emissary. Land of Sanz."

"The north, huh. So you're the replacement."

"Vice. Former emissary. Let's just say he had other matters."

"Matters? Total recall is what I heard. Vice was not—" She looks for the word. "Effective."

He smiles. "But you are."

✛ ✛ ✛

A nod, a handshake, sometimes a few words.

One day outside the soaring tower of the Enclave, she hovers as he waits for the Zone 9 shuttle. They stand beside a crystal fountain, perfect spray.

Her lips open, close.

He waits.

"Maybe we can . . ." she tries.

"Be effective?" he helps.

She smiles. "Drink sometime?"

"Yes," he says. "Sometime."

"All right. Then."

✛ ✛ ✛

One day, he kisses her.

He takes her to *La Japonesa*. Broiled calf, cured innards, servers a clap away. She eats without reserve, sweet meats in a tender glow of light.

"Hurting for calories?" he says.

She laughs. "Just effective."

Later, much later, she does not protest when he engineers a coach.

✛ ✛ ✛

A week. Oyster Street fair. They laugh to an exhilaration of speed shuttlers.

Wolf burgers at Centro. Down shooters at the Vortex under pink, yellow and green strobe lighting.

He confounds her with questions: about herself, her family, her work. Yes, mostly her work. She talks: about shuttles, no siblings, geo magnet. Yes, little of her work.

"Come." He pulls her to a swirl of lights, to new music.

Her dance is raw, electrifying.

✦ ✦ ✦

He invites her to Solaris, an island.

They meet by the sea. She is wearing a flowing dress dyed in patterns of rivers and dawn. His shuttle docks into a beautiful and private world. Hands clasping, they climb up hilly terrain, to the tip of a hillock. They gaze at the tossing sea.

When the air turns gray, blustery, as eagles vanish into the darkened sky, a sliver of moon, thin as a snake, casts its glow to the ground.

Torvill sits. His feet are stretched toward the sea.

"Tell me about the Enclave."

"What about it?" she laughs.

"The signals you encode."

"Let's not talk shop."

As they move to kiss, a beam from his eyes sears the gold in her eyes.

"Stop. What are you doing?"

He touches her memory, feels it.

"Stop. Torvill. Hurts—"

"Silence."

She fights him, physically, mentally. He stills her to the ground. But he can't read her. She is masking semantic data. Each download dimension from his beam strikes a call back routine. Success equals zero.

She wrestles from his grasp.

Moot! She is a fighter.

"You cannot decode me," she breathes.

"No one is that—" Torvill rolls, pins her again to the ground. "Effective."

"Get away from me you, you f-fossil, you."

She kicks, rolls, knocks him with a fist.

"You are well trained," he calls after her as she runs. "But I get what I want."

He is a hunter. He stalks, circles. He trails her fear, clothing caught in brush. A twig cracks near him. He pounces, grips her ankle as she flees.

"Get away from me you, you foul smelling, loose-livered, degenerate rake!"

"Good. Fire in your belly."

"*La Japonesa*! Oyster Street! The Vortex! Didn't any of those, us, mean anything?"

"I have a mission."

He hauls her by the foot.

"Torvill! Torvill? Please . . ."

He sits on her, knees astride her chest. Her prises her eyes open. He focuses his steady beam to the hippocampus of her brain. Start stimulation implant. Establish neural connection. Convert memory to transferable data: 5 %, 6 %, 14%, 41%, 43%, 43.01%, 43.17% . . . She is blocking him.

It weakens the decoding; shifts his access from her long-term brain hippocampus to short-term amygdala memory. Engrams of data show him the clip of her surrender in his arms that night of *La Japonesa* . . . He relives it: a conscious experience full of sensory data, parsed.

Smash!

✛ ✛ ✛

Rainbows in his focus . . . Torvill sits. He raises a hand to the back of his head, winces. Moot! A rock to his cranium? Volcano in that belly!

Somewhere in the distance, racing with wind and a murmur of sea, his shuttle roars away, away. He pulls a beamer from his back pocket, groans with effort. Mission failed, his syntax to Sanz. Fail, fail, fail hammers in his head.

Unlike Vice, former emissary, total recall is not his to embrace.

Despite soreness, he smiles, half-bemused at his new instruction from the planet up north: "Win her to our side. Make her a double agent."

"And if I fail?" he asks.

"You disintegrate."

# A MAJI MAJI CHRONICLE

*Maji! Maji!* Myth or legend
Or a scheme of fads, ideas embedded
One battle, one struggle.
Freedom! Freedom!
Painted features, glistened spears.
*Maji! Maji!* Myth or legend?
Sanctified water skims no bullet.
Grave, the lone stream bleeds scarlet.

*1905 AD.*

A copper-breasted sparrow circumvented the tree line. Flapping, he savored the natural scents of Earth that lingered in the wind: coppice, flora, even rain, beneath layers of clay and loam soil. Milk of woodland saplings blended with compound complexities of bodily secretions from nocturnal creatures marking territory or warding off peril.

The little bird surveyed the silence of twilight within a new smell of burning that explained a curl of black smoke in the horizon. He fluttered lime-mottled wings and landed on a branch tremulous from tepid wind. So this was Ngoni Village, the warm heart of German East Africa. He reined himself with the tips of his claws, leaned his body with a subtle shift of weight on the bough. His face twisted skyward, where an eagle soared in a battle dance overhead.

Broad wings slowed. Gleaming eyes angled at the limb of the thorn tree. The eagle swooped with power and a wild cry, talons outstretched with skill and focus.

*Schwash!*

The eagle and the tiny sparrow toppled in a downward shred of branch, twigs and leaves, and a curtain of red and lime-mottled fluff entangled in silver eagle feathers. The little bird floated out first. He preened himself and hopped two steps away in good recovery on firm ground.

"Surely, Papa!"

Papa was Zhorr, the grand magician of Diaspora. "I did not mean to loosen your feathers, younglin." He looked around, cleared his throat and said, "Well!" A gust of something burning swept into his nostrils. It grew stronger and wilder in the air, wild enough to push rain clouds away.

"This bird thing won't do," Pickle, his son, said. "Now what? Mmhh? What?"

"We go to the village."

"Like this? As birds?"

"And that troubles you, I see. Pretty much everything displeases you, ingrate lad."

"Having traveled back in time to build a picture of history, we'll be dinner in a human's pot before we catch up with that past. Imagine the possibilities: skinned or feathered, how will they eat us? Apprentice, guinea pig or bird, Papa, I do not goad fate."

"Relax. We won't be birds long. But we need to observe before we can morph and fit in."

"Fit? We could have fitted in better had we done the vortex. Churn, swirl, a blast of color and *schwash!* Right into this world in our normal forms. Why come as birds?"

"No mess, no structural changes," said Zhorr. "The black hole causes atomic fusions and chemical transfigurations. Flying in was safe. Safer! I understand your frustration. You must appreciate that 3059 to 1905 AD is a hell lot of years."

"No kidding. So why birds again?"

"You make an awful sparrow." Zhorr regarded Pickle for a moment. He swirled. Monster wings flapped and a swell of rapid air slapped Pickle to the ground. "That better?"

Pickle lifted on two legs. He sniffed around, scratched his ear and landed back on fours—a reddish brown mouse. He scurried into clumps of grass, dragging his tail.

"No point sulking," the magician said, now transformed to a gray squirrel himself. He gnawed his forefeet and shaped his nails. He rubbed his whiskers and sat on a bushy tail.

Above them, the dazzling eyes of a shadowy owl picked bustle in the shrubbery.

"Either way, Papa," came Pickle's voice from the brushwood. "In all these shenanigans, you leave me silly and game. If humans don't gobble me, that darn owl up there will."

"I'll do something. Maybe. At dawn."

They veered north, eating miles away in bristle undergrowth on a forest walk. Shadows peeped in and out between leaves and soft moon glow. Zhorr and Pickle steered by thick smoke curling in the horizon. They found an open field dazzled by white stars. The meadow closed to unfenced farmland bulging with blonde ears of maize. Yellowing grass trembled and snapped at their chins. Pickle legged it out. But digging, scratching and sniffing at whim, he simply couldn't keep pace with Zhorr, who looked fine and strong.

Pickle struggled, out of breath, way out of legs and famished. This is some adventure, he thought. A sudden nostalgia for Diaspora overwhelmed him—its gold and rainbows and snowcapped crags. In this godforsaken past, the wind looped and whined with speed and ferocity. The trees murmured and loomed tall like mountains to Pickle's modest size. A whisper ran across the grass and nearly scared him out of his fur. A dried leaf raced near his cheek. Behind the leaf's rustle came a gasp from a rousted and irate cricket. It, *zinged*! past Pickle's muzzle.

Zhorr and Pickle traveled over a dirt road stippled with clumps of dung in various stages of drying. Hungry, they paused and nibbled sprouting maize shoots by the roadside. Further north, a golden carpet of millet and sorghum fields spread. Fallen stems by the roadside crumbled at their feet.

"I'm still hungry," said Pickle.

Zhorr shook ears of grain into his paws and they had another meal.

Finally, they came upon sporadic huts. Zhorr and Pickle moved along a cattle fence and into a forest of mango trees laden with fruits. A narrow footpath led to a mud hut with thatched roofing. Beside it, they ate their way into a food shed where they huddled in sound sleep on a golden bed of drying grain, malleable as a waterbed.

Zhorr awoke to the crow of a cockerel and transformed himself into an old man. Drums echoed in the distance. The staccato beats left Pickle's sleep of light snores unruffled. The grand magician appreciated his son's exhaustion from a flight across years. The great land of Diaspora stood eons away from a small African village invisible on the global map but visible in a magic bowl with special effects.

He contemplated washing his face. He perused the compound and took note of a well that had seen better days. He prayed it held a trickle or three, else he'd have to cast a spell. A tin pail lay beside the well . . . all seemed hopeful. But before he could stir or rise, within minutes of the cock's crow, hinges of the hut's wooden door groaned. A boy with tight hair and bark loin came out. His lazy hands rubbed sleep from his eyes. He lifted the empty pail and took to his heels, swinging the handle, presumably on his way to the river for a day's ration of bath, drink and cooking water. That trampled the well's possibilities as a washing place for the magician.

Zhorr waited until the boy was out of sight and clapped his hands. Pickle woke up—a human boy. He was chocolate skinned and naked. He gazed in wonderment at his father's new form: a salt and pepper wise man with ancient eyes.

"No need to look so pleased, younglin," he said. "I never thought you'd eagerly embrace childhood. Being human, of course, afflicts you with all their scourges."

"Such as?"

"Disease and incontinence." Zhorr pointed to a rickety shack gated with maize stalks. "Pit latrine right over there."

Zhorr applied a sprinkle of sorcery and fashioned garments for them: Pickle in bark loin and Zhorr in dried cattle skin and a single-shoulder robe. A clap from the magician, and they soared to a new home, their very own, wetness still clinging to its fresh mud walls.

Pickle eyed two beds of elephant weed and covered his face.

"Breakfast. If you'll excuse me—" Zhorr vanished and appeared seconds later with newfound knowledge and ingredients, having completed an observation tour of Ngoni Village. "Twigs. Fetch me twigs, younglin."

Twigs, three stones, a conjured pot and a wooden spoon—the magician stirred sweet potato powder into lukewarm water in the pot. He mixed it well and removed lumps. The concoction came to a boil. He pulled out twigs and lowered the heat, stirring the porridge all the while.

"Ah, bowls." He scratched his head.

Clap, and half-moon gourds appeared.

He served the porridge. Pickle made a face but, in the end, licked the inside belly of the gourd with relish.

Replete, Pickle had one question: "The villagers don't know us. How will we fit in?"

Zhorr clapped again. "They know us now."

Sure enough, they were warming chilled hands over a twig fire, burning morning breeze from stiff knuckles, when a rap came across the wooden door. Chief Ngosi—whose wives, huts and extended family Zhorr had perused earlier that morning in his three-second flight—stepped into the hut. He led a dozen reed-thin elders, their walk too slow, too careful for the limited amounts of grays on their heads.

"Greetings Zhorr," Chief Ngosi said in a dialect that Zhorr and Pickle seemed to fully understand.

"Greetings, good Chief."

"I trust you and the boy are well?" Chief Ngosi asked.

"As well as can be."

Zhorr nodded at Pickle, who rose and left his coveted spot beside the fire and leaned by the mud wall, as the elders huddled around the merry flames. They were wiry-haired men with blank faces that carried eyes as still as a swamp. One elder bore wrinkles as numerous as the tales of the dead. There was no doubt that, behind their retinas, those elders carried wealth of culture that seasoned them with much knowledge. But theirs was a wisdom merged with gloom.

Chief Ngosi drummed his lips with a finger to call for silence. He glanced at the elders, then at Zhorr, completely ignoring Pickle, and delved into the focus of their visit.

"Zhorr," he began. "We all know that you and medicine man Shona are the most powerful sorcerers of our land." He sat on the ground, his knees thrust upward. "You know what happened to the village of Tumbi."

"Toom-bee," Zhorr repeated, rolling the consonants. The elders watched him closely. He cleared his throat and nodded, having no inkling of Tambi or Tompei, or what had happened to it, although Ngosi's tone indicated something awful. He hoped someone would tell him the headlines or the whole village thing would become pig's ass for Pickle and him.

The chief pulled a small twig from the embers. "When Whiteman came from the sea, we welcomed him with a feast. We gave him our wives and daughters to warm his loins. What did he do? He brought more white men. Soon, we didn't have enough wives or daughters to go around. To add insult to injury, Whiteman spoke of a thing called cotton and how much better it would be in our farms. Cotton. Better than millet, maize or cassava, Whiteman said. When we refused Whiteman's request, his soldiers came with magic sticks that threw fire. So we grew cotton, only a little at a time, in small portions at the corners of our farms, to make peace."

The chief poked the twig on the ground and made small holes. "Now this cotton does not feed the stomach. Our children need grain. Instead of being satisfied, Whiteman wanted half our farms to grow sisal. Then he introduced coffee on the Mount where the gods live. Before we could cough, he called himself Imperial Commissioner and demanded land tax."

"Yes," said Zhorr, not much enlightened. "Yes, indeed." So what happened to Tongsey again?

"Whiteman took our young men," said Chief Ngosi. "He forced them to work in his plantations. We gritted our teeth and bore it, for the gods were unhappy with us, and there was nothing we could do. Finally, unable to take it anymore, the people of Tumbi asked Shona for help. They wanted something stronger than spears to fight Whiteman's stick that vomited fire."

"And Shun . . ." the grand magician cleared his throat. "Shona helped them?"

"Why do you test my knowledge, Zhorr? Of course Shona helped them. He told them to mix millet seeds, water and castor oil, and he blessed the potion. He said the magic potion would turn the hot pellets in Whiteman's stick into water."

"If you ever heard a load of boloney—" began Pickle, leaning forward from the mud wall, arms folded.

Zhorr silenced him with a look.

"Village warriors drank the potion," said Chief Ngosi. "They wore headbands and waved spears. *Maji! Maji!* they cried and burst into Whiteman's compound."

Zhorr nodded. "Whiteman's bullets did not turn into water."

Chief Ngosi spat. "They did not. The wails of the women," he spoke slowly, "the children's crying . . . My ears are still ringing."

Zhorr touched the Chief's shoulder. "What do you want me to do for you?"

"Trouble is brewing. White soldiers are moving through the country. They are burning millet and maize. Tumbi is no longer a village. It has been reduced to an orange blaze. The soldiers are moving inward. In the village of Tana, they raped girls and mutilated men. Soon they will invade Ngoni. If we do not die of the Whiteman's stick that spits fire, we'll surely die of famine." Desperation scorched his eyes. "I am a leader and a warrior. The bones and blood inside my body cannot stay silent. If I sat like a stone and did nothing for my people, I'd be alive but dead. No one would sing of my creation, my story, my journey. There'd be no fire, wind or kingfish song. Not even a frog song. No one would tell stories to my children and their children's children."

"And you think I can help you—how?"

"If Whiteman's medicine was more powerful than that of Shona, then only you can defeat him. This morning, we beat drums to summon young men. They have formed gangs to rip cotton off Whiteman's plantations, burn his cattle and capture his women. In order to fully succeed, we need your magic."

"But Papa, you cannot interfere!" said Pickle.

"Silence, boy."

Zhorr pondered. Finally he spoke.

"If you promise not to harm the children or kill the women—they know nothing of your war—maybe I'll help you."

"We'll shed no child's blood or lay a finger on any woman. We'll banish them to the gaze of the sea where they came from."

"And if they can't swim?"

"We'll give them dhows and then banish them."

"Return to your huts and wait there until dusk. When the moon casts its light, summon your warriors. Meet me at the door of my hut and I will speak."

"Speak? Is that all you'll give us? Words?"

"I'll give you more than words, more than immunity to bullets with plain water. I will give you," he paused. "Magic."

After the last of the elders had shuffled out, Pickle rushed to his father. "You have not well thought through this. Surely you can't!"

"Primarily because?"

"You'll change history!"

"So it would seem." He scratched his head. "We shall see."

"But—"

"You'll know the outcome in due course." His mind slipped to a hidden place. Nothing Pickle said could reach him.

✦ ✦ ✦

"The first stir of twilight brings scores to our door," said Pickle.

Zhorr raised his brows.

"The entire village of Ngoni," said Pickle. "And gate crashers."

The chief's wives wore cowry shell bracelets and heavy gold anklets that clink-clanked with every stride. The rest of the women balanced, without finger support, fat clay pots on their heads. The men built a fire.

Everyone danced.

Ngoni Village had brought feast and dance to Zhorr's door.

Faces shone with body paint: ochre red streaked with white clay. Bellies distended with banana brew, roast goat, cassava and millet.

Seed rattles and bead-filled shakers tied to dancer's arms and legs chimed in tempo to the drum's *poom! palah! poom!* Necks swayed. A sky dance, a river dance, a new rites dance, a war dance. Expression, transition, choreography. Someone double looped through a ring of fire. Triple flip. Loop. Loop. It was more religious than anything else.

Pickle moved away from prancing feet in a ceaseless sequence of pace and loop, and walked toward Zhorr, who was seated in close vicinity to a banana leaf carpet piled high with food. In one hand, Zhorr clutched a gourd of mulled fruit.

Pickle touched his father's shoulder and knelt on the ground beside him. "I don't see how this will help my learning, Papa."

Zhorr took a swig of brew. "They rot fruit to pulp, crush it with feet, and ferment it to make this." He swirled it. "Clear water that boggles the mind."

"But Papa—"

"Look," Zhorr pointed.

Chief Ngosi stood fine-looking in ceremonial robe. Tails of peacock head-dress fell to his shoulders. He stood tall in paraphernalia, leopard skin and gold anklets. A strong white moon in the shape of a plump woman's bosom caught the shine of dark skin rubbed with fresh sheep fat.

The chief raised an arm and waved his people silent. Zhorr unfolded from the ground and climbed to full height. All eyes turned toward the grand magician. The people observed him with curiosity. "Today is a day of reckoning," said Zhorr. "I will give you—" Animation danced in charcoal eyes. The crowd shuffled. "I will give you ghosts!"

Children heckled. Men and women looked at each other and howled. Elders shook their heads, scratched their cheeks, muttered under their breaths.

Even Pickle's jaw dropped.

One wave of the chief's arm, though he didn't look reassured, silenced the jostling crowd. The elders still hummed.

"Before you throw bananas at me," said Zhorr, "swallow the import of my words."

Pickle folded his arms.

"We're listening," said Chief Ngosi.

Zhorr scanned the chief's entourage. "To defeat the enemy, I'll make you," he paused, "vanish at will."

✦ ✦ ✦

The first attack on the homesteads of the white men at the sleeve of the Mount came just before dawn. A servant later narrated what happened:

A burst of war cries trampled army fencing. Startled, white soldiers jumped from their beds in pajama-striped bloomers and snatched their guns from the holsters on the walls. They sought with their eyes for the enemy and saw flying spears every this way and that, catapulting from invisible energy fields. Four or five volleys of shots, and random bullets caught a few unseen targets who cried out. But, blind to their enemies, white soldiers lost their fight to stay upright. Ghosts slashed white men's throats open, knocked guns from their hands and fired back at them. At the end of the attack, women and children huddled in dreadful stillness inside cotton plantations.

Zhorr and Pickle saw all these events on the surface of still water inside a clay pot.

"Is this the initiation ritual you promised?" cried Pickle. "The one that would turn me into a 'made' magician? If this is it, I don't want it! I don't want to be part of this anymore."

"This is a lesson that supersedes spell recitals from *The Book of Magic* in the comfort of a floating castle in Diaspora. Now stop talking."

Pickle turned toward the grand magician. "You brought me halfway around the galaxies to witness men die? Your magic has created phantoms."

"Mouth all, younglin, I am not conflicted by it. If the Ngoni have become smitten phantoms, they are phantoms by choice."

✦✦✦

A wall of soldiers stood on guard outside the courtyard. One appeared, from his headdress, to be in command. Zhorr approached him.

"I must see Chief Ngosi," he said.

"Who are you?" the guard said.

"May your gods take pity on you, for I shall grant you none when I am through answering that question."

The warrior stepped aside. "Chief Ngosi is with his first wife." He pointed toward a distant hut with brand-new clay.

After a wait, Chief Ngosi emerged.

They sat under the shade of a banana tree whose leaves spread like an awning. Zhorr declined a gourd of millet wine. Chief Ngosi indulged. He wiped his lips with the back of his hand and suppressed a burp.

"What can I do for you, my friend?"

"I am concerned," said the grand magician.

Chief Ngosi regarded him.

"Since the massacre at the Mount, your warriors powered with invisibility potion, an ability to appear and disappear with the wind at will, continue to plunder Whiteman's farms and kill indiscriminately. They have forgotten anything about amnesty to women and children."

Chief Ngosi nodded. "I will ask them to show restraint. Is that all?"

"At this point, yes."

"Good. Perhaps you will join me for lunch. Fresh caterpillars from Yassa land."

✦✦✦

A week later, Pickle pointed at the water gourd. "Look, Papa."

Zhorr observed Ngoni warriors on rampage outside the tribal frontiers.

"Kill! Kill! Kill! White is white!" they chanted. "Kill! Kill! Kill!"

They marched past the Great Lakes to the coastline and left in their wake vultures looping the air in hordes.

"Greetings, Chief Ngosi. I wonder—" Zhorr began in their next visit to the chief's palace.

Ngosi's face tightened. *"Emperor Ngosi,"* he corrected. "I'm a very busy man."

"So I see."

Emperor Ngosi would speak nothing of his warriors' actions. In a stab of whatever modest hospitality he had left, he showed Zhorr his newfound treasures. Inside one hut, metal boxes, each carrying five hundred rounds or more of ammunition, stacked high. Another shed was a museum of gadgets from an Arab Sheikh: pistols, shot guns, machine guns, live ammunition and rifle silencers.

The emperor cradled a laser sight rifle in his hands. "A rarity even in the Western worlds, I hear. Isn't she a beauty?"

"Better than invisibility magic," Zhorr said through tight lips.

"This," the emperor lifted another item, "is a bazooka."

✦ ✦ ✦

In a third and desperate visit to the palace, Zhorr discovered that Emperor Ngosi was not so friendly anymore. He appeared out of mist and waved the magician silent. His court was now full of sorcerers whose powers he appeared to trust.

Emperor Ngosi locked his hands, his eyes dulled. "We are a master race," he said. He thinned into black fog where no one could see him. Invisible Ngoni soldiers lifted and tossed the grand magician and his son out of the palace.

✦ ✦ ✦

Lust predated greed that predated power that predated altruism. The emperor gathered a harem of one thousand wives whose shelter spread across three villages. Their feed took resources from twelve more villages now forced to pay 'protection' tax to the palace.

"You *do* understand the long-term outcome of this?" Pickle said to his father.

"Yes." Zhorr's smile was wistful. "What you witness is not genetic betrayal. It's not a modern phenomenon. It is simple quintessential greed. Recognizable as it is age old. Emperor Ngosi knows he can climb higher up the money cum power tree—that itch is powerful. He's obsessed in a rather clear way in a quest for continental supremacy that will only be a speck. In dramatic nuance, history will repeat itself, only with a new face."

"Yes," said Pickle. "A face called tragedy."

They regarded each other.

"The emperor has grown more powerful," said Zhorr. "Guns are no longer to him magic sticks that spit fire. He understands the mechanics, complexities and gains of advanced weaponry. Soon, his troops will invade Europe, Asia, Australia and the rest of the world. He will destroy opponents with weapons of famine, disease and bombs. The release of weapons-grade material will change the Earth's ozone layer. A tidal wave will unleash a tsunami that will kill millions. Changes to the Earth's epicenter will give rise to tectonic forces that will bend the Earth's crust. Earthquakes and lava bombs will kill millions more. Survivors and generations after them will become crippled with incurable illnesses far worse than mutable forms of bird flu, COVID-19, HIV or Ebola."

"And my lesson?"

"Clearly it works," Zhorr said in uncompromising attitude. "My method works very well. Too well, in fact, for the scoop of emotions it uncovers in you. Did you want me to teach you about galaxies and how a sprinkle of magic could keep them efficient? Did you want me to clap my hands and say: *Look at this world. Isn't it beautiful?*" Zhorr pressed his hands together. "This, my son, concludes our history session."

One clap and Zhorr regained his true form. Silver ringlets of hair fell to his waist. Jeweled apparel full of shadows, melancholy and river song wrapped around him. Onyx eyes glittered and lit the hut. The grand magician of Diaspora towered two heads above his apprentice son.

He laid a gentle hand on Pickle's shoulder, crisp with starched livery in lace, lavender and cream. "Tell me. What have you learned then? What have you really learned?"

Pickle's face shone with clarity. "No matter how strong the urge or goodwill," he said, "never use magic to flirt with history."

"Unless—" said Zhorr with utmost professionalism, "you have a rule to cover it." He ruffled Pickle's copper head. "Well done, my boy. With that knowledge, you have earned a diploma. Now we must depart fast track and travel between worlds to where we belong."

"Fast track?"

"Straight to the year 3059 and I will die in peace."

"What about the *no mess, no structural changes* that favored us flying as birds to the vortex? Atomic fusion, chemical transfiguration and what else, that's what you said."

"Pure gumbo." Zhorr toyed with tresses falling down his shoulder. He combed off tangle with a finger. "I always wanted to fly."

Pickle's brow creased. "But Papa—"

"Mmhh?"

"I am desperate to leave this world. My faith in you is restored. Partially restored, at least." He glared.

"Did you 'But Papa' me to fault my motive?"

"Can't we, must we not . . ."

"Must we not what?"

"Undo it?"

"Undo the flying bit or my dying in peace?"

"The damage. The course of history that you have altered."

"Ah, that. Course we can undo it. It's our obligation to do so. Yes, you must." Zhorr's strong fingers poked Pickle in the chest. "You," almost absentmindedly. "Yes, you. Put your wizard hat on. Quick! Time leaks perilously."

Before Pickle could lift a finger, the door burst open.

Zhorr and Pickle barely transformed to prior form—just barely!—before Emperor Ngosi fell in.

"I don't want it anymore," he cried. "I don't want it!"

Zhorr scratched his salt and pepper wise-man hair and regarded the emperor with ancient eyes. He took a step forward, laid a hand on Ngosi's shoulder, an action that appeared to carry calming effect.

"What is it you don't want, Emperor Ngosi?"

"The power. Take it. Take it!" He tossed down his staff. "It has made a monster of me. Oh, what have I done? My own people! Zhorr, I am a sick man. My forefathers groan in their graves. I see reason now. I don't want greater power."

"Do you speak from your heart?"

"All men are equal. There's no master race. Please remove your magic now."

"I am delighted you have found sense. I couldn't have enforced it without infringing your free will. Go home." Zhorr gave Ngosi an indulgent pat on the back. "We shall work some arrangement."

After Emperor Ngosi had left, shuffling his steps and carrying much weight, Zhorr and Pickle glanced at each other. Pickle spoke first.

"Your magic eyes didn't see that coming."

"N-no." He was back in his jeweled robe. "Time travel brings paradoxes and anomalies. That was an anomaly."

"Knowledge for the future. What happens now?"

"Ngosi has no need of us, really. Having seen light, his world will embrace him once more. The blood of a speckless rooster or three will appease the spirits of his forefathers. As for the powers of invisibility, he will no more use them for harm."

"Yet you hesitate, Papa."

"A small predicament really. Ngosi has no desire for greater power and he has already won the Maji Maji war. But, for the implications of changing history, although he is a reformed man, we must reverse the effects of my magic."

"Heaven forbid. Reversal will—"

"Different historical outcomes are not necessarily better that the ones that eventuated them. We cannot tamper with this world. Take us back to exactly one minute before Ngosi and the elders first entered this hut and sat around the fire." Fog touched his voice. It became hoarse, old as a museum. He glanced at his son with unwavering eyes. "You know what that means?"

Pickle nodded. "The calculation is simple." He turned away from his father. "A simple calamity, really." He stood still for a moment. "Ngoni warriors will use millet seeds and water to lose the war."

"I cannot stop it." Zhorr's museum voice trembled. "And neither can you."

"Yes." Pickle answered. "No one can."

In a flash, Pickle swished his gown. A glow of light on his forehead swelled in changing shape and size. It filled him with magical powers that lifted the grand magician's philter of invisibility on the Ngoni.

The cloak whirred again.

Zhorr and Pickle soared with outstretched hands into naked space.

Soft tips of Diaspora mist lifted and touched a cobalt line of hillocks. Crystal water gushed between pieces of boulder and cascaded downward in a waterfall. A snow-crested mountain ridge climbed toward a floating fortress with an iron gateway. An array of white lights in every arched window blinked. The flying castle sighed in welcome exactly three nanoseconds before a timid rap on the wooden door of a mud hut somewhere in Ngoni country.

# A GOOD BALL

"The game is alive," coughed the score worm. It illuminated with body shimmers who was winning. It was the Cyclops.

The amphitheater erupted.

An umpire blew his horn and the third quarter of the ball game started.

The way the game played was by each group of ten players dodging a ball that was a human skull hurled by the opposing team. Wear had nearly leveled the boned shape to a smooth oval. When it struck a victim, they were banished to the sin bin, sometimes for eons, unless a release deal was struck by song, delivered in prose poetry.

The first quarter had seen the Troika lose a trinity of players and one-third. A third because the precocious fullback was only a child.

During the break, the Troika had put a valiant effort to rescue their trinity, if not the one-third. Their lead siren, a third eye for the nose and fur all over her three bodies, understood the value of a trio. She sang in light waves that accelerated in orthodox lines across the one end of the amphitheater to the other and found refraction in the audience. Resonance jumped between bodies, patterns and frequency emitting a synchronous melody:

> *Earth stories oblivious to time and space are not our element. Like the boy with cowlick hair and a briefcase on his lap: he is a terrorist. A suicide vest caresses his chest. He smiles. His eyes are a palimpsest swollen with poems about phantom virgins floating in songline. They flow in monochrome, infographics that cascade into the working sea of his creed. No contrition or penance, just a magnificent white bird, yellow-beaked. It supplicates on bended knee but its droppings are full of calligraphy. Text ricochets from bird poop, hopping and skipping in telescopic trails of full stops, semicolons and em dashes. No adjectives as the bomb erupts.*

At the end of the tune, the score worm coughed and announced the verdict: "Your song was not quick to transition between notes. It was lacking in the depiction of humankind's diversity."

+ + +

The Cyclops were deft with the ball in the second quarter, but the Troika—a trinity and one-third down—put a brave effort, dodging the skull until the horn went.

The lead Troika siren put on show oscillating waves that cartwheeled in red and blue to generate diversity in her sung prose poetry:

> She sees a garden of commas. There's a curl on the crown. The sky is the color of baking cookies, but a pessimist would say it's the hue of sizzling bile, a task rather than a pleasure. There's frost growing in the gully. The kind of ice that doesn't drench thirst. And as she walks where punctuation is no taboo, she'll lace up her boots and remember to set expectations. Or beyond simple genetics and much like a novice who just might eat the dog.

But the home crowd heckled. Again, the score worm delivered a verdict.

+ + +

Things continued in pitiful fashion for the Troika in the third quarter. But when the faltering team's siren sang in EM spectrum that vomited gammas and infrared, the crowd listened:

> A soar of mercury [/ˈmər:kyə-rē/ n. a heavy, silvery metallic element] dries out stones until they burst to flame and scald the scorched Earth. No geometry on her face, just an interrupted purity of creation. No history of foreshadow, just a metaphor representing everything. There's a direct connection to a hippie bible that was never likeminded to revive an old relationship, ritual or a golden gate. A parliament of owls elects a blond fox to lead a charm of finches soaring to a spirit that's always here, decreasingly relevant as time goes on. But the fox is really a dog that came from the clouds beyond the epicenter of the city by the bay. It is an animal incapable of loving but thrives on heat [ready to mate] in an imaginary place where one day sooner—not Mother Nature—has the final say.

"That is a serious quest," shimmered the score worm. "I search the term to describe your song. And half a century and ten thousand lives after, I still know it's a great story. If the Cyclops have no challenge—"

"We have a challenge!"

"Let's hear it then."

The Cyclop singer was both ugly and beautiful. The blob of her face wore tiny eyes and a tubular nose that oozed blubber on the sulk of her lips. The softness of her fur reminded one of the Betelgeuse Star in its brightness and beauty. Her light was eye candy from space, a panorama that flowed like spice to quench the remotest need. Her song?

*At root we are leaders, helpers, destroyers. At the start of evolution, it was never on that we would check boxes to interrogate an internal question whose answer simply stalls a weightless black hole. As we search beyond the moon for what's left of an endless rain, a frenetic river smears fate into the night. The riverbed is a shadow whose shape is alternate art. It performs a hip-hop ballet that runs out of pirouettes. Our ancestors' dreams never looked like missing, but we're the wick and they are the flame. Together we burn. Encapsulated in a greater dimension that is unsightly and divine in this artificial world. You blink and it's there, then it slips into a whisper of silence—did you see?*

The amphitheater cheered in trickles, distracted by the blob and blotch snailing down the singer's face and sliming the echoes of her prose.

"It is a brave intercept," coughed the score worm. "But it's dislocated to pose a decent challenge. This means the Troika one-third is released from the sin bin."

✦ ✦ ✦

Much was at stake in the final play. The precocious Troika child made a grab for the skull and knocked down two Cyclops. It worked angles, pushing and shoving. Suddenly another player on the ground. It was a Cyclop—dislocated joint.

Nearly matched up now, the game quickly degenerated into a bloodbath. Players slipped on gelatinous fluid, an earnest struggle for the last one standing. By sheer luck, not effort, a body bang severed a Troika's jaw and she retired injured. It was the lead singer.

Unlikely that song would rescue the trinity, all understood they were condemned to the sin bin for eternity. But duty demanded righteousness in the score worm, one last call: "If the Troika have no challenge—"

"We have a challenge!"

"Let's hear it then."

The precocious child stepped forward. Her conehead, unrecovered from birth, was bald, blemished with yellows against a skinless pink. She studied the crowd, shifted from one chubby leg to another that could sprint with the velocity of light.

Her song generated weather. The amphitheater lit with two suns:

*The shadow on the wall is an unquiet memory on home ground, choked with the dreams of refugees who'd crossed lands, traveled wars in chants of darkness and light only to find a wall built of humanity's absence. How confusing their entanglement in the imperfect story of a better life that is a syncopation of deleted riffs nowhere seen. Just endless echoes of shadows in repetition.*

*Repetition.*

   *Precisely different.*

   *Ripped.*

      *Notes in the mailbox.*

         *Raped.*

The crowd look at her, silent. As the two suns dimmed, there was a roar. Encore! Encore!

"We were quick to transition," coughed the score worm, "as we evolved past lesser beings to our current states. Sometimes we must kill frail creatures for their skulls, we must kill them to balance the universe. But the human story is one that needs us the most. This child has reminded us of it. We've seen a good ball. The verdict is a draw. Release the full Troika trinity from the sin bin."

# A CASE OF SEEING

4:00 am. East Wing King George Hospital—opposite Durham Harbour. Sydney. Detective Chief Inspector Lawfer McDaniel climbs tall from an old Passat and steps into a crime scene.

A forensic analyst takes a moment to regard Lawfer. It's Tamyka: low thirties, slender face. She is wearing a navy vest inside a windcheater. "That hair, your rush to get here?"

Lawfer smiles. "Still roughly good-looking, yeah?"

"Stop fishing for compliments."

Lawfer is unprofessional in lean jeans and a long-sleeved shirt rolled up at the cuffs, unbuttoned at the neck. Unpolished leatherwork boots.

Gray fog clouds the dawn air.

Forensics crew are setting up equipment in an area enclosed with blue and white tape that reads: *DO NOT CROSS. POLICE LINE.*

Lawfer surveys the scene. She nods at two constables in spanking new uniforms gazing at a crushed body on the gravel. One of the constables returns Lawfer's nod. Low twenties, bald. His uniform is a size bigger than he needs.

"Boss." This one's face looks fresh, a kid plucked from his mum.

The other constable is fidgety.

"Ants in your pants, mate?" says Lawfer.

"Got to pee, boss." He coughs, something chesty. Wipes the tip of his nostril with a knuckle, then rubs his hands to warm them.

Lawfer restrains herself from touching the blood. She sees through touch. Sometimes the seeing is crystal clear, as if she is watching a film. Sometimes it's foggy: silhouettes. It is her gift. Or her curse. As early as she can remember.

✦ ✦ ✦

A toddler went missing. Child's mum, the woman next door, cajoled, hollered and wailed up and down the street, eyes broken, hair a jungle. "Thalia! Thali?" Clutching in her hand a teddy. Somewhere in the woman's fever, she forsook the toy. Little Lawfer had picked it up, fallen by the gate. Just then: a flash of memory—torn jeans and a T-shirt, a man wearing a jacket the color of dirty trees. Thalia's tiny palm wrapped in his fist.

Her charcoal curls, his gray mop. They vanished to the trees. No one saw Thalia again. Not alive, they didn't. The water-drenched body face down in the creek was nothing like Thalia. For days, Lawfer beat herself. She had tried. Grownups refused to listen, batted away her beseeching. Her words spiraled away to no home run. She tugged a police officer's sleeve but got no more than a tolerant smile. "Go home kid, this kind of mess—not for you." How could Lawfer tell about the man who escorted Thalia inside the tree line where the thicket swelled? Even so young, Lawfer analyzed her motives. Explaining her knowledge meant explaining the seeing: she touched a fallen teddy and saw. A gift unaccounted for, populated with hits and misses. Sometimes she saw right, sometimes just blurs. Lawfer didn't know how she did it. She just did. After the finding, she determined that she would grow up and join the force, make a smarter cop than the sleeve who found Thalia too late.

✛ ✛ ✛

Lawfer smooths the frown creasing her forehead. She takes in the crime scene. Her upper lip twitches, a staccato lift at the left edge. She pulls on gloves, lifts a shard of glass from gravel. She sees the smash. Pumpkin-like.

"One bad fall," she says.

"Just another crime scene, Lawfer," says Tamyka.

"Not when this goddamn lip tweaks. First time it did, my mother passed. Next it twitched, Glenda was gone, yeah."

"Shit happens," says Tamyka. She flicks a single long braid that falls down her shoulders to her bum. High cheekbones. Striking hazel eyes on a clean complexion. She likes Lawfer, you can tell.

Lawfer scrutinizes splinters of wood merged with more shards of glass on crimson-spattered gravel. "Blood trails tell no big tale."

"Not at first glance, no," says Tamyka.

At first touch, yes, Lawfer knows. She lifts a splinter, sees through the gloves. She staggers at the impact. It is like a hammer on her head. It is the seeing, a distant memory now: the splinter was part of violence—something hit someone. What? Who? Lawfer looks up the building.

An hour, the clean-up crew is still going. After the botch-up of Thalia, Lawfer kept believing, enough to sign up as a copper.

Now she taps the shoulder of the fresh-looking baldie. She sees a woman's face: a wasteland. The woman is related to the baldie. How? Sometimes Lawfer wishes the seeing would stop.

She says, "I remember you, constable. Always eating something. Guts don't worry you, yeah."

"Boss. Burger?"

"Please no, germs everywhere. And your name?"

"Robert Dale."

"Robbo. Missus pack that burger for you?"

"No missus yet—might wrap more than a meal if a missus did pack it. Nah, mum wrapped this up." He licks a crumb off the side of his mouth.

A dog howls in the distance.

"Crime scene snack?"

"Boss."

"Why not. Keep the bile in. Recall you chomping tacos at that shooting in Bellstown."

"Solved that quick—how do you do it?" Robbo's ocean-blue eyes below bushy brows, part silver, meet Lawfer's.

"Secret is to listen, yeah. People talk. Someone says it's a duck, it's a duck."

"Solved them all, crime sprees in Moe, Colander, Riverdale, Marsh, Kingsdale. Guns, knives, cleavers, lethal force. That guy that got necked. Reckon ducks there too, boss?"

Lawfer keeps her gaze steady. "That mouth be your downfall." Oblivious to forensic crew bustle, she puts a solid arm on Robbo's shoulder. She stands taller. "It's like this: Reckon I got you now, kid. Making you my right hand in this investigation. Top more odds. Will you, Robbo?"

"But Tank always . . ."

Lawfer raises her brow. "Tank? That roughneck can do paperwork in the cop shop in Abbey Wood. Do him some good. I'm picking you to work with me. Handpicked, yeah. Problem, Robbo?"

"Nothing major. Just . . . Why me, not him?" He nods his chin in the direction of the snotty constable back from his pee.

"Snotto there will contaminate my crime scene." Lawfer regards Robbo. "Relying on you, son. Reckon field expo will shape you."

"Reckon . . ."

"Reckon stakes are high. Less mouth kid and we get along, yeah."

"Boss." Robbo moves off, heads toward the forensics crew. Hand in pocket, Lawfer watches him go.

Lawfer scrutinizes the crime scene. She wonders at the surroundings and the possibilities. "Shit way to die, yeah."

A light mist threatens rain. It dissipates. Robbo returns. He is holding in gloved hands a crimson-stained ID card. "Says here victim is Professor William Banjo, forty-one. Brain surgeon at the hospital."

"Say why he kill himself?"

+ + +

6:13. Outside East Wing. Lawfer rubs dry eyes.

"Not much sleep?" says Robbo.

"Things not sweet, yeah. Today, as all other days." A quiet morning breeze, shifting and sporadic, worries Lawfer's hair. She surveys the gravel.

"Thoughts on it yet?" Robbo.

Lawfer straightens. "No, I won't speculate." She looks at Tamyka, shrugging off digital equipment. "Crime scene look ok?"

"All good," she says. "Glenda your dog?"

"Ex-wife. Yes."

The other forensics guy is packing bags into the back of a police van by the gate. He takes out a new kit, heads to the crime scene upstairs.

Lawfer strokes her chin. Gazes up the lofty building with rectangular blocks growing out of a central block.

"Why not just walk to a window and jump?" Lawfer asks Robbo.

"Trick question or rhetorical?"

"He jumped through glass, not a window. I say impact, and he fell through it."

As Durham Harbour begins to stir, Lawfer looks upward and sees the shadow of monstrous feet stalk the sky.

+ + +

6:24. Inside room, thirty-first floor of East Wing. The walls are gray and granular. Lawfer's gaze moves to the desk in Professor William Banjo's office.

She touches an empty glass on the desk in the main office, near a computer. She sees a happy face. The professor loved life. "Havana Club."

"How do you know?" Robbo.

"Try the smell." Lawfer points to another glass on a side table beside a pitcher of water. "Looks like our professor had a visitor, yeah." She lifts the glass. Flash: a hazy image of a man, not the victim. An earnest feeling, not violence.

Robbo seals the evidence into a plastic bag and leaves the room. He returns. "Forensics lifted two sets of prints."

"Tops, need all the help we can get," says Lawfer. "Make sure the lab hooks into those right away."

"Boss."

"Fast track."

"On it."

Lawfer examines darkened spots in sections of the broad office: dried along the table surface, a splotch on the carpet and a sprinkling along broken edges on the window where the body apparently crashed through. She feels the violence with every touch. She feels a third person. Someone else was in this room.

"A spray of luminol will sort that," says Robbo. "No blood it can't catch." He nods at the computer. "And forensics on that thing. Better visit his home."

"Kid, let me do the directing. Witnesses?"

"Deaf cleaner on the thirtieth floor. Loud colors, apron full of roses. Tried to interview her; not much English."

+ + +

7:47. The forensic crew has left. Lawfer is looking out the window down below, a long way down. She is pensive, hands in pockets. She watches a crowd gathering outside the police tape.

She turns, again inspects the room. She gazes at a wall portrait of a slender sandy-haired male with almost regal features. Posed before copious light, smiling into the distance. He holds in neat hands and with tenderness either end of a white scroll. Red ribbon on the scroll contrasts with the black of his gown. A crimson cloak loosely wraps around Banjo's shoulders beneath a jet-black mortarboard on his head.

As she moves her gaze, a newspaper clip on Banjo's desk catches her eye.

Robbo returns with coffee. He is gobbling a pink-iced donut speckled with a rainbow of sprinkles. Lawfer stays him with a raised hand. "There's an unsolved case. Pollute my crime scene, you and that donut."

"I swear, boss." Robbo holds out a gingerly balanced tray with two plastic cups on it.

Lawfer meets him at the doorway, lifts a cup and sips. She turns toward the sun rising beyond broken glass. Her gaze returns and settles on Robbo. "Get DNA on East Wing staff."

✦ ✦ ✦

8:49. Abbey Wood. Lawfer arrives alone to her workplace. Parks the Passat in a carpool near the police headquarters. Despite a bitter morning—the bite of breeze up her nostrils, its sweep in her hair—the sun is out.

Lawfer passes a woman in the driver's seat of a parked Ford oblivious to the dire morning. Two teens in hipsters and hoodies lean against a side wall, swap puffs on a ciggie. A waft of white cloud glides toward Lawfer.

She strides over to a building that has the abandoned look of an old bottle shop. Solid stone, peeling red paint. It is, in fact, an old bottle shop. A sign near the roof says so. Somebody forgot to sort that when they relocated from CBD to the suburbs. Lawfer smiles.

Chemist warehouse next door, then a barber shop and a bunch of somber, dilapidated council houses near a children's playground. Fratellino pizzeria and a news agency stand opposite. Next, a stack of unmarked shops—all empty—one with *CLOSING DOWN SALE* in white bold, then a car dealership.

The Ford starts and the woman pulls away.

Across the road, word is already out on the tabloids. Big captions. Lawfer crosses to read a news item on the paper stand outside. She steps briskly into the news agency, grabs a paper from a pile below the counter.

An Indian owner, full head of salt and pepper, regards her. "Hi Law. What you reading paper for, not catch criminals?"

"Classified's full of crims." She picks for change in her trouser pocket.

"Don't miss them two outside."

As she walks past with her paper, the hoodies refuse to meet the ice in Lawfer's gaze.

Lawfer steps into the old bottle shop. Inside, the building has seen renovations. A line of security barriers cordons off a dull interior from the public.

At the far end of the security gates is a horse-shoe desk. The guard behind it perks up at the sight of Lawfer. Short all-over curls, olive complexion. Small eyes and a big upper body.

"Still fooling druggies with that bottle shop gumbo?" says Lawfer.

The security guy laughs, his mirth rounding his chin even more. "Watch them all the time. Totter in, joints in the mouth, hunting two-penny booze and witching for something. Moments before a cop sticks them up: *You have the right to remain silent.*"

"Whacky tobacco kids, they're everywhere. Like an old woman's washing. Kids with knives, they'll stick you. Sometimes you don't want to arrest them; you just want to cock back a fist and let it fly, yeah."

She swipes her card, walks down a narrow corridor and climbs short stairs to her office.

+++

9:35. Lawfer—still in jeans but her hair combed neat. Her work boots are polished.

She strides into pathology, touches her nape. Sniffs the *eau de toilette* on her fingertips.

A plastic sheet covers a cadaver on a trolley in the middle of the room.

Senior pathologist Zea Caine is setting tools, readying for a procedure. She lays flat a scalpel on the trolley's side tray.

Nearly as tall as Lawfer, handsome with dimpled cheeks. Zea is wearing little makeup. Dressed in overalls. She has a russet crop and coffee eyes large as a deer's.

The eyes light up when they see Lawfer. "Got your message; I'm up to my ears. What's unusual about this case?"

Lawfer silently hands the newspaper, finger on the bolded caption.

Zea takes the paper in both hands and reads:

### Nobel Plummet to Catastrophe

Brain surgeon Professor William Banjo, who only a week ago was named Nobel Prize nominee for his contribution to neuroscience, was today found dead. He is believed to have leaped from the thirty-first floor of the King George Hospital, leaving behind a faculty in bewilderment.

Zea hands back the newspaper. "A Nobel Prize doesn't label one suicide-free."

"He didn't jump. You do the autopsy or not?"

They face each other.

"Not much left of the body from that height. Chat in due course."

"In due course?"

"Do the best I can." Zea lays a gentle palm on Lawfer's hand.

Lawfer tries to see the men in Zea's life. Nothing. The seeing is selective, non-optional.

"Aren't those eyes just hanging out of your head," Zea says.

"Probably stressed, yeah."

"Drink later, maybe?"

"Nh'nn."

"Can't or won't?"

Lawfer's eyes feel prickly. "Got a kid tagging along."

Zea frowns. "Constable Robert Dale isn't exactly a kid."

"I can't answer." Lawfer shakes her head. "Entire world know I got a new sidekick?"

Zea laughs. "What's wrong with that?"

"Gaaah. Gotta look after him the same, yeah. They don't teach kids nowadays how to take a bullet."

"And can you? Take a bullet?" Cool fingers on Lawfer's hand still. This time Lawfer feels the staccato of Zea's heartbeat, a pupil-dilating kind of beat.

"Last one had a name. Glenda."

"Sob story, DCI?"

"Fact."

"Someone's mending a heart."

"I'm just a fucked-up cop. I tell anyone will listen." Lawfer touches Zea's chin gently and her tone goes soft. "You got a face on you."

"But . . . ?"

Lawfer smiles. "My bullet—Glenda. She had a face too."

Lawfer strides out the door and a cold blast hits her face. Her smile dissolves in a whistling wind.

+ + +

12:05. Back in Durham Harbour, three floors above Banjo's in the east wing of the King George Hospital. Robbo gobbles down the last of a meat pie outside an office door.

"Still hungry?" Lawfer, cynical. "What's your past?"

"Nothing black, boss. I'm just eating."

"Eat your Ma yet?"

"Boss!"

Lawfer raps on a door that is ajar, pokes her head. She steps into the room. Robbo follows. Professor Syke Patterson is a worried little man trying to look tough. Well-fitted bespoke suit, his eyes the color of fresh algae.

"Got a moment, Professor?"

"No."

Patterson looks down his nose at their approach. The kind of look that tests

Lawfer's mettle. The professor has the scent of ylang-ylang, marjoram, sandalwood, jasmine and a complex floral nectar.

"May I?" Lawfer sits herself on a traditional visitor's chair of black leather and sturdy wooden frame opposite Patterson's desk. She shows her badge. "I am here to find out about a nomination."

Patterson recovers from his startle. "Are you arresting me?"

"No one's arresting anybody. Done my research, looks like Banjo was married."

"Three ex-wives."

"Like I said, done my research. You were a brain surgeon way before Banjo. You took a liking to him, quite a liking. Took him under your wing then he outdid you. You wanted him dead."

"If you're asking whether I killed him—" Patterson begins to rise.

"Sit down, professor." Lawfer reaches into a side pocket, takes out a notebook. She leafs to the middle, rips out a clean page. Slides it across to Patterson. "Ex-wives. Names, please."

Patterson scribbles.

"Last night. Where were you?"

"At home. With my wife."

Lawfer leans forward, her gaze intense, places her palms atop Patterson's hands on the desk. "She know about you and Banjo?"

A flash: crimson on Patterson's face.

13:21. Outside her office in Abbey Wood, Lawfer gives instructions. "Get a car, Robbo. Be here in five."

Robbo revs up with a white Falcon ute.

Lawfer opens the passenger door and slides in. "You see me drive a Passat? That's my car."

"That's a car from the pool. Not yours."

The Falcon travels several minutes along an improbable landscape—thermal springs and rock art—within the sprawling homestead in Saltair. A bright yellow 4WD Cheyenne is parked easy on the driveway.

A costumed maid by the doorway of Professor Patterson's house offers molecular food, sounds like *mozzarella di bufala* the way she says it, accompanied by pastries some Michelin chef might have made.

Lawfer declines. Robbo grabs a palmful.

Inside a glass cupola, Fidelis Patterson clasps Lawfer's palm a second too long. Flash: Fidelis in a curl, face down on a sofa, chin on hand. Eyes bottomless longing, or is it sorrow? But this Fidelis now greeting Lawfer smiles. Small and wan, in her late forties, speckled hair in a fringe around her face.

"Your husband, Mrs. Patterson, where was he last night?" Lawfer.

"A particular time?"

"Did he leave the house at any point?"

"Not that I recall."

"You're not sure?"

Fidelis's face, lit by orange sunshine, bears for the moment the hint of a secret before another smile dissipates it. "Course, I'm sure."

15:49. Inside Lawfer's office.

"Call up some cops, your buds, yeah. People who get things done," she tells Robbo.

"Boss?"

"Find out something on this Banjo."

A ring, Lawfer's mobile. Zea.

"Glass breakage on the window consistent with his fall," Zea says. "Injury on the body consistent with falling."

"Anything else?"

"A lump on his head, something struck him."

"Tops."

Robbo returns with lab results.

"Three sets of fibers in Banjo's clothes. One like a piece of carpet, one definitely animal hair—dog, maybe—the third is a piece of wine-red lace or chiffon."

"That all?"

"Lots of dust and black hair."

17:23. Out the window, the fading sun burns scarlet.

Three ex-wives: Rachelle Pitman. Grecian blonde with sweet dimples. Owns a pug that matches the dog hair. Channel Wheeler. Gym instructor with large, gray eyes, auburn tousle. Has a Javanese mat in her bedroom that matches the carpet fiber. Francine Will. Brisk and professional, neat boyish figure. Mauve head. Owns a cocktail chiffon with plunging neckline. Wine red.

Lawfer rubs her brows, feeling in the woods, helpless, like Thalia. "There go our clues. Bar the ebony tress."

"Fella was obviously plugging his ex-wives," Robbo says.

"Not obviously, but a possibility that cannot be eliminated. Chase those blood and computer results."

"Fast track, boss."

Lawfer contemplates. You can't get them all, the baddies, but like heck you try, yeah.

✦✦✦

Phone rings inside Lawfer's office. Robbo with lab results:

Blood samples taken from Banjo's office: not Banjo's.

Computer report on Banjo's desktop: nothing unusual. Report on Banjo's laptop at home: porn—men, women, gang bang, bondage; and multiple emails to Patterson.

DNA of swabs taken of East Wing staff at the King George Hospital eliminate all but Patterson. He matches the blood in the office.

Lawfer sits pensive, fingers a blue packet Robbo has managed to procure. Flash—suddenly Lawfer has a seeing

✦✦✦

19:18. Lawfer bursts into Patterson's office. Behind her, Robbo.

"Don't you have a home to go to, detective?" Patterson looks haggard.

"Don't you?" Lawfer tosses the blue packet across the desk. "You wrote it. The research—you bloody wrote it."

Patterson gazes at his hands.

"You were lovers," Lawfer.

"Banjo was a wonderful lover," Patterson speaks to his hands. "But he loved women too."

"What's the deal with the research?" asks Lawfer.

"I'd been working on a microchip that imitates living tissue in brain damage," says Patterson. "Emulating cellular metabolism around astrocytes. I told Banjo. I'd applied for funding, they needed referees."

"Explain the research."

"The microchip served as a neuroprotective agent, reducing toxic reaction on dead cells and emulating metabolic simulation that activated spontaneous blood flow in the inner core. This triggered recovery in working brain cells, albeit slowly. Inbuilt artificial intelligence in autosensors generating cellular growth during the recovery phase, adjusting electronic stimulation into that part of the brain to double cell cycle time."

"And Banjo stole credit?"

"He took it to the medical board unbeknownst to me. Claimed it for his. Imagine my shock when I found out he had a Nobel nomination from thieved intellectual property. Such audacity. He understood my compromise—how could I expose him? I confronted him; he said: 'You had your moment. It's not enough to lead a race; it's important to win it.' It seemed ages since I loved him. I wanted to kill him."

"Did you?"

"What do you think?"

Lawfer outstares him. "Forget DCI. Put Director in front of my name. Director of no bullshit."

Banjo broods at manicured nails.

"Tell me about the blood." Lawfer.

"Banjo, he struck me."

Lawfer touches him, suddenly it is clear. "Your nose bled. Banjo sobbed, he was sorry. He offered you rum. Then you went home, left him in his office."

"And in the morning," Patterson's voice is small, "Banjo was dead."

✦ ✦ ✦

22:45. Outside East Wing at the King George Hospital. A white half-moon with gray shadows shares few secrets against a blackened sky.

"There goes another clue," says Robbo.

Lawfer feels the way she did the night she arrived to find Glenda was not home. Lawfer threw down her jacket, put her head, then her hands, on a pillow. And flash—she saw: Glenda straining in a beard's arms. The ginger had fingers like feathers, trailing along Glenda's inner thigh. Glenda's breasts coned with need, her nipples swollen raisins eager for butter. The unseen fist that punched Lawfer's belly took her breath away, such was her shock. First there was empty, and then a swarm of angry bees in her thoughts: How? Why? Where else?

Lawfer cursed her gift that day, the knowing she would have given her life to erase.

But she has long unsheathed Glenda from the pouch in her heart where she resided too long. The kind of pouch you put someone you flew 12,425 kilometers for an Elvis look-alike to wed you in a Las Vegas chapel, whose floors are splattered with freshly picked hybrid tea roses, whose walls are columned with drag queens in sumptuous costume, whose ceilings are splashed with graffiti of baby angels, Indira Gandhi and an opal-eyed basilisk. Took Lawfer eons to whisk back to solid the scatter Glenda's betrayal put inside. And tonight ... The allure of the moon, its beauty and myth, shifts something inside. *Take a leap,* she thinks. *Damn you, Glenda.* Tonight Lawfer sees different. Glenda's shine in her head has waned.

One with Zea, what's wrong with that, yeah? They'd drink Durham dry.

As the car reverses, Lawfer spots it. Opposite East Wing, above the library, a little blinker on a camera angled toward the crime scene.

"Well, well ..."

Robbo sees it too, the CCTV. "Reckon I'm topping your odds, boss."

"Shit yeah."

✦ ✦ ✦

Lawfer touches the tape, sees it all, way before CCTV footage.

Banjo, glum in his office. The ajar door opens. A petite Asian woman in khaki uniform—an apron sprigged with a pattern of scarlet petals wrapped around her waist—enters with a vacuum cleaner.

"That's—" begins Robbo.

"The deaf cleaner," says Lawfer.

"But how—you didn't interview ..."

"An unfortunate oversight."

"Yes. Explains the dust, the black hair."

Just then, snow lines. The tape goes blank.

"Holy sh—" Robbo holds back the swear.

But Lawfer's touch has seen. She knows what happens next.

"What do you reckon?" asks Robbo.

"I reckon the cleaner whacks Banjo with the vacuum handle, breaks glass with a chair, pushes the concussed Banjo out the window."

Robbo whistles. "Some reckon. That kind of strength, be a psycho or a woman just sick of rinsing glasses?"

"Mother of a student Banjo was banging."

"That kind of motive gives you strength." Robbo looks at Lawfer. "You're just guessing, right?"

"Guessing, yeah. Or a case of seeing." Lawfer smiles. "We got a cleaner to interrogate. Not much English you said?"

# THE ENDURING

She remembers landscapes, the history of silence loud in horses wearing blankets in a lush green farm near the Yarra Valley rodeo no longer in use. Vision remembers scent, the car's "sweet lily of the valley" in a fragrance leisurely releasing from a hung freshener on the indicator stalk of a custom-made dash.

K steered with one hand and fiddled with the radio, his eyes off the road.

"What's in your head?" she asked.

He didn't answer.

The color of words was gray in the stereo on full blast as the car whipped into Wandin and its white and yellow flowers near a graffiti-walled toilet named Lost Trains.

Nothing in the mood was changed inside a community park where the car pulled up, or near the parking machine labeled *FRAGILE. NOT IN USE* and goons had wrapped it in cling wrap so it couldn't swallow coins.

The camphor-scented bar that was also a restaurant across the road hosted a waiter with the body of Apollo and a face both devils and angels would love.

Vision avoided both, the body and the face, knowing K's caliber of jealousy. She focused instead on the waiter's voice when he took their order of a flat white.

"Murderers have killed for less."

She looked up startled to have spoken her thoughts out loud on the waiter's constricted vocals, but K refused to notice.

"Are we fighting?"

He still didn't answer but his silence never left the table or the saucer or her heart—it lurked everywhere it could hurt.

Vision dipped her thoughts in K's coffee and sought for answers buried in dates and resentments in the muddied froth.

As the waiter busied himself shining glasses, a ruby-haired mermaid winked inside a framed photo of an island and a coal-dusted tower reaching for an otherworld along the wall.

+ + +

She remembers the locating.

One way is a bell miner's *tink*, sweet and musical, just before sunrise and finishing on a hiccupping note just after sunset. One way is the poet's limerence, verse upon verse in gravity and circles, black-billed gulls in smoking puddles on the burned sand waiting for the whitewash in rhyme. One way is wintering in the northern hemisphere while the patios in the south grow hot and hotter, the flies *zang* as opposed to *zing*, beating at heat until they collapse, and Vision, sunstruck in Sailor Falls, said, "I do," to an excerpt.

One way is albums and camping and everything in between that sirens warn against in songs full of rain. One way is the rumble of wind from his bum in the dead of the night, half a gallon of air condensed into fair dinkum toots. As he turns in his sleep she wonders about forever.

One way is the road to Lost Trains and locating that you're dead.

+ + +

She remembers the enduring.

His was the kind of jealousy that vomited a sizzle of green, silent as an ogre but just as mighty. It was no surprise when just days ago he reminded her: "Twenty-five years."

"What?" She lifted her eyes from the manuscript and its proofreading mark-ups, but his face was a wall.

"All gains make for nothing."

She raised her palm in exasperation, presenting him with the animation of an oak that wore the portrait of an old woman with cross tattoos on her face, each line of ink shaping a history of stumbles.

If K saw it, the portrait etched in air, he said nothing. Or perhaps he was immune to her gift of the preternatural, or was it simply to the characters in her manuscript?

In the worlds of her stories there were systems and plots to deal with green-eyed monsters, but in the world of K . . . She wondered what he saw as gains in their shared years and why they would make for nothing.

His suspiciousness of her beauty or her literary triumphs or both had the eye of an osprey spotting fish in a lake, the giant bird swooping with talons stretched, shaking water off its wings in slow motion and soaring skyward with the fish secure in its grasp, all the way to a feeding perch where a hungry beak tore into pink flesh.

Only in hindsight did she understand that twenty-five years was a milestone, the landmark of a dying, a dawning of the day he would shape out her beating heart with a kitchen knife to quell his need to possess.

+ + +

She feels the writing.

She wrote herself into the story and transported her spirit into a quokka. She did consider a selkie but rather liked the furry macropod and its ebony button nose and jolly temperament, despite the selkie's shiny seal coat and superior gentleness, let alone the advanced swimming. The quokka doggy paddled out of the manuscript, just as K finished the carving.

The critical incident response team, all sirens, arrived in a panel van blinking orange and blue. As K cradled Vision's disconnected heart somewhere on a blood-bathed floor, the quokka opened the door, shook its head at the bewildered response team and said, "He was not a mouth."

Men who rage out loud, the talkers, they are harmless. It is the silent ones . . .

But Vision was not a mouth either.

+ + +

She relives the dying.

She allowed herself to feel each slice of the blade, and was still thinking long after the response team arrived. She wondered what the team might do next, if they understood the precipitous nature of unwisdom that had already sprayed Sailor Falls in the lead-up to the new year. What with gangs raping shops and residents, lotto megadraws going unclaimed and sexual abuse scandals hitting yet more politicians, would one more slaughter make a difference? Such was the world of detachment, the response team arrived and saw and departed, without doing a thing.

She determined that, unable to keep what the team had witnessed—not the blood-soaked floor or a husband holding his wife's beating heart, but the sight in Sailor Falls of a quokka that spoke human—one siren in the incident response team might write an anonymous op-ed without getting a stint in the psych ward.

+ + +

The history of silence was loud in horses wearing blankets in the lush green farm near the Yarra Valley rodeo out in the warm rain.

Unpunished and uncuffed, K had wrapped her in a shower curtain, hauled her out the door and lowered her and a spade into the boot of his car where her blood crystallized into gemstones.

Her quokka sat next to him, riding shotgun into a wail of cicadas soaring in circles etched in daylight, bothering the landscape now quiet after the response team chased down a different emergency. Vision was not surprised when the cicadas fell aground as dogs, and they ran away barking at K's approach to the boot. She considered that they, too, were her animal spirit.

He buried her right there in Wandin and its white and yellow flowers near a graffiti-walled toilet named Lost Trains.

The end?

Not quite.

Turns out one siren in a whole team did write an op-ed.

The quokka watches K's life in monochrome inside a prison that is an eternity, the husk of him shriveled to a gnome trapped in ancient skin.

If you listen closely, you will hear a faint scratching of nails long as a Komodo dragon's on somber walls licked by a wash of tide, whispers from ashore in time after time inside a fossil tower on an island so unexpected, you'd be astonished anyone goes there.

And if you work more characters into the story, you'll find an important writ both fascinating and disturbing in the profundity of prison house faces never too disarming to distract the photographer. The shutter *clicks*, *clicks* to stir the silence unwashed in coal dust scattered over a short story with an old woman full of cross tattoos on her face, where a ruby-haired mermaid winks in the shores of what bodes inside a frame.

# FIVE-SECOND BUTTON

"A what?!"

"A five-second button," said my mother.

She pressed a pale blue object into my palm. "Your father gave you a dream. Here I go, it's a button, my gift to you. Call up favors, use them wisely."

"But—"

"The button is special. When my mother gave me mine on my nineteenth birthday, I thought I owned the world. Then I learned to be careful. The goodness it brought . . . your father . . . at a time when—" Her eyes clouded for a moment.

"I don't know, Mamma . . ."

"Flow with what happens, when it happens."

"Oh, Mamma."

"Abella, dear child. You will gain wisdom." She pressed the button with her thumb, dug it into my skin, and it vanished.

I stared, astonished. "There is no blood—"

"Questions, my child. Just your palm there now, harmless as a button. Press it and your future, whole or in part, slows down to five seconds."

"But . . ."

"Once you push the button, there's no unpushing. Remember that."

Three feet away, the rest of the family waltzed, drank fizz and ate shanks of roasted calf.

+ + +

My younger sister Amy, newly a teenager, always a tease. "Why so glum on your birthday?" she said. "It's a rave, not a funeral."

"I am thinking."

"About what?"

"Boys, boys, boys!" Jeanie, her twin, piped in.

"Keep that up and see what happens," I said.

"Must be true, so true. Abella likes *boys! boys! boys!*"

"Oh, shut it."

The twins dodged my reach as they laughed.

"Stop that racket, Jeanie, Amy!" boomed Mamma. "Whatever is happening, forget it."

"Dr. Phil here," said my brother Micky, pointing at Jeanie, "knows all about boys."

"Lennie!" Mamma, distracted already.

"Boys! Boys! Boys!" sang Amy and Jeanie.

And the hullabaloo went on. A food court in the living room. Music like a rock band come to visit. Our family, big enough for a football team in staggered age groups . . . yet I felt alone.

I thought of my button. *Your future, whole or in part, slows down to five seconds.* The future seemed a whole lot brighter than loneliness at your own party. I touched my palm and pressed.

My head swirled. Time rolled as I lifted across seas and lands.

*One second.*

+ + +

Summer was here. *La Bonne Nourriture*, an eatery sign said. Another road sign indicated I was in a town in the South of France.

My gaze beheld a gentleman's weather-beaten face. A thousand creases danced on it, and his smile went on forever, warming those wrinkles. The object of his smile caught my eye. A dainty woman in her early fifties. A silvery carpet of short hair framed her head with as much intimacy as her fingers clasped his.

*Two seconds.*

+ + +

She led him up steps to a raised floor of the outdoor restaurant toward a vacant table. As they passed, I caught the question in her soft, dimpled voice: "Where's Beau, darling?"

What he said didn't matter, just his voice: husky, reassuring.

*Three seconds.*

+ + +

I sat by myself at a table for two, drinking a glass of house red on promotion. Peals of laughter rang out somewhere in the distance. Wine flowed like a sea, ruby, gold, and white. It twinkled in polished goblets, sizzled and spat in champagne flutes. Tables away, servers ferried platters of culinary art. Food like wild rice, consommé, duck liver pate, camembert . . . in intricate flower arrangements. Chef's chop, slice, whisk and mix transformed into bouillabaisse, fresh onion soup, Marseilles sabayon, raspberry fool . . . garnished to perfection.

*Four seconds.*

✦ ✦ ✦

Laughter . . . it seemed a million years from my world within the boundaries of one small table. I yearned for a soul mate, someone who *got* me.

Rustle, a jacket whipping past, then a clatter of cutlery. I wrenched my thoughts to the present, and a face came into focus. The gentleman with the weather-beaten face had now emerged with the flawlessness of youth, with river eyes that ran deep.

"Pardon," he said. "It was my fault completely, Madame."

He retrieved the fork from my feet where the edge of his coat had brushed it from my plate. He beckoned for new cutlery.

A tinge crept to the corner of my eye. I bit my lip.

"*Ou la la,*" the young man said. "It was not my intention, Madame. I did not mean to upset you."

His commotion was clumsy. He started for the tablecloth, then a napkin from my lap, abandoned the idea and drew a crumpled handkerchief from his trouser pocket.

"*Ce n'est rien,*" I said, a tremor in my words. "Nothing at all. *Rien à voir avec vous.*" How vague it sounded. "*Choses sur mon esprit,*" I continued in poor French, and figured I'd better translate: "Things on my mind."

"Not nothing. It make you cry, Madame."

"*Je ne ai pas l'intention pour cela.*" From his baffled look, I decided to repeat: "It was not my wish to cry."

Our gazes held. His eyes softened. For a moment, I thought he would say something.

*Tell,* my heart begged.

His hand still cradled mine.

*Five seconds.*

✦ ✦ ✦

"Abella? Bella!" It was Mamma. I was back to the present.

I glanced around. I was home, laying out plates for melon puff and vanilla lush. Three feet away, the rest of the family drank, ate, bustled . . . When melon puff crusts became bullets that Lennie shot, when it crescendoed into a fight and my thoughts darkened, I pressed the button.

✦ ✦ ✦

This time I was in a room with a man, a naked man who had spring in his eyes. Fine lines on his face, features that brought out his beauty. I touched the back of his neck below the hairline.

"Silky," I said. "Soft as Kleenex."

I kissed the silk.

*One second.*

✦ ✦ ✦

Dawn through a sway of curtains into a room dimmed with pain, such pain. It shot in splinters from toe to spine, and my insides collapsed.

"It's a boy," said the midwife.

"Aviva," said the man with spring in his eyes.

*Two seconds.*

✦ ✦ ✦

He dangled from a tree. I knew at once his name was Fergal. I was sad with the knowledge that he was a man in my future, and that was all I knew.

*Should I? Could I? Would I?*

In that terrible moment, I wondered whether and how I might lift those dead eyelids to see if the dangler was my man with spring in his eyes . . .

*Three seconds.*

✦ ✦ ✦

A funeral, mine. *God, I'm dead.*

There was Amy, Jeanie, Dad, Lennie, Micky, me . . . Me! But where was Mamma?

Then I saw her behind a veil, her arms folded across her chest inside a mahogany coffin, her face gray ice. Flowers: wreaths of petunias, daffodils, jasmine.

Smells: sodium, ammonium, formaldehyde. Mother no longer bustled and bossed and loved and hollered.

She was gone.

*Four seconds.*

✛ ✛ ✛

Dad lay in bed, in a room dull with stillness. He gazed at tomb gray clouds out the window. The sky opened and it poured. The minute arm on a wall clock ticked. Purple leaves of a bougainvillea swayed with moisture above the windowsill. When drizzle stopped, and gray lifted from the cloud, a drop of rain glided down the window. Outside, a frog croaked. Then the birds: a rolling tweetie from a singing finch, a sparrow's twinkling peal . . .

*Kroo! Kroo!* soon joined the merry chirp.

By the bedside, I watched Dad.

✛ ✛ ✛

Later, when I came in with a meal tray, he was crouched by the bed, next to the lamp stand. He rocked, sang to himself. His voice was withered.

Suddenly, I felt tired. The space in Dad's eyes, lackluster eyes with no curiosity, told me that wherever my father was, I could never reach it.

*Five seconds.*

✛ ✛ ✛

*Tap, tap.* I was home. Right here. Now. Away from those dreadful years, that terrible future rolled inside five seconds. What had taken me there? The darkness in my thoughts on the button press? It didn't matter, I was gone from that godforsaken world. I was back in the present.

"Got a minute?" Dad poked his head round the door. "What's this?"

I pressed my wet face to his chest.

After he left, I looked at the dial of my watch. Five hours had passed since my mother pressed that goddamn button into my palm. Five! Was there time to undo that sordid future? In that instant I determined I would set out to find the man of river eyes who had cradled my hand.

*Press.*

✛ ✛ ✛

As if reading my mind, the button faithfully delivered me to France. And there he was, right there, in the restaurant where wine flowed like a sea. He sat two tables away opposite the woman with a honey voice and the man with a thousand wrinkles.

I sat at a table.

A girl with big lashes, big shorts and braces in her teeth took my order of veal and house red. I looked at the older man's shoulder, its honesty and straightness. The younger man, the one of river eyes, had the same honesty and straightness in his shoulder. He was watching me. When I caught his glance again, the puckering of a smile told me we had already met. I had arrived to the future a moment after he clattered my cutlery and cradled my hand.

How could I change this future now?

When I looked up, the older man and the woman, and the man with river eyes . . . they were gone. I signaled for the bill.

The girl bobbed over, a curious look on her face. She placed before me a saucer with a folded note.

"Your bill, Madame," she said. "It has been paid."

I opened his note, and read his lines:

*This feeling of déjà vu—roaches, doves, or wolves? Perhaps two quails in the wild, soaring to the moon. Beau*

And a telephone number.

+ + +

*Call up favors, use them wisely*, Mamma had said. That night in a motel, I called up Dad's birthday gift. The dream he gave me for my birthday:

*I was in the garden, chasing rain with a man like my father—it was him, yet it wasn't. Water pelted against our faces as we laughed and splashed about with bare feet. My father lifted me to his shoulder and swirled me around. A little boy about my age, two or three years old, waved from the distance. "Come," I called out. Wind carried my words above the rain, chased by a stroke of lightning. The boy smiled. He spread fingers through his hair, pushed water from it. He ran toward us just as darkness swallowed him.*

+ + +

The next day, I lifted the receiver.

"I knew you would call," he said.

"You don't know my name."

"But you will tell me."

"Abella."

"It mean breath in French."

We dined at *La Bonne Nourriture*. His smile caused my heart to flutter, pounding harder every third beat.

We dined the following night and the next. The harmony in our togetherness, in our friendship, in our desire . . . it was more than chance. Was this a parallel universe?

Suddenly I had to know. I wanted to see our future—was it a wedding, kids, Beau and me growing old and stupid together? I slipped my hands under the table and pressed the button.

+ + +

My head swirled. Time rolled ahead: One second. Five minutes. Ten. Three hours. Thursday night. And time stopped—not a lifetime or years ahead, just two nights away . . .

+ + +

I opened my eyes in the future. We were at the restaurant.

"The haunting in your eyes," he said in the glow of dimmed restaurant light. "It comes and goes."

I reached for his hand.

*One second.*

+ + +

"Even me," he said. "Sometimes I was haunting."

"What are you saying?"

"My mother, she go with my baby sister. *Poof!*"

"Where did they go?"

"*Ma cherie*, I was a boy," he replied. "My father, he tell me they die."

"Do you remember the funeral?"

"He protect me. My father."

I squeezed his hand. "You sad boy."

"My father, he marry, no more sad."

I thought of the woman with silvery hair and the honey in her voice as she eased a forelock from his face with the intimacy of a mother's touch.

"She loves you," I said. "Very much."

"She has enough love for two." He held me in a searching gaze. "For three, yes?"

*Two seconds.*

+ + +

Outside the restaurant, he kissed my throat.

"I like when you smile," he whispered to my hair. "The light in your eyes."

A clap of thunder sliced the air. Sheets of rain fell upon us, cold, hard rain. Droplets filled the space between us and the car. We ran holding hands then shivered a few minutes as the car heater kicked off.

*Three seconds.*

+ + +

Beau ran his fingers through his hair, pushing water from it. "I have a picture," he said.

"Of what?"

"My mother, my sister."

He pulled a box from the glovebox and took off its lid. He unwrapped a black and white photo from soft tissue. I looked at the sweetly posed mother and child, and my heart fluttered. I put my face in my hands.

*"Mon dieu,* what is this?"

"The woman in the picture, she's your mother?"

"Yes—"

"She's my mother, too!" I hiccupped in his chest.

*Four seconds.*

+ + +

The boy in the dream . . . Fate had found us. The light in his father's smile, the magnetism that drew me at a restaurant the first time I saw him, his was a countenance immortalized by a dream. Dad was not my real father.

My grief fed into a great and sudden anger.

*Five seconds.*

+ + +

Beau squeezed my hand across the table, smiling at me.

"Abella?"

*The present! God. I'm back in the present. His present.*

My distant eyes hauled from the future. Softness of dimmed lights and a flickering lamp touched Beau's face. I looked at him and saw him anew. Beau. How could Beau, this Beau, be my sibling? What did Dad know when he gave me a dream? What did Mamma know when she gave me the button for my birthday?

"Something you don't like *ma cherie*? On my face?"

"Oh Beau, I'm sorry."

"So deep you travel. What is this faraway place?"

"There's no such place."

Outside, he drew me into his arms. I nestled into his embrace.

"I like when you smile," he whispered to my hair.

"Come," I tugged his arm."

Beau could never know. At any rate, he would never know. Not from me, he wouldn't.

"Come on," I said.

"To where?"

"Doesn't matter." Briefly, I wondered about my other world, the one of bustle with Amy, Jeanie, Dad, Lennie, Micky and Mamma. I shook the thought, caring for the moment, now was now, later I would ponder the rest. And a future that had changed.

I steered Beau away from his car and its glovebox. Rain came down like a monsoon. We ran.

"There," I pointed. Tepid water raced down my lips. "See those lights? It's a motel."

And our feet splashed in the rain.

Away, away . . .

# DIMINY: CONCEPTION, ARTICULATION AND SUBSEQUENT DEVELOPMENT

*Londinium. 1905 AD.*

"Better be good," Professor John Bates thought aloud.

One hand rested on the brass clutch of his new Edwardian mobilis, open roofed and one of 250 automobiles of this brand in high Londinium society, and the entire universe. And though the "vanishing principle" of travel that the cosmic beings applied was faster, allowing a sweep of vast distances in half a pulse, the mobilis was fashionable this summer.

John Bates's hand tapped a staccato on a stick handle that served both as a steer and propeller pump. A single-horse carriage aligned itself to his left. Automobile and stallion waited for a lollipop man herding a group of students three-boys thick along the school crossing.

Watching them, Bates recalled his own youth. From his mother's worrisome eyes to his father's speckled mustache. His Pa's somber eyes could harden into cobalt icicles that promised nothing but a rod that lay at the top of a chiffonier; a polished cane with "John Varon Bates" engraved upon it. Bates smiled. A stick with a child's name. "Each punishment executed," his father said between strokes, "is an act of love." When that act was due, Bates had to himself stand upon a stool, stretch and blindly pat until he touched and retrieved the very instrument of love. And, as his mother watched with broken eyes, he would take the gleaming cane to his father. A single nod would permit the pulling down of shorts, and a bending across a chair, desk or bed for chastisement. And so Bates had always wanted to be a mentor, the caliber of teacher his father wasn't. Unlike Pa, Bates saw promise in young folk. But there was one young chap . . . !

As he chug-chugged along, Bates shook the troubling thought and instead considered wheels. He contemplated other advanced combustion engines already on advertisement but not distribution, and dismissed them. The mobilis was doing fine. He had neither intent nor purse to replace it.

Perhaps, with accolades for his next article, "Arousal and Instruction of Infantile Minds toward a Path of Greatness," funding would accompany universal acknowledgment of his intellect, and Bates might allow a trifle indulgence on a newer car. As for now, rather grave matters in the West End commanded his utmost attention.

Unfortunately, those matters pertained to Freudo Brio: the young man who worried him. Bates should have known the student was trouble the moment he stepped into King's College clasping papers that flew from his hands, armpits, teeth. Jungle eyes, flustered hair and matchstick legs under handmade trousers. Students snickered when he approached, called him "Gawk," "Gangly" or "Clod." They booed—until he started asking questions. His arguments left fellow students astounded to silence, and lecturers floundering for words. He graduated seemingly in months (or was it days?) and set about stunning the scientific world with his novel, usually irrevocable findings.

Not only had Freudo's latest experiments proved Bates's theorem of Cognitive Antecedent wrong (and how skillfully done!): the batty young man had now summoned him for a trifle display. Demonstration or not, today Bates had it measured. He was going to wrap up the young enthusiast and package him to his rightful place.

He parked off New Oxford Street, near its intersection with Charing Cross, about the same time that a young female in a summer dress climbed out of a carriage. He stepped out of the mobilis and pulled a monocle from his side pocket. He surveyed a mold of dress that mocked the tiers, drapes, frills and trains of the time. Ocean green in color, a pattern of water swirls hugged close a nipped-in waist without corset, the element of style both flattering and youthful.

The garment was a true headliner if not a scandal. Not that Bates thought so; to the contrary. But many a citizen would raise more than a brow contemplating it.

The woman looked exquisite and chic in that ankle-length piece; a rather ostentatious number that set his mind roaming. He felt a melt in his mouth as all exclamation evaporated and he could nought but gawp. The simplicity of that dress, the sophistication of its outcome . . . Minimal drapery; silver buttoned shoes, three inch; a choker of pearls on her neck, and the creamiest ankles he had ever seen—the sight was enough to stall a war. The female was almost ethereal, something delicate made in the stars. Behold! Here she was now, recreating the very beginning of him.

Camellias, hellebores and cyclamens invaded his nostrils.

Crack! Crack! heels down the pavement. Hips drawn back, bosom thrust forward, she switched away under a sapphire sky and a tease of breeze. Crack! Crack! Swagger. Sway. Must have diamonds in those soles, Bates was sure. He stood by the roadside, much distracted, until the hourglass vanished round the corner, parasol, plumed hat and all.

Inside the Science Clinic tucked in an offshoot of Tottenham Court Road, in a laboratory that was the largest in Londinium, young Freudo was bent at his desk, poring over paper and a fast-moving pen.

"I'm a busy man," said Bates.

"What?" Freudo Brio. "Ah, yes! Professor! Marvelous, marvelous!"

Bates determined that Freudo's madness was twice grown compared to last they met. He untangled himself from Freudo's embrace, uncoiled the younger man's hands from his waist and retrieved his fallen hat.

"You have an experiment to demonstrate?" He brushed his lapels.

"Course! Of course. Yes, Professor, I understand your commitments. But this . . . !" Freudo moved to clasp Bates's hand and found space, for Professor had without hesitation tucked it into his waistcoat pocket.

"I would rather you expounded the idea to me first, Freudo."

"Oh, my, yes. Good, good. I can't wait to show you my findings."

"Being . . . ?"

"Relating to your motivation theorem."

"I wrote a few papers. Which, pray, do you refer to now?"

"Eh? Ah yes. Persistent Behavior, sir. A gem for sure."

"And you have come up with an opposing theorem." Bates stated, not queried.

"Inverted Motivation, good sir. You made a supposition that response to persistent stimuli, complex or otherwise, is proportional to operant conditioning. Good, good. But an episode, yes, a little trouble, that's all, in the laboratory, questioned this analogous principle of ecological or other influences—"

"Show me."

"What's that? Ah, yes. The experiment. Come with me, Professor. Do."

✦ ✦ ✦

The laboratory, as Bates remembered it from a visit before his retirement, had contained a practical tally of gadgets. Now, chamber after chamber bespoke psychosis, spilled with equipment Freudo referred to as transmitters, transponders (or was it transgressors?). Wildness, not control, ruled the lab. Rooms held human subjects exposed to various stimulants: alternation of volcanic roar to distant purrs that slipped away; bold wealth in the form of modular furnishings in gold or velvet to bone-hard scarcity; tropical rain, lightning and thunder to blanched sand under blistering heart; amputee trees with gnarled waists alongside fat, healthy ones pregnant with fruit . . . something in a glass compartment wobbled like consommé jelly.

One experiment fed to another, rooms large as stadiums. Bates was not eager to ask how the earthlings were got; more than a rumor indicated human snatchings from Earth. The developing cells of humanoids made them adequate if not perfect candidates for trialing new concepts.

Bates pointed at two females in what looked like a field. One girl warmed up on the track, as if readying for a race. The other huddled to the ground with pulled knees.

"Prison camp did this?" he observed in disapproval, especially of the condition of the bony lass.

"Ah. Eh. These earthlings have been subjected to the same diet, environment and external conditioning as near as possible. But they have each experienced different motivational spurs."

"Spurs?"

Freudo turned a key in the lock. "Eh? Yes, yes. The stimulus is implied. Perceived. Come, come." The door snapped open. He pushed Bates into the room, led him to a podium with a view to the track.

"That is Ego," Freudo pointed at the girl built like a Spartan. "Vabe," he indicated the latter who was malnourished, raggedy as cured salami. "Each subject is conditioned to respond to exact external stimuli but each carries different perception implants that we turn on and off. Vabe's metabolism is adversely affected by the stimulus of the most recent trial but that is a temporary adjustment, a pure matter of tissue reload easily remedied."

He leaned forward with head gear, goggles and ear plugs.

"Put these on for me, will you now, Professor?" Freudo fastened the apparatus. "Now, we're going to watch a race."

Freudo pressed a button. A horn sounded in the field. It was a stimulus that both Ego and Vabe immediately responded to, albeit in different fashion: Ego burst to the starting point, muscles rippling in anticipation. Vabe, a wimpy thing in big shorts, faltered every two steps to the line.

Bates, in exasperation, fumbled for his pipe.

"Not here, Professor. Please don't smoke in my lab. The atmosphere's controlled. Everything in this experiment bar you and me is controlled." He spot-checked his equipment.

Bates leaned back and spread his legs, resigned for the talent drop to amaze him. He pried loose from his thoughts the woman with a sheath dress and dramatic heels.

"On your marks!" chimed an automat in the air. The girls responded. "Get ready!" *Bo-wow!* The sound of a starting gun.

Ego exploded from her blocks. Vabe twitched, climbed to her feet and careened. She toddled like a person without control of motion. Ego was already round the east bend and Vabe had barely made two steps.

Freudo flicked another switch. "Internal stimulus increase by 170 percent."

Ego flew on a new gear. Vabe's limbs grew more uneven: arms wilder, legs ever more desperate. Shoulders drooped, then dragged. Her face drew closer to the ground.

"She looks just about to collapse," observed Bates. "You had better stop this experiment."

Click! Another switch. "The stimulus is above threshold now," Freudo proclaimed.

Ego, now three-quarters of the way down the track, staggered and appeared to slow. Vabe, in turn, lifted from her stoop. Her shoulders broadened, strengthened. The arc of her back went straight. With a new pump of arms, her stride lengthened. She flew down the track, zapped north past Ego and lifted the finish ribbon with her chest.

Bates sat upright, eye straining through the monocle. "That is—!"

"Motivation," said Freudo.

"Please explain," said Bates.

"To do so, I must first demonstrate the girls' stimuli."

Freudo flicked a switch. "This is Ego's stimulus," he said.

Bates found himself viewing a crowd that filled the stands to bursting.

"Go Champ! Ego!" they cried. "Ego! Ego! Champ! Champ! Ego!"

"And this is Vabe's stimulus," said Freudo.

The same crowd but it hollered: "Boo-woo! Boo-woo!" Rotten eggs flew down the stands. "Boo-woo!"

Bates lifted his goggles. "Very well," He said at length. "It's obvious to me what you've done, you switched stimuli, haven't you? Ego got the rotten eggs and Vabe the cries of Champ. Negativity blanks motivation." He smiled. "Nothing is new in that theorem. I wrote it, swelled it, notarized it. The one and only thing that amazes me is the miraculous recovery of Vabe's muscle tissue. Is it some metaphysical construct arising out of a refreshed mental state? I had miscalculated the supremacy of motivation."

"Sir, if I may. The amplified stimuli are not a reversal but the very same that each individual was already subject to."

Bates swallowed. "I do not understand."

"The mind is complex, amorphous as an opal. Easily ruined without nurture. One can flirt with it but not fully control it. Amplified stimuli on preconditioned operants result in mental disintegration of those very stimuli; the mind can grow muscles of its own to produce an effect that heartens survival."

Bates sagged. "Please explain."

"Eh? Good." Freudo rubbed his palms. "Any faster, Ego would have died. Her body is not yet equipped for that degree of velocity. Any slower, Vabe would have collapsed. Her mind is not yet accommodated to that level of rejection." He paused. "What you have witnessed is the application of inverted U-shaped behavior. The individual can respond to increasing complex stimuli to a point. By augmenting that trigger to above threshold, an inverse reaction occurs to decrease operant conditioning and produce an opposite effect."

Staggered, Bates fell out of Tottenham Court Road, faltered like a drunk all the way to New Oxford Street and threw himself into his mobilis. He took toward the Thames along Victoria Embankment and chug-chugged all the way past the docklands. Riding home under a darkening sky, John Bates acknowledged that the young scientist was more than a showman. The prat had once more disproved him with experiment.

Bates turned, wheels bouncing, off the main road into a dirt path. He headed in a ride of wind toward his farm in Greenwich. The sky roared and broke loose. The mobilis hopped in an increase of speed as the first eastern droplets chased its progress.

Damn Freudo, he cursed. Damn, damn you!

Thunder bellowed. An orange stick of lightning broke into a zigzag. Bates thrust his thoughts from Freudo and focused on his wife Mabel. She would by now be worrying for him. Or perhaps trussing yet another of her pies that did little to narrow a waistline once needle thin inside a bunching of bustle and soft fullness of garment.

He thought of a thigh-skimming skirt crackling with movement. High inch heels that carried a woman's walk as she swayed, swayed in his head. John Bates would do well in his next life to come half a century later and leave the darn enthusiast of a Freudo to neurotic trials on proven principles as ancient as Rome. Bates had met his match in the young maverick. What Bates needed was a leap into the future, into a career change. Perhaps he could, instead, slip into fashion. He would invent thigh-grazing style, something diminutive, a micro skirt that accommodated a gleeful cha-cha of hips and long, long legs that vanished into steep, ivory boots. Oh, behave!

Diminy. He smiled. He would call it a diminy. He closed his eyes and imagined a black, black dress and kitten heels. Bared midriff and climbing hem. Click! Click! The music of seven-inch heels danced in his head.

Clippety-click! Click! Click! Clippety-click! He did not anticipate the towering chariot that slammed into the Edwardian mobilis. Nor did he imagine the shot of pain that carried him to a dark eddy of cloud and white, white stars.

✦ ✦ ✦

He swirled. A bout of exhaustion caught him. Inside shadows, he heard a voice, one ever so familiar. *Finest, finest, finest*... Freudo was saying within the labyrinth. *Mind... mind... mind.* Bates allowed the cloud to float him. *Rare, rare, rare...*

Freudo's words faded, leaving Bates with white pain and blinking stars. He tried to isolate the pain, to understand it. But the ache pulsed, and he was not sure what part of his body was broken. His awareness coasted into a burst of luminosity that compelled him to reflect upon beautiful things. *Cha-cha! Cha-cha!* a woman's walk. He was still pondering the movement of hips in a miniskirt above long, long legs when he opened his eyes to a burst of light.

He panicked. Was he in an alternate world? Part of an experiment? Had Freudo set him up? The chariot... was it Freudo's doing? His alarm grew. Was he, Bates, dead?

"Sir," the face of a girl leaned toward him. Starched cape. White collar. Brown eyes regarded him. She looked human.

"How are you feeling?"

"Is he awake?" another voice in the distance.

"Yes, doctor."

"Sir," sweet brown eyes. "Do you remember your name?"

"Bates," he said.

"Weights?"

"Bates."

A man in white, the doctor, approached. He was young. Familiar jungle eyes and flustered hair.

"Eh. Ah yes. Good, good, for sure. My name is Dr. Brio."

"Fwodo?"

"Oh, my, yes. Your head injuries are affecting your speech. But you know my name?" He looked at the nurse.

"Sci... Kinic... Fury." The doctor's gaze was baffled. Bates gave up. Nothing he said was sounding like science, clinic or theory. But one thing was clear: this *was* an alternate universe. Perhaps the collision had opened a doorway to another realm.

The doctor leaned forward. "Who are you, my good fellow?"

Bates's smile hurt. He wanted to say, "I am the distinguished Professor Bates." But his mind was swamped with *Cha-cha! Cha-cha!* a woman's walk. A miniskirt above long, long legs. His mind soared with purpose, a newfound passion. Yes. He would name the garment a diminy. No more would Freudo Brio—not even the one of this world—collapse his theories. So instead he said, "My name is John Bates."

"Weights," the girl again.

Bates tried to sit up.

"Dear fellow, please," the doctor.

"My name is John Bates," firmly. "Inventor of the diminy."

"Wiminy, sir?" the girl.

"A fashion statement," said Bates.

# MAHUIKA

She fell from the sky, a daughter of the sun. She was many forms, how fiery. In Phoenicia, she wore a flame of feathers and lived as a phoenix. In Persia, the thunderbird built a nest and burst into fire and regenerated as a cosmic serpent. In West Africa, she was first a leopard and then a goldsmith who forged an iron sword for the Fon people, before she destroyed the divine tool in a blaze. In Greece, she found logic in the bed of Apollo, and then illogic that caused her to make fire in a sacred place that was the Oracle of Delphi—it melted. In her fifth birthing, she took the form of a human, and found a website.

Scorcher sat behind the wheel on Coral Bay along the peninsula. Winding roads swept past Kauri trees and kopi, and toppled toward the coastline. You faced out the window, silent, as the car juddered after a van with a sign: *How's my driving? Call 0800 BE AFRAID.*

*Basque*—her online handle. No spas, massages, spooning or watching DVDs on the couch. She adored sunlit beaches, a hearty laugh. She sought someone who didn't stress the small things, her profile. She didn't ask what you were wearing within nine seconds of your instant chat. There she was, a brand-new someone in blonde shades gazing at you right there on your screen. She was hotter than your ex. A whole day eyeing your cell phone, Beethoven's Fifth: the arrival of her text.

On Little River Bay you sank bare feet through the opulent gold of hot, wet sand. Sweat made silhouettes of the contours of Scorcher's skimpy undies and her braless torso through her ankle-length sarong, enveloped by shimmering air. She was *Mahuika*, your fire goddess. Her fecund laugh accompanied malevolent surf that washed you toe to crown. You tried swimming in a humping sea but the water's resistance, the mercury in your shoulder, the mallet in your head . . . it was a swim through a rock. Ashore, one look at Scorcher and your sun shone through her eyes. Life without her didn't bear thinking.

✦✦✦

But her temper! First time she roared, a pillow away, a boulder entered your stomach, and cuddled. You stared at the roar like it was a stray animal, a jackal or a serpent, wilderness sprung into your world. You gazed at the night long after the roaring. You questioned "in sickness and in health," asked yourself over if you were ready. You understood, with her, you didn't know what you were getting. As your mind formed the right answers, Scorcher laid her head on your chest, shone stars through her eyes.

✦✦✦

Moon—a powerful arbiter of relationships. The astrocenter assured compatibility. There you were, two water-signs in the Western horoscope: Scorpio and Pisces. In touch with your feelings. The Chinese zodiac told the story different. Scorcher was a fire tiger, her personality intense. You were an earth monkey, your nature playful. Your witty barbs speared the delicate ego of a tiger. Yet within your cosmic elements it was an affinity relationship: fire generates earth. You listened to your soul and behaved young again.

✦✦✦

Her rage! Second time she roared, you stayed away three nights, five hours, thirty-six minutes and one second. Rewiring put such rapture in your body, it was minimizing to think of it as a melt in your thighs and your buttocks and your big toes, but you did.

✦✦✦

On the way to Track Bay in a ferry, you watched as sweltering wind whipped Scorcher's sand-speckled hair. You walked hand in hand a mile down the cliff and gathered oysters, scallops, mussels and pipi—bleached as Scorcher's hair, fair as her eyes. Later you wore towels around your waists, wolfed eggplant chips with the shellfish at the terrace bar with pohutukawa trees, pheasants and tui in bush clad hills out yonder.

✦ ✦ ✦

Her vicious! Third time she roared, on a narrow and twisty road, her unreachability made you ravenous.

But you said, "Stop the car. Put me on a beach."

"Your best work right here," she said.

Tears stuck in your eyes as you walked barefoot with mercury rising, the sand heating. You were like a cat on a tin roof when Scorcher chased after you, promised stars with her eyes.

Soot in your heart, you kept walking. You wondered how it was that she burned everything she touched. Out in the horizon the *cheet cheet* of a piwak-awaka; no sight of the bird anywhere.

# BEING MARCUS

*This was no ordinary crime, nor one of small scope. It was committed unexpectedly against a friend; ungratefully against a benefactor who had shown mercy after a war; lawlessly against a sovereign; in a senate chamber; against a pontiff wearing his priestly garb; against a ruler who was unique and useful beyond all men to his country and its empire.* —*Appian,* The Civil Wars, Book 4, section 134 (cited in Lewis 1983, 58)

*Ting!* A visitor's bell chimes.

Marcus lifts his head from behind the shelf, from stacking flyers warm still from the printer. The pamphlets announce new membership rates at Fitness Studio.

"Do you do stretch classes?" a brunette asks across the counter.

"Yes." He watches her without interest or dislike.

"How much?" She blows a perfect pink bubble with her gum. "For the classes?"

Silently he slides a leaflet across the chipped wood.

"Boxing," she reads, manicured finger on the line. "I want to do boxing. And Pilates. Do you do personal training?"

He looks at her, wordless.

"Here it is," she laughs. "When can I start?"

"Now if it suits you."

She is taken aback. "It's not like I'm fat-fat but Shannon—my partner—she thinks . . ."

She yap yap yaps about her need for body shaping, reasoning aloud with her conscience why she should do it. Fingers her hair as she yaps, until Marcus cuts into her self-dialogue:

"Discuss with Shannon, see what she likes."

*Ting!*

Marcus considers the new one. She is flustered by his beauty. Men and women melt like snow to its fire, forever enslaved by his splendor. Like Claudia Pulchra, his first wife.

She lit up like a diamond the first time he stepped into her father's court-yard . . . Allowed his fingers upon her flawless cheekbone, did not protest when those fingers slipped the belt off her sleeveless *tunica* to find the coolness of her thigh. She followed him unbidden to his house, loosened the straps of her leather *sandalia* (such perfect toes, she had), kicked off those thongs that knew no dust and curled, feet tucked, on his bed. She would not think to return home and so, to dignify her name, he wed her. But she contaminated him with her jealousy, tart like maderized wine the moment his eyes set upon another woman. Her beauty dulled and all he saw was a shrew. When he jilted her for youth, desirable as it was flawless, in the face of Portia Cartonis, the daughter of Uncle Cato, Claudia went mad.

"I, um . . . . You do fitness evaluation?" the new one says.

He hands her a flyer.

She enrolls for assessment and dietary planning. When she trundles out, he does not return to arranging leaflets. That one needs more than evaluation and planning, he thinks. What she needs is a cuddle bunny.

He sighs. He's not on a good day today. Reminiscing has squandered any goodwill he has. Today, he does not bear the persona of Marcus, the fine gym instructor. He feels like Brutus. And most Brutuses he's come across in this world are canine. "Here, Brutus! Fetch!"

So today Marcus feels like a dog. Same one that bit the hand off its adoring master. Same one that joined the inner circle centuries ago in a conspiracy that shore an empire of its hero. Caesar was a god. He could have saved himself. Almost did too. With a single sword, he could have taken them all, sliced their treacherous hearts one by one. But the moment he saw Brutus approaching with a dagger, "You too, child?" he said, and covered his face. Heartbroken and resigned.

But Marcus is changed. He is not Brutus anymore. After Caesar's death, he traveled from Crete to Philippi. Torn with guilt and defeat, he fell on his sword and gave himself up to the spirits of his gods.

He smiles wryly.

Fate tricked him. Of all the immortals to attend his dying ground, it was Caesar who came, regal in his toga. Not his favorite white *candida* that symbolized purity of intention, but an all-lilac *sagum* cloak, a symbol of war embroidered with gold. As dying Brutus writhed, impaled on his own weapon, Caesar stood tall and handsome, a resplendent general of the new world, the ghost of a true emperor. He took a step toward his betrayer and Brutus cringed.

He understood that Caesar was not there to grant pardon and otherworldly amnesty to his once beloved, as he had forgiven him when Brutus made enemy alliance in that civil war between Pompey and Caesar, the Battle of Pharsalus. With Pompey crushed and Brutus cornered, Caesar gave notice to his officers not to harm Brutus. Not only did the emperor immediately forgive Brutus's perfidy: he invited him into his inner circle and made him governor of Gaul, and then *praetor*. Never before had Rome seen such affection. But the face that Caesar covered with a toga as Brutus and his cohorts committed murder was now intolerant.

"I believed you with all my heart . . ." His voice trailed off. "Who rinsed the blood off my cloak?" He smiled sadly. "Not you, Brutus."

He stood there dazzling, as he had that last *Saturnalia* festival before his death when drunken crowds paraded the streets of Rome, and there was feasting fit to burst. Wild fruit. Suckling *porcius-pocus*. Cress, mallows, ducks and pigeons . . . fresh heart, liver and lungs from calves at the sacrificial altar—all poppy seed-, anise-, mustard- and fennel-marinated, of course. Cranes, grouse, partridge, snipe and woodcock. New fruits too: apricots, pomegranates, peaches and cherries. Wheat bread, rye rice, ewe's cheese and curds! *Mulsum* wine, apple cider . . . So much wine, new and old. An orgy of dining. Caesar had sat with members of the senate in their crisp white toga *virilis* and purple sashes, sprawled in the raised area, partaking in jollity, inebriated eyes shining like pearls. And Rome was exposed in all its glory . . .

But on the day of Brutus's judgment, Caesar came without scroll or senate to declare verdict.

"You demean yourself, dear Brutus," he said almost gently, "attempting suicide like this. But death for you, my friend, is not an option. You will live forever," eyes sad, "in the shadow of my name."

And Brutus did live forever. He found himself not dead but filled with youth and eternity. Ashamed of his past, he traveled the worlds as Marcus, boundless centuries of world after world, from one galaxy to another, finding no peace.

A shadow . . . If anyone spoke his name, it was in the same sentence as Caesar. Never just Brutus. They came up with ways to remember the emperor: Caesar salad, cesarean operations. Brutusean? Unheard of. Brutus salad? Laughable. Even the Germans had their Kaiser, never a Brutuser. Men spoke great things of Caesar; of Brutus they studied only his shameful betrayal. Shakespeare wrote a play; it was not about Brutus. Master novelist, Dante, wrote a book; the only Brutus it portrayed was one being chewed by Satan at the vilest point of Hell. Along with Judas Iscariot. Never consumed, no—that was too light a sentence. Eternally chewed . . . Caesar's right-hand man: that gent was forgotten. History forgot the real Brutus, the soldier who fought alongside Caesar to transform a Republic into an empire: great battles fought and won from Alexandria to Tiber to Ponstus to Thapsus.

Fifty-seven times, tired of wandering aimless, a half-damned soul, Marcus plummeted down to Earth, shed his wings and pulled out his feet.

He lived simply, settled. Picked up women and saw them blossom. But none of those women possessed the beauty and quiet strength of Portia, his wife in the days of the Empire, the one who would have breathed her last for him but didn't. Couldn't, because he was a renegade on a woodland hill when he came face-to-face with dying. Not that death took him.

Afterward, plagued by the curse of timeless living, he knew that he could never go back to Portia. That going back would mean adoring her freely and without fear, and then suddenly watch her age, wither and die. Frankly, he didn't want to bring himself to experience that. He loved her, Portia. Too much. Fifty-seven times, when he succumbed to coupling need, he had no difficulty finding it. A lovely woman opened up like a lily to his charm, letting him love her, a handful of years of bliss. He always ended up watching her, and then one by one her offspring, grow old and die. Each instance of a loved one's demise brought with it a new, sharp dagger to penetrate the cusp of his heart, the ache infinite. So he vowed solitude. To never get close to a woman because she would die and leave him clasping in two hands the wreckage of his heart.

Although he was astute about commerce, the means by which he amassed wealth in Cyprus before returning to the Empire to join the senate in those days long past, he understood that one cannot teach an old dog new tricks. He was nostalgic for the wealth of the Empire: the gold, the pearls, the amethysts on walls, furnishings, togas and Flavian-styled hair. Patrician antiquity and luxury that, next to birthright, defined people and their place in society.

Now he trains people to fight their demons. For most of them it is weight. But others simply need balance and stability. For the lonely, he suggests yoga, a team sport. Or fitness boxing, a contact sport. He is Spartan in weight resistance training, body shaping regimes. Faultless in the diets he prescribes; rigid in the discipline he enforces. He doesn't know how long he will stay in this world until his mind sets roaming way before his feet, and wanderlust yet again takes hold of him. But right now, he makes soldiers of people.

A young female comes to the counter holding an exercise mat. He remembers her name. Jade. Matches her eyes.

"Hi," she smiles. Sea green eyes, calm. Amber hair, dyed. There's a softness in her poise, the way she tilts her chin for him.

"Early today," he says. "Yoga class starts in ten."

"I'll just warm up," she says.

She is dressed in tank top and hot shorts, not the ballet chemise and three-quarter flare pants of yesterday. Her body is feminine, toned: belly six-pack, tiered. He imagines her in a silk *tunica*. A plunging neckline caressing her breasts, running downward to meet a waist sash; Venus hair finely woven with gold wire; chandelier earrings, gold anklets, pearl brooches merrily singing as she walks; slaves fanning her with peacock feathers . . .

How stunning she would have been in the days of the Empire.

Yesterday during yoga, she sank on her knees and spread her palms. Her toes turned and her heels gradually lifted away from the floor. Watching her, Marcus felt a shadow of the urge, the yen to be with a woman again. To feel once more like a man, to swell and spread until he swallowed her cry of pleasure with his lips. He thought about it, how he might make her soft and receptive; slip in and out of her in ways to tease her, heighten her pleasure; impregnate her even.

He's been with other women before, so why not now? he questioned himself, as she reposed on her mat, right leg parallel to the line of her torso.

He is a superior lover, he knows. But he also knows that, while he can elicit response, he can never himself feel that expansion, that conflagration of the loins that explodes into a musical fugue of the senses. He is, after all, not real flesh. He is immortal. Cursed to forever be a fragment of the man he once was, a shadow of the hero he loved.

Now Jade shifts, ready to leave the counter. Pauses. Faces him again. "You . . . er . . ." she hesitates. "Wanna do dinner sometime?"

He regards the tremor in the periphery of her lower lip, her uncertainty of his reciprocation of her interest. She is, to him, simply a whim. A new ballad before he is once again thrust into lone vigil, the permanent kind. Drifting unnoticed, powerless to pry himself from undying odyssey. Moving in and out of worlds, beyond lands of different shape, color, light. Some dull as a swallow's nest; others more radiant than the tail plume of a peacock at the height of courtship.

"Sure," he says. "Dinner. Why not."

# SCARS OF GRIEF

*The story starts here. This is a work of fiction. The author is struggling, he finds his story rigid. He wants to write about a thing he once read in the paper, an article about a bad tabloid that gained from victims of murder, hacked into their phone lines. Anything for a juicy caption, right? Wrong. The tabloid marched into trouble. Frankly it was shut down.*

*The author wants to build a set of events. Not around the tabloid and its shut-down, but around the families that were harmed. He makes the choice to write about the families because he understands his talent. He has a knack for people stories, no aptitude for institutions. He wants to be true to his learnings on the art of suspense. He wants to make sure that all is not revealed at the start. He worries. If he manages the use of suspense well, what if the reveal comes too late? He is nervous. What if he runs out of story? He is restless. What if the reader gets unhooked?*

*He looks at his cast.*

✦ ✦ ✦

Ralph.

Ralph Patton avoids their eyes. His wife Trinity sits haggard, listless. Withdrawn into herself. Marble Norman handles it best. Her husband Dane cradles a tempest. Time leaks perilously, frightening and consoling.

It is a common grief, reborn. It unites two couples who lost two little girls nine years ago to a murderer. Trinity finds her question. "Why?" There is a dead twig in her voice.

"Because journalists are knobheads," snaps Dane.

"Cookie . . ." Marble reaches across the table to calm his fists. Despite her composure, Ralph knows, her anguish is undiminished. Her grief is the kind that spills inward.

It seems minutes since Detective Vera Downs came to see them, first the

Normans, then the Pattons. To alert them to the phone-hacking, to stress again her regret at finding the girls too late. Yesterday. The detective came yesterday; brought them a day that opened up grief, that awakened the one thing that stirred the Normans, the Pattons, to seek each other out. Now they sit together at the Norman house in Halls Gap, Victoria. Same way they sat those many years ago when tragedy snatched their children.

Trinity lets out a sob, rises from her chair, flees the room. Marble chases behind.

"Bleeding freaks," Dane Norman says.

✦ ✦ ✦

*The author pauses at this stage, feels like he is scratching an itch. Should he dump the Normans? He notices that, with this story, he asks himself a lot of questions. Regarding the Normans it's . . . it's not that he is insensitive to Dane's rage, his despair. But he . . . he wonders if the story is better served focusing on a single family. A typical short story has a small cast at a single point in time. The author feels he can achieve more fleshing out the characters of Ralph and Trinity Patton.*

*Undecided, he continues typing.*

✦ ✦ ✦

Ralph understands the freaks. They are monsters bold as gold but septic inside. That same tabloid, a glimpse of hell, already once prospered on a story, the Patton and Norman story: two six-year-old girls curled ten-foot deep in a ditch at the mouth of Mount William ranges. How the press bled it.

The curtain flaps. Slowly, Ralph understands it is raining outside. A determined drizzle grows into slanting rain. He has never set foot near that bushwalk in the Grampians again. Neither has Trinity; they both want to forget. But Marble visits it annually like a shrine. Ralph never thought he could feel a knife so deep, so twisted in his breast.

He doesn't know why the news scandal has thrown him into the pit again, why so bottomless. But it has. Each word the detective said curved the blade deeper. "I am sorry they targeted you," she said. "There may be more families."

The press stopped at nothing, disregarded whose privacy they breached. Just the ready money a hot yarn cashed. The tabloid's ugliness is personal. Stolen conversations of trauma, of gloom, distorted on front pages. Intimate words shouted to the world, vilifying everything, sparing nothing. Ralph wants to climb to an edge and leap from the world.

✛ ✛ ✛

*At this stage the author pauses. He has hinted about the tabloid, about the children's murder, more than hinted. He has unveiled that a grief almost healed is now again torn open. But he is not sure . . . Is he indicating well what exactly is doing the tearing? So the press hacked the parents' phones, nosed into their grief. All for back story. But the coppers just found out now titbits of press data. Leaks, like how Trinity wanted to down a palmful of pills. Like how Dane was going to quit the marriage. It was all too thorny for them, barbed enough without the press. The author wants to show, not tell. He wonders how much detail to contain, how much to tell. Should he spell out what the tabloid did with the conversations it stole?*

*Less is more, he decides.*

✛ ✛ ✛

Ralph.

With the phone-hacking scandal, *Hot off the Press!* has slashed open scars that began to heal after that trial in August 2005 at the Magistrate's Court. Ralph thought the torment was abridged when Chief Magistrate Gray handed the monster two life terms. But what he feels now is wolfing him alive.

Even so, those same shock-and-awe tactics that saw the tabloid thrive since 1901 have proved the tabloid's own undoing. 113 years of scandal flushed down their rotten drain. That infected ink will never hurt anyone again. Not after one week today, the publication date of their last edition ever.

The end.

✛ ✛ ✛

*But—wait. The author sees how this ending moves away from the parents to the tabloid, how it is rather rigid. How can the story be over?*

*The phone tapping is part of Trinity's sorrow. The author wants to build on this, make it her recovery. So he deletes "The end".*

✛ ✛ ✛

But the tabloid's disgrace, and then closure, cannot patch what has happened.

It cannot fix open scars. The Normans and Pattons part yet again as they did years before, no longer allies, no longer able to feed as one the grief that joined them in the first place. It is as if they can no more bear looking at each other, being together.

Weeks after that parting, fog remains in Trinity's eyes.

Ralph takes to writing. He sits at his desk by the window. Trinity pours herself into works of charity: baking, resourcing, fundraising, publicizing . . . Now with the Salvos, the Vinnies, the Givewells. Philanthropy. Bugger that. Ralph types, types, types into his computer. Ideas jotted down on a shoddy notepad in the dead of the night, in that stretch between midnight and dawn when sleep eludes him the most.

He writes about Apple and the swell in his heart the first time his eyes set upon her. As he writes, the child invades his dreams. She is so tiny, so rosy, her face scrunched like an old woman's. Now it's a strong little mouth, she smiles. She is so vivid, her baby smell, still now, apricot and honey soap. She doesn't say a word, but chuckles when he ruffles her furious curls . . . a tangle right there on the crown of her head, an island of red.

Sometimes, gazing at windswept grass in the fields beyond the gate—it needs new paint—he thinks about what to write. Other times, he presses his nose against the window and an eye toward the horizon and can't think because his mind has slipped off. Just as well. He gets stuck in his head too much. But often, words swirl like waves and he cannot type fast enough.

His writing this morning is charged, stimulated. A whiff of melting butter, lime rind and fresh blueberries fills his nostrils. Trinity is baking. The waft of cookery is like a therapeutic balm. The smell stirs fond memories. Apple loved cookies, macaroons, turnovers, brownies . . . gobbled chunks whole without chewing.

Now and then, on difficult days, a sting of tears escorts his writing. Other times like now, memory massages his heart, lifts something inside him. Elation swells his being. He feels merry, surreal even.

Apple, always a scrawny thing, no matter what. Always wandering, investigating her world full of butterfly, ladybird and garden snail surprises. He watches her dazed expression at each find . . .

"Look Papa! I gots a new friend." The trapdoor spider escapes but Apple finds a Goliath stick insect to replace it. "She hungry, Papa. I ask Mama for a cookie."

"Why not, kiddo."

The moment her eyes, and then hands, lock on Jojo Norman, their love is instant. Without question, as if destined, Jojo reciprocates. She follows Apple everywhere. They toddle with hitched up skirts in grasslands near home, run—their delight giddy as summer rain.

"Me and Jojo see a wolfie near the park, Papa." Ralph experiences again the fork of fear in his gut, but it's a neighbor's European Wolfdog—completely tame—on a run.

The girls' lust for adventure steers them into trouble.

+ + +

*The author pauses. Is there a better story out of building the characters of Jojo and Apple? Then bringing in murder? Or maybe . . . How about looking individually at Ralph, Trinity, Marble and Dane now? How each responds in a different way to news that their privacy has been breached. Maybe exploring if that breach is as important to them as the way their daughters were treated in the original news reports. Yes, emotions directed at themselves, at their feelings of exposure, instead of at their daughters loss.*

*Still . . . he questions the angle, understands that this kind of feeling may not be true of Dane. Or Marble. Or Trinity. Or Ralph. After all Ralph has been writing, a cathartic way to deal with loss.*

*The author asks himself why he cannot put away "The scars of grief" for three months, give it another look then. It is too raw right now, he knows. But, then again . . . He is in a hurry to bed it down. He likes where he is going with Ralph.*

*Look behind you, Ralph, he says. Forget the blinking cursor on my screen.*

*Thanks.*

+ + +

"Do you remember when Apple made toast in your brand-new stereo?" his wife speaks quietly to his hair. She is right behind him. "How you lost it and scolded her to tears but stopped short because Jojo bawled so loud?"

Ralph looks up from the computer, startled and then awed. Fog has lifted from Trinity's eyes. What brings about her change? Is it reading his writings?

"Clearly it works," she says softly. "It works very well." He stares at her. "You bring her back each day . . . Apple, she is right here." She presses his hand to her chest.

"I missed you." He nestles his head against her breast.

"And I you. Dreadfully."

Their coupling is . . . animal.

Later, Trinity showers his face and throat with kisses that cool and burn. Wrapped in her arms, Ralph speaks against her wet skin, bedraggled hair. "I thought . . . maybe . . . Marble and Dane . . . I thought maybe we could go and see the Normans tomorrow."

"Okay."

# THE ANIMAL I AM

"Millet brew?"

"Thank you, Nisa. Mmmhh—sweet water from the gods. Makes everything else taste like hyena piss."

"I told you about champagne and all that, Freya. You and the high life."

"When in Rome . . . ?"

"Stupid saying, and it's Melbourne we're in."

"It's the concept, Nisa. It's how we enter stories."

"Concept or not, how is that daughter of yours? She and the white man she married."

"K and C? They are separated."

"Ayah? It was raining goals at the stadium, the day they married. Though the good team was winning, I knew it wasn't a good sign when K tore out of the house in that ivory gown of hers and started digging holes in the backyard. Do you remember what she said?"

"She said, *How do you last years with a lunatic in your face?* She cried inside her veil as she clawed. *He will Peter Pan me to death!* she said. But you and I both knew C was no Peter Pan. But that didn't make him a no-good husband, Nisa."

"Do you remember what you said to your daughter as she cried and dug with her nails?"

"I said, *Bend your fucking knees when you dig.* It's called tough love. The astrocenter assured compatibility. There they were: Aries and Gemini. A great match, right?"

"Wrong."

"Mmhhh—this millet brew is something else. Why don't you pour some more? Stop squeezing it from that calabash like it will kill you to serve it."

"Freya. You tell me where to get fresh millet in Hawthorn, then maybe I'll get more generous."

"Have you been to Footscray?"

"And let myself get mugged? These ancient bones will not survive a tackle to the ground."

"Nonsense. I was lollipop woman to little urchins in Footscray like forever, and none of those rascals ever attacked me."

"It's the big ones I'm worried about. I'm not in a hurry to cast a spell and zombify some idiot with an idea to rape me. So this thing with K and C. You should have listened to her tears. They fed stories to the soil. What you thought was a great match was nothing but trouble. That's what you get when you go with white-people thinking."

"You call Western astrology white-people thinking? Don't you know Aries and Geminis are made for each other?"

"Then their marriage should have worked. For all those wonderful horoscope prognostications, I could have told you already: your daughter and her husband had never been unhappier! You should have matched her on the Chinese zodiac instead."

"Ayah! I thought you'd say I should have consulted the gods of the baobab tree."

"You believe in that rubbish?"

"Better than Chinese witchery!"

"Let me tell you, my dear Freya—I have known you a lifetime. And I know a good thing when I see it. Not you. Of course I love you. But this Chinese calendar is a gold mine."

"Nisa. Our ancestors are turning in their graves."

"Turn your mind to accept this truth. Had you looked at the Chinese horoscope, it would instantly have said K and C possessed differences that did not complement one another. Conflict and tension were to be expected. Together was not meant to be."

"Hrrmph!"

"I should have told you about the twelve signs—the Horse, Ox, Goat, Tiger, Rabbit, Dog, Dragon, Monkey, Rooster, Rat, Snake and Pig; and the five cosmic elements—Fire, Water, Wood, Metal and Earth . . ."

"Horses and snakes? If you weren't my blood sister—we rode on crocodiles to travel oceans and find ourselves in this pale land—I would have cursed you today already!"

"I should have told you about affinities between the elements. Like how fire generates earth; and earth generates metal; and metal generates water; and water generates wood; and wood generates fire."

"Spit quickly, Nisa, and wash your mouth from blasphemy. Venerating Chinese charts!"

"I *should* have told you about resisting relationships between the elements. Like how fire dislikes metal; and metal dislikes wood; and wood dislikes earth; and earth dislikes water; and water dislikes fire. K is a Water Pig, you see. And C is a Fire Rooster. Overall compatibility: 50 percent."

"Can you just tell me how you know all this?"

"My blood sister, Freya. Not so many years ago, right here in Melbourne, I set out on a quest. The lions and the leopards of the Savannah having failed me—there are no lions or leopards: the black men I met were hyenas and wild dogs. Pack animals with no heart. Legged it from their own shadows. Tails between their legs when there was no pack to muscle for them."

"I won't argue with that, the banana heads you picked. A bunch of phone checkers sitting on the bones of their bums. What happened to your second sight?"

"It slipped into old habits. Goes silly when it sees a third leg. Completely blind when the pestle pounds the mortar."

"Hehe! Tell me about this quest of yours."

"I was curious: would the animal I am find compatibility (or not) with others?"

"Animal?"

"Will you just listen—I'm telling the story. As it goes, I turned on my sixth sense and went gallivanting for love—in Chinese astrology."

"Go figure!"

"Well. I found a few bastards. And some good folk. I made some notes—can you read tea leaves?"

"You wrote in a teacup?"

"So easy to fool you, my Freya. I didn't bloody write in a fucking teacup. Here's my diary."

✛ ✛ ✛

### The Spirited Horse

*Colt was a Water Horse. He was his own person, independent. Galloped into my day when all I wanted was a simple trot. The Water Horse, he flowed like a current: adaptable yet indecisive. Got stuck in a loop deciding whether to go out with me for a Japanese or Italian dinner.*

*When I saw a hint of cunning, reckless or impatience in him, "There goes the horse," I mused. The tantrum that exploded every now and then, like when he lost a footie tip, that was definitely the stallion. Our compatibility: sixty percent.*

### The Serious Ox

*I found Nandi—he was a Metallic Ox. A policeman Ox. It wasn't the uniform or* the boots that wooed me, or was it? All he had to do was quip, "You have the right to remain silent!" and whip out a pair of handcuffs . . . I'd have mellowed in rapture.

That never happened. The Ox's approach to tasks was methodical, most productive when he worked alone. Conservative, I liked that. Chauvinistic, didn't like that. He was more obstinate than a mule. Passionless too: kissing him was like kissing a hearse. And he wasn't reliable as Oxen are meant to be—he left. But I didn't chase. Not a shred of emotion in that Ox. Should have gone for a Water Ox—he'd have understood what I felt. Our compatibility: seventy percent.

### The Dreamer Goat

Billy was the Fire Goat. Oh, how he threw me. Fire-balled straight into my life, ninety percent compatibility—that's what the charts said. He was curious, a dreamer—loved theater. I watched Pan with him, and he gobbled all the chocolates. "Are there—baaaaaa!—more?"

Didn't fare well with that one. Pumped, stoked, incredibly high-strung. He was an anomaly. Must have been the elements. Ninety percent flop was more like it. Nowhere near sensitive as Goats ought to be!

### The Charismatic Tiger

Cait was a she-Tiger. Expressive, vibrant, a Fire Tiger. Unpredictable, a touch eccentric, oh what a girl! When she loved, she loved with all her soul. Hot-headed, competitive—there was always a new challenge.

Like when she just upped and offed, went backpacking in Bocas Del Toro, found herself in the Galapagos, and then somehow in Zanzibar. A need to be independent fueled her restless feet, and she explored sometimes dangerous worlds. We were kinda lovers; not the best ones though. Our compatibility: seventy percent.

### The Sentimental Rabbit

Jackalope was a Wood Rabbit. Affectionate, obliging—the sweetest thing. So quiet and unselfish, not a fighting bone in his body. Spent half his time doing stuff for others—lent you a hand and donated a kidney, just in case you might need it.

But the Rabbit has a quiet love for daring that caught me off guard. Out the window flew timid and he shacked up with a woman more than twice his age. Our compatibility: ninety percent.

### The Steadfast Dog

Adlet was a Metallic Dog. Threw himself into work and our relationship, unlike the Water Dog I once knew, whose commitment to relationship was incomparable to her attitude toward work. That Water Dog stayed close to love, was a most relaxed sort with her colleagues, never delivered a milestone on time! But it could have worked with either. Our compatibility—both Adlet and the She-Dog: seventy percent.

### The Leader Dragon

Morse was an Earth Dragon. He came from yesterday and was a natural leader. Rooted, level-headed, gave personalized cards to people on their birthdays. He was powerful, lucky too—did I tell you about that lottery ticket? Our compatibility: eighty percent.

### The Hedonistic Monkey

Satori was an Earth Monkey. Held a PhD in metaphysics, teemed with magnetism and lived a life full of turmoil. Our tryst dithered for loss of trust—mine in him. I had no time for smokescreen loyalty. Riotous ardor soiled his odds of commitment to one person. Our compatibility: seventy percent.

### The Shrewd Rooster

K's husband the Fire Rooster, oh, what an ego! His image of himself was flawless. He held priority in his own eyes and the self-aggrandizing tales he crowed should remind you why you are not fond of pride. Our compatibility: fifty percent.

### The Charming Rat

Freya is a Water Rat. I understood from the onset she holds a prominent position in the Chinese zodiac. She symbolizes curiosity and wit. She's charismatic, mysterious. No drama, practical too. Quietly full of feeling, loyal and attentive—yes, she listens. Our compatibility: eighty percent.

### The Seducer Snake

Monty was a Snake, that mysterious shadow on the moon. Snakes I am wary of be they Fire, Water, Wood, Metal or Earth. "Snakes eat Pigs," the Zodiac says. Our compatibility: forty percent.

### The Earnest Pig

Now you know. I am a Metallic Pig. Enthusiastic about love. I fall in love quickly and deeply, maudlin to the core. Don't let my tough shell deceive you, because I am tolerant—judging by the frogs I've kissed! I will trust you straight up and ask questions later—merely to reaffirm our relationship.

But if you think to pull one over me, my sixth sense will read you, miles before you see me. Might just be the Pig, sniffing for truffles.

+ + +

"Ayah, Nisa. It reads like a fiction. How is this a diary? It says who we are. A Rat and a Pig."

"True sisters. Eighty percent compatibility. No wonder I put up with all your rubbish."

"Then give me your recipe for that millet brew. I don't care that you never found a husband—or a wife—in that Chinese zodiac gallivant of yours! Who can live with you if you're so stingy with your wine?"

"Go away with your complaining, Freya. I still love you."

"And I you. Have you ever thought of friends with benefits?"

"Woman. You can't hold your wine. Without millet in this godforsaken place that has no yams or proper maize, corn, my foot, I used a chant—"

"Ooo-weee! You want to kill me? A chant!"

"Stop it now, you hysterical cow."

"RAT. Not a cow. Never a cow!"

"Don't get hysterical, that's all. Just remember what I've told you about K and C. It didn't matter that C was a Gemini."

"Might well have been a Virgo or a Piscean?"

"That's right. K's ideal partner was a Rabbit or a Goat; a Rat, Pig or Dragon; even possibly an Ox, Dog or Horse. The Tiger or Monkey might have needed some adjustment, like a sprinkle of the juju I poured into the wine."

"But most definitely not a Rooster or a Snake. In particular, NOT Fire ones! My Nisa—did you just say juju?!"

# ACE ZONE

Showers. Lightning. The night is momentous. She flirts with it: dusk. Drizzle joins forces with the black sky. Nightfall transfigures her. She is Ace Zone. Beautiful . . . in a subterranean way.

Her arrival into the land of Meteor is seismic, as is the downpour she commands. Rain: she loves rain. *Step . . . swish . . . step . . . swish.* She walks in its curtain. She has beckoned winter; a night so dark, it chases poltergeist. She cannot tolerate summer. Not since the battle in Sanz, when Ur butchered his own brother Opac, her husband.

Ur's cruelty has urged Ace Zone to respond. She remembers the good judgment of Opac, may the gods rest his spirit. But she also knows that to triumph in her war, to depose Ur and his iniquity, she must fight blackness with blackness.

A tongue of lightning. Wind spits a wet spray from the tip of Ace's hat. Moisture finds her nose inside a veil. *Splash!* A slipshod road shuttle swerves. Rain like flecks of silver. She crosses Kings Plaza. *Step . . . swish . . . Step . . . swish.* She comes to a Y-junction. Traffic, shuttles headed to the city, to the mountain, to the marina. On the other side of the intersection she follows the *Bridge Ahead* sign. She goes up a lone alley. Her hips sashay to the music of fat rain.

She waves a hand, and rain fades. A purple cloud swells on the horizon. It draws near, nearer still, pushes the last droplets of drizzle away. Bats drift across the firmament. Twin moons peek off the cloud; tentative honey-gold eyes in a lilac spread above.

Ace walks under a banshee tree with foliage that twists into the sky. Remnants of rain whisper in the dark leaves. Lowermost branches hang leafy fringes to the ground. The bough trembles. A lost spray slides down Ace's forehead. Puddles, more puddles. A baby cries in the distance. A hinge groans. The lane is fogged, deserted. North-east, a group of girls is bunched around a streetlamp. Bohemian tops; pencil shorts. They quit talking, stare at her. A door slams. *Step . . . swish . . . step . . . swish.* Ace skirts around the hoarfrost women.

She finds him at the end of the road, at the corner of Little Boulevard and Stellar Street. He is standing outside Saturn Inn. His eyes are loud. They shout interest.

"What are you, sixteen?" he says.

"Ace," she says. "Ace Zone."

He is visually pleasing: fine height, muscle and focus. Marks of a soldier. His burgundy waves are drenched. His smile is bold.

He does not understand her kind. His eyes seek only pleasure.

She loosens her hat, removes her veil.

He sizes her toe to lip, takes in the ankle-length boots; the dark cloak. Her tourmaline eyes are the color of watermelon; they shift between rubicund and jade. She knows he is stunned by the rubellite in her hair: how it casts light from tresses that fall to her hips. She opens her cloak.

"You are wet," he says.

She is beautiful . . . in a subterranean way.

She rubs her hands. "Take me somewhere."

"Saturn . . . " he glances at the inn. "It has . . . rooms." He licks his lip.

The inn's rowdiness explodes behind the doors. A shout of ribald laughter.

"The river crossing," he says quickly. "There's Maunder. It's 7-star."

She smiles. "Show me."

He leads in silence. Squish. Squish. Squish. His wet shoes.

*Step . . . swish . . . Step . . . swish.*

"Do you have a name?" Her voice is like an oboe.

"Selenius."

"Good," she says.

Selenius finds the foot of a tunnel. Down stone steps, then up, up in a twist into a gust of fresh air. Hotel Maunder is like a castle: it climbs. Vultures emboss its marble walls. A velvet carpet stretches long.

Up a gilded balustrade, dragons crown the parallel pillars in the suite. A bronzed effigy, naked, glorious, holds a chalice.

"Drink?" says Ace.

She digests his youth, his magnificence in the play of chandelier light. A careless fringe sprays down one side of his forehead. His nose is fragile. His mouth can be mean.

She steps out of her gown. His lust for her: the energy of its score fills her with chaos. Creation. Chaos.

Later, much later, she holds out a hand. "Dance," she says.

"I can't."

"Wagner."

"Please—"

"Imagine Wagner. Tchaikovsky. Brahms. Chopin. Verdi. Einaudi." They dance to Earth music.

Complete strangers. Or are they?

She glides in and out of his arms. She twirls, twirls, twirls . . . His face is softer now, the meanness in his lip gone. He sees a future: his and hers. He caresses the rise of her cheekbone; the flute of her nose . . . She glides in and out of his reach.

"Pharaoh," she whispers. "You look like a Pharaoh."

He is hesitant with her play. "Are you hungry?"

"Famished."

They gobble scorpiurus flowers and amethyst worms with saffron rice. They wash it down with wine and russet cheese, grilled and served with sweet radish.

He is to her more than a seasonal interest. He is a prospective soldier.

She is unrushed. She feeds him a truffle. Port. She swings a leg over him. He trembles as she strokes him. Her eyes blaze like comets. She bares teeth, injects her potion.

When he wakes, she will be gone; perhaps already to Planet Ishtar, or Lune, or Rigolith. She has little time but ample to do, drafting soldiers into her battalion. Selenius might note the bite mark on his neck, but he will not comprehend it. He will remember little of the night, nothing of Ace Zone. But for Sanz, its new emancipation battle, he will give everything, *everything*, when Ace commands it.

# A PINING

She has lips like the bows of a ribbon. She climbs a seesaw in the park and rocks; it doesn't budge, weighty for her frame.

"I can't do it," she says. Her coffee eyes are wide, gazing at you. "On that end," she points. "You sit."

"Me?"

"Yes, you."

"Couldn't be."

"Then who?" The little girl laughs. Her youthful eyes are unmarred by life experience. She is wearing a turtleneck inside a pinafore dress. Butterfly socks to her knees.

"See?" she shows, the unrocking seesaw. "I can't do it."

"Keep trying," you say.

"Why?"

"It's a start."

Every dawn . . .

✦ ✦ ✦

"Ellie!" a woman calls out. "Who're you talking to?"

"That's my momma." Ellie. She puts a finger to her face.

"Picking your nose?" You.

"I'm trying to put it back," she says.

You smile. You are easy like this with girls: little ones, big ones. You genuinely like them. Without ulterior motive, you find fascination with them. Perhaps they remind you of Rocket. You see them, you see her, your demeanor warms.

Rocket, before she died.

So precious, so easy to lose.

Every dawn, each dusk . . .

Your own mother never recovered from the loss. Barely brought herself to set eyes, let alone fingers, on the lone breathing child. If she'd had her way negotiating with Death, obvious which child she would have offered first. But cancer is random, unpicky. There is no negotiating with it. The odds . . . like Vegas. When the house wins, it snatches everything.

Stepping into Rocket's private room at the Royal Children's was like entering a den filled with rot. Her stool: tarmac-black goo in nappies. Hair gone, bone-thin, she never lost her belief in you. The feeble squeeze in her palm when you held it told you of her trust in your devotion.

+ + +

"Seesaw with me," Ellie pleads.

"Ask your momma." Your tone is gentle.

The woman stands by a swing, her meerkat eyes alert to strangers.

But strangers do not hurt you like people you know.

You shiver, not from a late evening breeze. Pepper's betrayal was heartless. It takes a certain kind of person . . . A tinge at the side of your head hammers to a migraine.

Every dawn, each dusk, clutching the pillow . . .

+ + +

Pepper lay on top facing you, rubbed her body against you, sat when you put hands to her waist. Her mouth fell open, the muscles of her face relaxed. She took a breath. Watching her, your head felt lighter. You put fingers to her face, closed your eyes.

In that silence, as you lay consumed by her scent, she spoke. "He's a dentist."

Your body betrayed you, ignored the conflict of her words and your desire. When she hooked her legs around your waist, you rolled, uncurled her leg and raised it to your shoulder. You took her with a cry and, for the first time, you led. When your lips caressed her breasts and she gripped your head, you pushed her against the pillow, gazed into her eyes and thrust again and again and again.

Later, much later, she untucked from the bed, traces of you on her thigh still. She tossed her fringe. Door open, door slam. The roar of a shower. She snatched scattered clothes one by one from the bed, the floor, atop the chiffonier. Lace stockings. Slid into leather boots. You locked eyes for a moment. She opened her mouth to say something, thought better of it. The silence between you was one that shouted. It was an unusual kind filled with different energy. The kind of silence before a bullet.

She grabbed her purse, exited without makeup. As a door snapped you wondered about her dentist, if he had an opinion about the levels of propylene glycol in the whitening toothpaste, minty fresh, in your bathroom.

✦ ✦ ✦

Long after you pushed off the park and strolled hands in pocket, walked against the rasp of weary wind beneath a setting sun, you remembered Ellie's smile, genuine and big.

When Pepper left, clicked the door and abandoned your house, your heart, you thought you would stay proud and strong. But all you remembered were three words: He's a dentist.

Couldn't she just have said: "His name is Jack?"

Or: "I'm done."

Why did she have to bring up a profession? Was it a white-collar thing, a comparison: you're a plumber, he's a dentist? Didn't she . . . was it not . . . how she said over and over about loving the sand in your hands? Coarse from plumbing, rousing on her velvet skin. A single touch and her whole body came alive.

Yet how swift, so strong, those three words from her mouth.

But they were not enough to kill your desire. Every dawn, each dusk, clutching the pillow against which you held her . . .

✦ ✦ ✦

Finding solace in the park is different, much less primitive than your first instinct to go as far as possible, to Africa, to a place you could sleep with lions, swim with crocs, at sundown in some wildlife lodge. Perhaps it was a death wish. Hippos are the biggest killers of humans in the wild.

You'd even got a brochure from the girl with canary-yellow hair and gazelle legs in shimmering tights at the travel agency. She was dressed like a teenager. Easy rapport. You allowed her to talk you into a cultural experience in the heart of some jungle full of trails and hills and a meander of rivers.

"It's more than scenic," she cooed, oblivious to the sudden tears stuck in your eyes.

She was on a yarn about how the safari escapade would make you happy, breathless, safe and wild when you shot to your feet, hands balled into fists.

But your voice was full of implore: "Could I please not?"

Every dawn, each dusk, clutching the pillow against which you held her as you claimed her one last time . . .

The whip of wind on your face was a welcome distraction from the shock of solitude that suddenly struck you.

$$+++$$

You circle a few blocks, hands in pocket still. The night is red, angry. A side street. The creak of a door. A cat drifts out like a ghost. Shimmers of rain . . .

Every dawn, each dusk, clutching the pillow against which you held her as you claimed her one last time, you swallow the fullness of her lips, interlock your legs with hers. Something snaps, explodes.

You walk until your headache washes away.

You arrive at your apartment, filter through the door. In bed, you wonder about the streets. People. There must have been people. But you cannot remember them, same as you cannot remember how heavy the rain. You weren't drenched when you got home.

You wonder if you'll ever find Rocket.

After Rocket, her passing, and then Pepper, her betrayal, something tipped inside you one dawn. You gave up trying to remember, or to forget, and gave your mother her wish.

Like Vegas and its odds . . . you snatched everything.

$$+++$$

You enter the bathroom. You step back into your body.

It is sprawled, wrists slit, its resting place a crimson bath. You wonder when someone will find him, if his mother will find him, or perhaps it will be a stranger . . .

Strangers don't hurt you like people you know.

It is a stranger who will rescue him from his water tomb.

$$+++$$

Together you think about the girl in the park, her lips like the bows of a ribbon, her eyes wide with the curiosity of childhood.

You wonder how she will turn out. Will she grow into a woman with long, long legs that climb out of boots to her navel, who wears a musky rose fragrance with a hint of cedar, who likes gold highlights on a sidewise fringe, who loves with no borders and then in a twink whispers three words of change: He's a dentist?

# DYING

It hurt each time he died. The first time it happened, Bluey was on his way to
Kinetic, the insurance firm he worked for. That morning he woke up to the alarm
at 6 a.m. Showered, cerealed, took the lift to the ground floor. He was crossing
the road to catch a No. 78 tram into the city when he went splat, flattened by a
truck. A mural on the pavement: flesh, blood, brain and bile.

+ + +

6 a.m., the alarm woke him. He sat up in bed, scratched his head. He looked
at his torso, his feet. Everything was there. Perhaps it was a just bad dream. He
showered. Chewed a bowl of cereal soaked in milk. He took the lift—gray floor,
blinking mirrors, steel walls as usual. He walked through the sliding door of his
apartment building to a whooshing wind. Cobblestones. Trees on the sidewalks.
A kid wearing a yellow shirt and green shorts whizzed past on a scooter. To the
side of the street: parked cars. In the street: running cars. An Asian woman rode
past on a bike, headed opposite.

He reached the main road. He took extra care at the intersection. A tall thin
man in a tar-black cloak crossed with him. He was safe on the tram platform
when a fire engine all lit, full siren, roared past on the street. It was headed to
the city. The tram was six minutes away. Bluey thought for a moment that he
should ditch it, leg it all the way to the city. The tram came, he took it. As did
the tall thin man. In the city, there was the lollipop woman at the pedestrian
crossing with its zebra lines. Bluey got to work carefully, without incident.

At the ground foyer of Kinetic, he walked on a polished floor, all marble.
Wall décor: climbing vines snaking to the ceiling. Up on the ivory-white ceiling dappled with baby angels were blinking dots: smoke alarms. There was the
receptionist behind her desk, even faced, cobalt haired. Round wide eyes, all
lashed up. Potato cream suit. Bluey smiled. She smiled back.

He took the lift to the ninth floor.

"Mornin' Bluey," said Geoff Coles the team lead, approving claims at his desk.

"Morning, Joffa," he said.

"What's going on?"

"Nothin'. Glad to be alive, I guess."

"Golly gum. First time I heard a ginger say that," said Coles. He pointed at Bluey's carroty curls. "Always so uptight."

They laughed.

Coles was a gun whore, always yabbering about some weapon or another. Sometimes he brought guns to work, sneaked in a drawer: rifles, shotguns, semis—harmless things really, Bluey was sure. Coles was a brag. A gun-toting brag. Sometimes Bluey called him Indiana Jones.

Bluey sat at his desk. He looked at the yellow phone. It never rang. All day he stamped insurance claims, approved some, rejected some. Day in, day out. That was his job. Stamp, stamp, sign. Today was no different. Or was it? He refused to think he had died. Pushed it out of his mind. Someday he would joke about it with Coles. He and Coles were tight. Coles wasn't just a gun-flashing brag. He was also a giver. Last Christmas he gave Bluey a nutribullet. Who named a juicer something close to a gun? No wonder Coles fell for it.

Their eyes met.

"Change your mind about being alive, I got a Colt 45 in my drawer."

"Sure thing, Joffa."

"It's got a grip safety and a thumb safety."

"No shit, Indie." Stamp, stamp, sign.

They ate sandwiches in the kitchenette. "Nana's brisket," said Coles. "Grainy mustard."

"Wilco that." Bluey licked his lips.

Coles wife was a grand cook. Bluey had never met her. But he'd met her sandwiches: tomato, basil and mozzarella; super steak; apple and blue cheese. Today Nana's brisket. Back to work. Stamp, stamp, sign.

The lollipop woman was still at the pedestrian strip. He was on his way home, about to cross the road, when he tripped on a shoelace, fell into traffic. A racing motor bike leaped to avoid him. Its revolving wheel struck and decapitated him. His head rolled seven meters from his body.

+ + +

6 a.m., the alarm clock. He woke up in bed. He touched his head. It was there. Shower. Cereal. Lift. He thought about cycling to work, decided against it. The bike, a nine-year-old thing that had seen better days, was in the basement of the apartment building. He called up an app on his phone: Uber.

The Uber guy was chatty. "Turks and Dutch at it now."

"Turks?"

"All over the news. Godamn politics. Hibernating or what?"

"Or what."

He smiled at the receptionist with her cobalt hair, lashed up eyes and potato cream suit. Baby angels and sunbathed clouds on the ivory-white ceiling. She smiled back. Ninth floor.

"Headache," he told Bluey. "Yabbering Uber chap. Couldn't shut him up."

"Exercising his freedom of speech. Next time just shoot him. Trams not running?"

"Mid-life crisis, I guess, Joffa."

"Roger that."

Bluey approved some claims, rejected some. Stamp, stamp, sign. They had lunch in a new joint two blocks from Kinetic. Coles got a plain risotto sprigged with truffles. Bluey went simple: a beef pie. Back to work. Stamp, stamp, sign. A mild cramp in his stomach came and went. A wall clock chimed. He stood up.

"Golly gum. You clock-watcher."

"A man's gotta be something, Joffa."

"Headed out to the horizon?"

"And beyond."

"Not so far a sniper can't hit."

They laughed.

Ground floor. Receptionist. Uber. Out in the street, he saw a woman who looked like the one who rode a bike outside his place. Wilco that.

His stomach was knotting by the time Bluey arrived home. In an hour, he was passing watery stool. In another half, it was bloody stool. By the time he thought to reach for a phone, his body caved, the agony excruciating. This is how he died of diarrhea.

✦ ✦ ✦

6 a.m., the alarm. He touched his stomach. It hurt no more. He swung his legs off the bed. Pondered a moment. Shower, no cereal—today he was changing it up. He pulled the nutribullet from under his bed. Tore it from its glitz and ribbon wrapping. Rinsed it. Plugged it. Tossed in a few carrots from the fridge.

Healthy living, hey? He flicked the switch and the blender hummed, hummed, exploded. Hot sticky sauce leaped toward his face. He dodged. A vomit of carrot spread along the tiled kitchen wall. There was a splatter on the floor. He looked at the mess, the mess looked back at him.

He grabbed a mop and a bucket. Took him an hour to clean it up. Finally he sank to the floor against a wall, wrapped his arms around himself and shivered a whole two hours. This was more than coincidence. Death was actively hunting him. He started laughing, laughing. Rolled on the floor laughing, laughing. This is how he died of loss of oxygen to the brain.

+ + +

6 a.m., the alarm. He thought about the shower, decided on a bath. He was climbing into the tub when he tripped on a floor mat, hit his head on a shiny faucet, zonked out and drowned in the stagnant water.

+ + +

6 a.m., the alarm. Outside it was pouring. A bolt of lightning licked the window. Bluey wrapped a nightgown around his pajamas. He went to the basement, unhooked the bike. He rode out into chopping rain. No kid on a scooter. No woman on a bike. He rode against the traffic. Cars swerved.

A flash of lightning lit toward him. He started laughing. "That's right. Do it. Get over with it now." A clap of thunder. Cars horned.

"Death wish, you fucker?" someone yelled.

Bluey pedaled faster in the rain, madly laughing as he rode. He aimed for an oncoming car. The driver braked. "You outta your head!" the driver yelled. He pedaled on and on, on and on, away from the city, toward the mountains. No bolt of lightning struck him. It stopped raining. The gray sky turned milky. He rode past a beach. The water was a turquoise blue. He pedaled until his legs hurt.

And then he saw it. A cliff! He huffed and pedaled toward it. The poison in his muscles was killing him. "Just one more pedal," he whispered. "One more. Just one. Here, baby, cliffie. I know you want me." The pedals refused to move. He was laughing, crying, his leg muscles stone. The bicycle tipped and he fell to the ground weeping. He was still sobbing when the coppers found him.

Soon as the hospital discharged him, Bluey hired a car. He drove out from the city, toward the mountains, past the beach. He arrived at the cliff. He sat in the car a moment, and then put the foot down. The car coughed, spluttered.

He floored the accelerator, again, again. Nothing happened. The car allowed him to turn it away from the crag. It sped him away from danger.

Suddenly he had a purpose. Yeah, purpose: kill himself. Not like there was anything to lose. Nobody special to leave behind, someone to miss him. Maybe Coles, as in miss him, not like he was that special. No, Bluey didn't have anyone who . . . loved him. He felt a bit sad at this thought.

+ + +

6 a.m., Bluey towel-bathed, chewed an apple. Didn't choke on it. Pity, he smiled.

He took the lift with its gray floor and blinking mirrors. The door of the apartment building glided and he was out into cobblestones. There was the kid, whizzed past him on a scooter. He took a tram to the city, a train to the countryside: Glen Ranges.

He walked, walked, walked, he didn't know how long. Finally he saw a farm with big black bulls chewing hay. He jumped the fence, lay on the ground by a huge bull's feet, goaded it. "Do it, fuckwit. Do it." The bull gave a lugubrious sigh and lumbered away. "No!" Bluey grabbed it by the tail but nothing seemed to agitate it much. The bull's kick was so half-hearted it barely left a scratch on his shin.

Distraught, Bluey returned to the city and hunted manholes. He'd read about them, lids giving way, loose crossbars and all. People plunging and drowning in twenty-one feet of human waste. Where were these goddamn holes with their loose lids? He found a few, lids clamped tight.

He fell into bed exhausted. He did not question his past, or his future. All he knew was now. He was Bluey, a ginger head who worked at Kinetics, an insurance firm. And now more than ever, he wanted to die. To die. To die. Didn't death want him? A big fat tear rolled down his cheek.

+ + +

6 a.m., the alarm. Out in the streets, just past Hade Avenue, he saw a milk truck. He ran toward it at full speed, eyes closed, arms spread. Nothing happened. "You got a death wish or something?" the driver barked.

The building that housed Kinetics stood tall, unperturbed by it all. There was the receptionist with her cobalt hair and potato cream suit. Sunbathed ceiling awash with heaven. She smiled back. Lift. Ninth floor.

"What's going on?" greeted the team lead.

"I'd tell all, Joffa. But you won't believe me."

"Shove off. Hospital thing, I heard. Take more time off. Work will wait."

"I'm good, Joffa. Ask you a question?"

"Shoot."

"What do you know about me?"

Coles's laugh was uneasy. "Messin' with me, boy?"

"I wake up. Every day. Come to work. Go home. Who am I?"

Coles scratched his head. "You do your job. I'm good with that. No questions."

"Then good for you! Me? I have questions. My life is the same, day in day out. Just the deaths. Now the living. I got questions!"

"Just go home, man."

"You and your Nana, you've got a life. My life's fucked-up."

"Man. Get a grip."

"I die and wake, die and wake. That's right. When I avoided death, I died and then I woke up. When I chose to die, chased it, nothing happened. What twisted fuck controls my destiny? Who is in charge?"

"You're talking like some TV guy, mate—"

"Am I? Am I! This ain't no drama!"

Coles was quiet a long time. "You're talking all over my head. I don't understand a word of it. But if dying is what you want—" He pulled a brown bag from his drawer. He put the gun in Bluey's hand.

"It got bullets?"

"What do you think?"

Bluey pressed the gun to his temple.

"Holy mother. Bluey. Thing's loaded!"

"Is it?" said Bluey. "I'd like to ask what you're doing with a loaded gun in the office. See, me, I ask questions." He waved the gun.

"Point. That thing. Away from me!" Coles's eyes were that wide.

Bluey dropped his hand. "You gave me the gun."

"Jesus Christ. I was just messing with you! Pushing common sense!"

A burst of ringing, the phone. Bluey looked at Coles's desk. "No shit." The ringing persisted.

Coles answered. "Hello?" He listened. "I didn't," he spoke to the receiver. "Some mix up, sweetie. Golly gum. Really sorry." He hung up. He looked confused.

"Well?" asked Bluey.

"Receptionist downstairs. Asks why I called."

"Strange."

"Roger that. What the—"

Bluey aimed at his temple and fired. The gun just clicked.

Coles had leaped, was crouching behind his desk. "Christ!"

The phone started ringing. It rang and rang and rang. No one paid attention.

"Thought you said this thing was loaded." Bluey fired. Nothing.

He pulled back the top of the gun, slid the chamber. It spat out a bullet that dropped to the ground.

"Shit, Bluey—"

"So it was. Loaded." Bluey laid the gun on the desk. "Told you. It's not our script. Ever wondered? About life? What if we're part of something bigger than us?"

Coles slumped against the leg of his desk. "You could have hurt someone."

"What if it's someone else's show?"

"You could have killed yourself. You, you . . . Larrikin. You."

"Ever wondered? What if that receptionist downstairs is a bot? And see those?" Bluey pointed at the ceiling. "Those blinkers, smoke alarm shit, what if they were eyes. Watching, always watching." He yelled at the beacon above his head: "That's right. You narcissistic fucks!"

Coles was looking at his hands as if they were snakes. "You want to kill yourself," he said finally.

"Now you get it."

"Would you? Try that again?"

"I'd try it again tomorrow."

Again Coles went quiet. "Your life is fucked."

"Sure thing, Joffa."

"What now?"

"Imagine scientists in a room full of monitors. Someone speaking to a recording: 'Computer, register this. Subject zero showing signs of reasoning capability beyond preconditioning.'"

"Ha-ha funny. Not."

Somewhere in the city, in a dilapidated pub named Crockers, a few people sat round a table with the angel of death. Among them: a kid in a yellow T-shirt; an Asian woman; a lollipop woman.

"Why didn't you let him blow his brains, boss?" the kid asked.

"To what end?" said the angel, the man in black. "It's more fun when he doesn't want to die. Just wish the Jesus chick didn't keep patching him up."

"Must have the hots for him."

"Yes. She loves him."

"Let's get another prawn," someone said.

"Yeah. That Geoff Coles goon."

"Jesus Christ," the angel snapped. A pay phone somewhere along a corridor started ringing. They all stared at the direction of the sound. "Coles got family," the angel said, quieter.

"What, you've got a conscience now?"

The phone rang out.

"Call it whatever you want," said the angel of death. "Everyone has to die some time. I'm just not ready to take Coles right now. That answer work for you?" He looked around. "No more of this shit. We have enough on our arses, like proving that free will is pure gumbo. Death comes knocking, we don't ask you about voluntary. Any more of you clowns got questions?"

They all looked away.

"And while we're on the topic of clowns. Stop calling *her* name in vain. Bitch won't stop ringing."

"Um . . . boss," someone said. "It was you that said Jesus Chr—"

"Sod it, the goddamn phone—"

*Ngrrrr-ngrrr! Ngrrrr-ngrrr! Ngrrrr-ngrrr!*

✛ ✛ ✛

At the ground foyer of Kinetic, the receptionist behind her desk, round wide eyes, all lashed up, cradled the receiver.

# WOLFMOTHER

Dragon and I sit at the bar. Tavern Terrafirma is chockers, bustle as drunks, punters and bartenders in baby aprons and carrying trays interlace with the crowd.

Dragon is on pristine behavior.

"Fire play, none tonight," I'd counseled. But a crystalline shade, pretty as a wish in his arms, not my warning, bears reason for his unspoiled manners. She has azure eyes, wide. A glitter of gems strokes her arms, throat and ears.

Dragon needs no notice of how her colorless skin could never endure his flames; never seen him gentler. He clicks his fingers. A barmaid, all bosoms, appears.

"One freezer for my beaut, one sequin double for Russo," points at me, "a pint of red lantern for me." Slips a twenty in the valley of her chest. "And one keep change for you, my dear."

The shade pouts.

I chow on chilled pheasant, and notice a spread of curls at the corner. "That, is who?"

Dragon shrugs.

A clink of coins in the haze of smoke . . . now the jukebox is playing. Spread of Curls faces us at the bar. Olive eyes sweep past me. I turn. It's a traveler. Tavern Terrafirma is the traveler's inn, attracts them like flies. This one treads his way to a stool beside Spread of Curls.

He smiles. She smiles.

I twirl to Dragon and his shade. "Again, she—is who?"

Dragon fingers a scar on his nape. "Diana Ferrari or her reincarnation."

"Puff out."

"That said with diplomatic caution," Dragon. "She's a moxie too, aggressive as they come."

Moxie or not, blokes are jostling for position, but only Traveler has scored. He's bought her a drink.

"Know each other, them two?" Me.

"Don't bet on it." Dragon.

"Puff out."

Falcon is behind the counter, tonight on duty. He is a hawk mutant, charcoal hair gleaming, eyes sharp as pins. His red-brown cloak matches the hue of his beak. He is glowing new glasses from the steamer with a towel. He notices me, winks.

The tavern door bursts open. Headless lurches in. A crust of crimson on his neck. His severed head under his armpits. A motley crew spills after him into the tavern. Skullface is with them, dressed all tar and pearl white. Hangman too, sporting burgundy tights.

"Lost it again?" Falcon, across the counter.

"Grow back soon." The muffled croak and echo is from somewhere inside Headless's neck. "How about a pint?"

"Straight down the throat?"

Ribald laughter all round. Only Traveler looks troubled, I note with liking.

The lads are guzzling away, raunchy jokes aturn. Dragon and Shade have vanished. Even Hangman is in jolly disposition and has said nothing of gallows or appointments with a headstone. Spread of Curls is working the traveler, or the other way round. Doesn't matter really, they are making out. Period.

"Bloke's whopper impressive," Hangman says. Hands me a joint.

"Shark—he sure is."

"I'd call him a dolphin," Dragon behind me. The shade's gone.

"Dawn climb to the mountains," he explains. "Come-of-age ritual, imagine that."

Traveler and Spread of Curls are heading out the door.

Hangman's head is clasped between elbows. He snores.

Dragon glances out the window. "Coppers, yellows and reds," he says. "Beware."

I don't understand. I don't really care. Actually, I do. But fuck.

Falcon is closing shop: stool over stool over stool. Place is abandoned, just the regulars now.

"Fierce storm," Falcon says.

"Splice, want one?"

"Why not."

I offer him a joint.

Tavern Terrafirma reeks of burning corn. A flicker of light through the window, then a spear of lightning. A burst of copper, yellow and red chases a white shaft of light.

"There," Dragon. "Colors of the night."

At first I think my hands have tremors. Then I notice the table.

"An earthquake. From where?"

The measure of shaking so intensifies I seize my drink.

A scream renders through the dusk, then quiet.

The tremors are gone.

Spread of Curls slips into the room. She pulls a stool beside me. I pretend to ignore her.

"Hey sweet girl," Dragon says.

"Hey Drags."

Her curls are in disarray, her face half-hidden from light.

I glare at Dragon. "Know each other. You two?"

"Long story."

"Puff out. Prick. Introductions, that's what."

"My dear pal, no one introduces his best mate to a vamp. Meet Wolfmother."

She faces me fully, olive eyes dark as a seer.

"Pleased to make your acquaintance," she says. Her voice is as caressing as the crimson drop at the corner of her lip.

# TOUCHED

She'd come to the end of herself when Flare stumbled on the church.

It was an innocuous little thing in the middle of a small street off Objections Place. A man and a woman stood holding placards. One sign said: *Put a boot on it*. The other said: *Kick it*.

She saw a cross on the wall.

You know how life passed you by and left you scattered? She moved toward the placards. The woman was a young girl with purple hair and chewing gum. The man was the kind you'd expect outside a church: suited and wearing tennis shoes.

Across the street a guy in torn jeans and a T-shirt that said Omega looked in their direction. People flocked into the little building, piquing Flare's curiosity.

"What's with the signs?" she said.

"It's a protest," the suited man with tennis shoes said.

"Against?"

"Despair," the purple-haired girl said.

But people were spilling with goodness. They looked at Flare with kind eyes and smiled like they knew her.

Going in was like walking into the Tardis. It grew bigger on the inside. She went past a buzzing food court, through a T-shirt attended book stall and stood by a rainbow-colored playpen. Parents were dropping off children. Most totties were happy for some stranger to take them, but one bawling toddler in pigtails, hands outstretched toward daddy, chased. Someone gave her a rose-colored bible and she sat on the floor, happy, flicking through pages, hair on her face, her daddy forgotten.

Three entryways led to what turned out to be a massive auditorium. It pulsed with disco lights and music that could only come from heaven. The lead singer was Miss Universe—she had to be. The rest of the choir comprised beautiful people loaned from bliss.

Flare found herself in a pew up front—somebody likely ushered her there.

There was goodness everywhere. Everyone was smiling and swooning and dancing. You could leave your stuff on the pew and go up front to sing with the choir or be prayed for and no one would steal your purse.

The music was like sunshine and rain, spring and autumn, magnolias and sweet peas. Something wistful and sacred wrapped around Flare, even as the sweet melody ebbed and Flare sank with the sound to her knees.

A pastor named Parrot—yes, like the bird—flew on stage. He was a tall, wiry fellow who hopped and pecked about the pulpit. He wore black-rimmed spectacles but only used them to quote from the bible. The rest of the time he bent his head and looked over the glasses at the crowd, smiled before he said fierce words.

There were serpents and dry bones in his sermon. And he liked to say: Hallelujah. I like that! When he wasn't raining snakes and dead bones at the faithful, he was spewing fire. As he danced on stage, he said something about angels and faith, and Flare saw three angels moving alongside the preacher. One was a baby with fat legs and black curls, and despite his nappy he was playing a harp. One was a girl with tattoos and a nose ring—yes, she was an angel too: she had wings. The third was this old guy with a bald head. He was good-looking in a Bruce Willis kind of way, but he was a person of color and ribbed like Wesley Snipes. He too was an angel—there were wings, see?

Embrace the process! The preacher was yelling. Contact with the Maker—have you had the touch? As the faithful fell out of their pews and spilled toward the preacher, Flare realized it was an altar call.

She had no time to think twice about it. Before her nerves could deteriorate, her feet, on their own accord, led her away from the pew and her purse and out in front toward Preacher Parrot. All she knew was she'd never had the touch but really wanted it today.

The preacher laid hands. People collapsed. She felt a presence and his energy neared. Her feet were jelly by the time he stood before her.

"Where does your story begin?"

She tried to tell him about her boyfriend, Amos, and his dad jokes, how he wanted sex every night. About her asthma that hadn't responded to preventers over twenty years. About the stupid workplace that took a pound of flesh but paid nickels and politics. No words came. She looked at him and he looked at her. And then he was mouthing something that nourished everything within and urged her to be born, find her essence.

The faithful were making an unholy sound.

"Hallelujah. I like that!"

She realized the preacher wasn't asking about her story. He was telling it.

"You're the favorite."

She felt whole. Now she was crying. He started to lay hands. She swooned. Gentle palms at the back guided her head to the floor. The light dimmed. Faint music seeped from heaven. Sunlight and rain. Magnolias and sweet peas. Two faces peered at her from above. It was the tattooed angel and Bruce Willis Snipes. They smiled. She smiled back. She wanted to rise but her legs refused to give. She wriggled some fingers and strong hands guided her up.

She walked wobbly to her pew, but it felt like a float, so light her head. Her chest felt like an adrenaline stream had scoured her lungs. Her purse was gone. She didn't recognize the people to her left or right. Was she in the right place? It didn't matter. She just felt . . .

The calming fire.

+ + +

She let herself in, the keys from her—what? she had her purse. It was a night of miracles.

Amos sat on her couch. He was watching footie, eating nuts. An empty glass of red on the coffee table. A news ticker was rolling at the footer of the TV:

*Police urge vigilance against a serial rapist who has strangled five women . . .*

The remote was scattered on cushions, the carpet littered with beer-nut skins. Amos looked up. "I think my ears have dropped." He laughed at his joke. "Haircut. Looks nice."

"I've been home ages. Where'd you go?"

"I don't want to have sex tonight," she said.

"Someone's in a mood."

She didn't take the dirty glass to the dishwasher. Buried the urge to vacuum. Oblivious, the aircon hummed.

"Shall I leave?" He ran a hand through his hair.

"You can go if you like. I just don't want sex tonight."

"You're the boss."

"Not the boss. Just no sex."

He stared like she was a new person. "So what time are you going to bed?"

"In a minute. I'll have a soak first."

"You want help with something?"

"Not really."

He blinked. "Okay." The sigh again. He looked troubled but didn't leave the unit for the pad he shared with his mates out east.

Outside, a murmur of cars washed down the street.

She wasn't angry or anything, just a little exhausted. She ran a bath and soaked in it for an hour. The calcium in the salts calmed her like the church.

Amos was waiting in the bed. He was naked inside the covers, checking his phone when she entered. Put it away, looked expectantly at her. She climbed between the sheets, pecked him on the forehead, closed her eyes.

He shook the bed with his foot. He was breathing hard. "What about a hug?"

"Just sleep, darling."

He didn't. She lifted away his roving hands from her body, over and over. Now they faced off like warriors, lying side by side toward each other. Her arms and knees were crossed.

Suddenly, the baby angel was with them, blowing Amos's fringe into his face. So was the tattoo girl: there too. She was smiling at Amos, who was flicking the fringe from his face. He didn't seem to notice any of the angels. Bruce Willis Snipes gave Flare a wink. Music like sunshine and rain floated the bed from the floor. Flare felt wistful and sacred. She hesitated. Put out a hand and touched Amos on the chest. He went off like a light, smiling.

Flare drifted off to sleep.

✦ ✦ ✦

Somewhere into the night, she opened her eyes. The angels were gone. Amos was softly purring. The room was black as poltergeist, no streetlight through the window. Her throat burned with incredible thirst. She took quietly to the kitchen but was startled by a breeze. The main door was open.

She stepped out into darkness, to an odd stillness. No garage doors creaking, or late-night cars stealing home. She stood, arms wrapped, by her doorstep staring at nothingness.

She smelled him before she saw him. It was the smell of the chemistry lab those many years ago when a prankster toyed with sulfur and something like sewer gas invaded the room. It was the smell of roadkill—she was six and in a school bus with loads of kids, they'd come from the zoo somewhere southwest of the city and it was night when she was sick with her asthma. Her coughing fit stopped the bus and Rebecca, the sub, helped her out—for what reason? Perhaps it was to administer her Ventolin in private. The bus was purring, pupils peering out windows, some putting tongues to the glass. Flare wanted something to swallow her away from the attention and was quietly fretting when she saw the dead animal. Its face a paste on the ground. A pink intestine trailed on the road. Even without a face, she knew it was a koala—who wouldn't? But it was the smell she remembered.

He wore torn jeans and a T-shirt that said Omega. The kind of lips you might see on a male model. She remembered him from outside the church.

"You followed me," she said.

"Stalked like a limpet." Soft words. Dream eyes.

"Why me?"

"You're the favorite," he said. "But you missed a bit of training."

He spoke near, like he wanted to kiss her.

He looked like he should smell good. Athletic shoulders, neat jaw. Fine nose, box cut. He was elegant and upright. But he reeked like his mouth and insides were festered with rot.

"You're the strangler." It wasn't a question.

They eyed each other.

And then she lifted her hand and touched him.

In hindsight—and she went over this many times—what really happened was that a version of herself stepped back. Another version levitated forward, finger pointed, and touched Omega on the forehead.

The energy of the touch bounced Flare off her feet to up yonder where she watched him burst into flame. He screamed and flailed as he charred. But there was no sound.

He collapsed to the ground, burning, burning and she wafted back to bed.

# HE REFUSED TO NAME IT

Winter. His toes always felt cold even with socks. But they had never frosted this much. He understood it was a haunting. Not the kind of a low chuckle, doors closing and opening when no one was there. This one took the form of ice in his feet. And he knew she was there. Right there in the darkness, as he lay in his bed.

Something else too: a sweet antiseptic smell seeped into the room. Not so much a hospital smell. This was more like the sanitizing, disinfecting smell that accompanied death.

The smell of a morgue.

✛ ✛ ✛

"She what?" They were standing at the reception, Calder and the bloke from Diggers Rest with torn jeans and a checkered shirt.

"Childbirth, mate. These things happen," said the bloke, his voice like a drum.

"Never seen you in my life before," said Calder. "You come all this way from Sunbury Hospital. Track me to my workplace in the city. All to tell me that my ex—not wife, not fiancée—my ex-girl is dead?"

"That's right," said the bloke.

"I haven't seen M in months."

"There's a baby."

"It's alive?"

"It's yours."

The receptionist with a weak smile and wearing dog glasses looked up from her typing.

"Twinx," said Calder. "We'll take a meeting room."

He took the man's arm. Bear, his name. Dragged him into the privacy of a thirty-six-seater boardroom—that's all that was available—sat him at the head of the table.

"Listen Hussle," Calder said in a gentle voice. He leaned toward the man. "You want some water?"

"I'm good."

"How about coffee? A latte or a long black—what type are you?"

Bear shook his head.

"Twinx can get you some. It's no drama."

"I'm good." Bear looked at Calder like he was stupid.

They were both stupid.

"This is a predicament, mate," said Calder. "How come I don't know you? M never mentioned a brother."

Bear shrugged and said in his boom voice, "All this nonsense, right?"

Calder put a hand on the man's shoulder. "Boss man. As you say, these things happen. Your sister's dead. Why do you think it'll give you peace of mind to go enforcing baby daddies? For all I know—"

"Please don't. She said you'd be like this."

"Like what?!"

+ + +

That's how it started.

Bear's visit ended with an address scribbled on a tear—seriously a scrap—in bloodshot ink. "Those are the digits to my pad." Bear said, voice inside a drum. "There's a wake tonight." His tone did not indicate an option for Calder. "You can find Sunbury Hospital yourself. Ask for the baby ward. It's the only newborn today."

+ + +

You know how things happen and it feels like a dream you're witnessing? But, somehow, you're also in the dream that is most thoroughly a nightmare? Calder looked at the sleeping baby wrapped in linen like a mummy in its sterile cot, the hospital's white walls soaked in iodoform.

"Such a tiny gorgeous," cooed a nurse or a nun in a tunic the color of summer sky and a cape imprinted from the crisp white of forbidden ivory.

There was nothing spectacular about the baby. Oval face. Even symmetry between onyx eyes, button nose, plum mouth.

Calder walked out of the room without a word.

He caught an Uber because he had not thought to drive—who does when things like this happen? But he didn't return to work. His Monday to Friday suit smelled sweet and sterile like the hospital.

It was windy and cold outside, the streets all gray.

His unit in Blackwattle was a spartan place that looked like the kind you get when Ma and Pa Kettle rented a spare room. But that wasn't even the owner's name. Calder had never met the landlord. He rented through a property agent. Each unit had its own backyard, fenced. Out the front, a communal car park. As for the neighbors . . . he didn't give a toss about them. Sometimes he saw them. Sometimes he didn't. There was a fresh-faced chap, the jogging type. He wore tight trackies and white tennis shoes. He also had a wedding band, but Calder had never seen the wife. There was a girl with hat hair—all coned with brimmed-out edges. Mauve. She lived with a bald teen who wore a mo and gumboots that, rain or shine, never came off. There was an old man with a walking cane and a beanie. He was always dragging a shopping trolley—it had to be empty, the easy way he pulled it.

Calder sat in the unit and thought about shopping. Not like that. You know how you go shopping and there's one thing you forget, remember it when you get home? Toilet paper. Washing up liquid. Cling wrap. M was like that—this is what Calder thought about. After they broke up, he forgot her and then remembered. In spurts. The workplace became his castaway island: he immersed himself in paperwork. Strategy and planning. Stakeholder engagement. He didn't go through denial and all the shit that comes with grief. He just occasionally forgot and remembered. But he certainly did isolate. Feelings. Sure, there was anger at the time of the argument. Then came a black hole and dust that filled it up. Heartache was too much of a gorge to consider. He refused to name it.

Now he felt a deep sense of aloneness. It was like grief attacking him in reverse. Something warm and wet snailed down his face. He realized it was a tear.

Before M, he'd never been the boy with the cool girl. Then pouty M came along with her spectacular cheekbones that contoured her face and evened the angle between her big eyes and thin jaw. She was a cool girl, stern but all pretty. She was his. Sure, sometimes she was a bit dizzy. Silly things came out of her mouth and got his goat. But not for long: who stayed cross when a woman that was a million stars lit your world?

She was more than a curtain raiser. She looked like a creature from another world, another time. She was a goddess from a temple far away who took him on a stroll along a hanging garden. It lasted only three months, but it was enough. She was the Milky Way, a sprawl of stars twinkling around his Sagittarius. She was the gravity that held him together. In her own right his nebula—bright and visible to his naked need.

There are people who're receptors. They open to an experience and find immersion in it. Calder was a receptor. There are people who're givers. They have power and sometimes power comes with love but is often devoid of it. M was a giver. Calder didn't think he was both a receptor and a giver; his touch never transported anyone. And M was never both—she was incapable of receiving. But she was most definitely a giver.

She had a key that gave him access to an invisible palace. When she kissed him, he tasted authority on her tongue. Each touch was like creation. She molded his clay, lifted him to unseen glory. Enlightenment. Their intercourse was edification: he opened to her tutelage. It wasn't a choice, it just happened. She molded. He was malleable.

He sat on his bed thinking about all this until night fell. And then the house talked to him. Usually it was silent, other than outdoor sounds of starting up cars or revving motorbikes. But tonight, it talked. First it was like a beating heart in the wind. And then a sway of dry leaves. He was astonished when he lifted his head from his hands to find a scatter of gum leaves on the floor.

He took a dustpan and hand broom. Chucked the leaves into rashes of grass in the backyard.

✛ ✛ ✛

He caught an Uber because he didn't want to search for Diggers Rest. The car pulled outside a gray townhouse with a cerulean roof and a wooden garage door. Calder checked the address scribbled on a tear. He put the scrap back into the pocket of his shirt.

The door opened before Calder finished knocking.

It was Bear, still in the checkered shirt. In his arms he rocked the baby from the hospital, still wrapped like something from ancient Egypt.

"They discharged it?" Calder made conversation.

Bear did not answer.

He led them into a lounge room full of character. Polished wood on the floor. A painting of roses on an ebony backdrop hung on a big white wall. A plush three-seater, all black, complemented the white and silver house. Every wall was white. Every fitting was silver. There was a modern kitchen with silver-top benches and matching toaster, microwave and refrigerator.

Calder dug out a bottle of beer.

Bear and the infant didn't seem to mind. They were rocking by the fireplace.

"Boss man. This is a goddamned wake. Where's everybody?"

"Just us, mate." Bear continued rocking. So charcoal, his eyes. "No murder of crows. That's the rest of them. Nobody gives a shit."

Calder studied a silver-framed photo of a small boy and his younger sister standing on the golden salt of some Bondi Beach. You could see resemblance. He was charcoal-eyed with a thatch of hair on his crown. Nothing like the full-haired bear he was now, fur crawling all over his face. The girl was stern and pretty, full of authority. She used her body beautifully. She was like an albatross in a swimsuit. Looking beyond the camera at something else.

Calder sank in the three-seater. "Well I'm here. So, tell me."

"It's about routine," said Bear in his boom voice. "Warm the bottle. Change the nappy. Repeat."

"I can't just take the baby."

"Yes. You can. It's yours."

"Give it a rest one minute."

For the first time, an emotion flickered across Bear's bearded face. An emotion like hatred. "Did you think for a moment about the consequences of leaving?"

Calder drained the beer and stood. "I think I'll just go."

"Yes, run. Like you always do."

Calder reached Bear in quick strides. He hauled the baby from the big bushy arms and nuzzled it against his shoulder. Slammed the door to the fuckwit from hell.

He stumbled into a shout of wind.

✝ ✝ ✝

He couldn't sleep, the baby by his side.

The house still talked. This time it was an endless flutter of bird wings. It sounded like a peep of chickens. Calder tried distracting himself with thoughts, but he couldn't shake the frost from his feet.

The pleasure of thinking about M came along with ice swords to his core. Would it have been easier had she been murdered? A bloodied body found in the bottom of a ditch? This was rough: childbirth. She'd carried a baby to term. Never thought to tell him. She was always secretive.

He remembered the mountains, a pulse of time. It was heart memory. Who forgot a getaway like that? He did. But now he remembered. The Briars cottage with bird-nest lamps. Waking to the sight of snow through the windows. M curled into the pillow that wintry morn. Rubbing against his leg like a cat. Her breathing soft on his skin. He remembered everything. Her spectacular cheekbones. Tousled hair on her stern, pretty face lost in sleep. Her taste of toothpaste in the morning. Her lusty gulp of freshly squeezed orange juice from Black Forest Café. An intensity in her scowl at the skinny flat white topped with a heart. But she thawed with the double-ladled pot of mulled wine at the Pig and Whistle where they stopped for lunch. The food tasted washed. But it was a glorious day despite the cold, not a single brow in the horizon. The sky was a giant blue lake. The boy who served them whistled all the time, a sound of birds from his lips.

Calder remembered the fight—how M let slip she had to get back to the city for a shift.

"You've got a job?"

"The odd hand here and there."

"Like where?"

"Fifteen."

"The *Fifteen*? That's top notch."

"You know I can cook."

"Then why have you been temping as a typist?"

"Because I went to culinary school, it doesn't mean people immediately see my potential."

"So now they do at Fifteen?"

"Geoff said—"

"Geoff?"

"He's a sous chef there. Sometimes you need connections."

"That kind of history?"

"Feels like a grudge match. Why are you so angry?"

Things tumbled from there pretty much.

As they drove back under the big lake sky, Calder tried to mend things. "Move in with me. It'll be closer to your work."

"Move in?" she spat. "Blackwattle is a shoebox."

"You could fit a whole army in there, still have room."

"An army of idiots."

He said it then: "You're cold in the heart. Incapable of loving anyone but you."

"I don't hate you," she said.

✦ ✦ ✦

He woke from a fitful sleep to a smell of bird. The window was open. A trail of fresh droppings led out of his bedroom to the backyard. He swept the droppings, sprayed the floor with antibacterial kitchen cleaner.

He warmed a bottle, changed the baby's nappy.

Only later, he frowned. He didn't remember taking a bottle, baby formula or nappies from Bear. He didn't remember buying them. Such was his rage he must have blacked out.

+ + +

He was straight about the break-up, pragmatic. Same way he was pragmatic now about the baby in his shoebox. He warmed the bottle. Changed the nappy.

The baby strangely followed him with its eyes, sometimes intensive, sometimes drowsy.

Now it was asleep.

Already it was dark outside, and the house started talking. A sound like rusty pipes. And his feet, so cold.

In the middle of the night the baby woke. It didn't cry—he just felt its eyes.

He held it in a stranger's hands. Borrowed feelings to feed it. Glanced without emotion at the child's greedy tug on the tit. Onyx eyes fixed on his face. Tiny palm around his finger. Rapid breaths on its ribcage.

It slept.

The house once again talked. It shifted, walls and floors humping. But it too fell silent and slept, sounds scattered to nothingness. Only Calder stayed awake, listening to the unbeating heart of the house. What had changed?

He was unconvinced it was him who had changed to this life in monochrome. Every day was night. Everything dull and noir.

The baby was still as a corpse. He didn't remember its face—it was a distant memory.

Suddenly the house spoke. This time it was the sound of a car endlessly rolling on mud.

Calder wasn't surprised to wake up from a doze to find a trail of muddy tracks with wheels leading out to the backyard. He noticed the tree for the first time.

It was shaped like a phallus growing from the ground.

+ + +

He hadn't seen the neighbors in a while. How many days had passed? Or was it nights? It felt like a post-apocalyptic movie where everyone was gone. Work hadn't called. Who was doing strategy and delivering on the corporate plan? But he was a manager. And managers, like sous chef Geoff, got away with things.

He warmed the bottle. Changed the nappy. The baby followed him with its eyes. What baby was this? It never cried. Now he wondered about the baby's tiny palm around his finger when he fed it. He didn't remember unbandaging the mummy wrap. And how the hell did he change its nappy?

Suddenly he was afraid. For the first time, he regretted succumbing to Bear's goading. How it made him take the baby. He worried that, if he looked, he might find nothing inside the mummy.

✛ ✛ ✛

It went dark early in winter.

He took his car, a sedan on good mileage he'd secured from a second-hand car city along Punt Road. He put the baby in the back seat, strapped it in the baby seat—who put it there? He didn't remember buying a baby seat. A curtain parted in Unit One—that was the girl with the hat hair and the gumbooted baldie. A peek of brows but he couldn't tell who it was. A flicker of television in Unit Three—that was the old man, the one with the empty trolley.

Calder set destination in the smartphone, pulled out of the driveway. A ghost of trees lined either side of the street. A man and his Labrador on a leash walked the crossing just before the main road. A jaywalking smoker dashed across the junction. The rest was smooth sailing. Lights that were red turned green as he approached.

He let the English-accented navigator guide him through the M1, down the freeway and along the M80. He drove all the way to Diggers Rest.

He leaped out. The baby stayed strapped in the humming car.

Calder banged on the wooden door of the gray townhouse. He banged like he was on fire.

"Yes, dear?"

A white-haired woman wearing a green cardigan and jeans peered at him at the doorway. *Hau! Hau!* A sausage dog, wire-haired, all tan with deep chocolate ears, barked at her heels.

Calder pushed inside. "I must speak to Bear."

"Gracious, manners dear." She faced him. "Who's Bear?"

"He lives here. Right here. See?" Calder pulled out the address scribbled on a tear.

He blinked. The scrap of paper was blank.

"No. This can't be right. There was a photo."

He searched the big white wall and found its painting of roses. He sought the boy and his sister standing on golden sand, regal in bathers. Nothing was there.

*Hau! Hau!* said floppy-eared Barky, all bowlegged in a lively trot.

"Oh, my," a float of the woman's words somewhere in his consciousness. "You look like you've seen a ghost, dear—shall I get you help?"

But Calder was already legging out of the front door.

The woman and her dog ran after him. *Hau! Hau!*

Calder bracketed the wiener dog's barking off his mind. Was powerless to unhear the woman's exclamation: "Jesus! Is that a baby in the front seat?"

He leaped into the purring car, roared away.

Cars rushed on either direction of the freeway.

In the city he parked off the road. He took the baby and entered the office building. Up the lift to the sixth floor. He swiped in. Twinx was there.

The receptionist looked up with her dog glasses, cast him a weak smile. "Hiya."

"Working late?"

"Something like that." Eyes fixed on him. "You've been gone a while. We haven't seen you since—" She looked at the baby.

"Do you remember the bearded guy with a checkered shirt . . ." He didn't know how to continue.

"What guy?"

"You booked us the boardroom . . . ?" Twinx stared at him. "Surely, you remember?"

"I book a lot of rooms for a lot of people." She eyed him funny. "Are you alright?"

He shook his head, laughed. "You're messing with me. You don't get to do this. Just don't. I'm not your bosom buddy."

"I didn't mean to upset you, Calder. Why, you're acting all weird."

"Tell me this—am I holding a baby?"

"What kind of question is that? Of course, you're holding a baby."

✦ ✦ ✦

He pulled into the communal car park. The jogging neighbor, tight trackies and white tennis shoes, crashed past on the way out. A thin black girl with slippery hair jogged nimbly after him.

It was weary feet that stepped into the husk of Calder's unit. Fatigue washed over him. He sat with the baby, studied her onyx eyes intent on his face. Doll fingers wrapped around his big thumb. She broke into a gummy smile meant for him. Cooed and blew raspberries. Fat legs kicked in the fluffy rabbit onesie zipped up front. Why in heaven had he thought it was a mummy wrap?

His heart swelled with sudden affection. Titian curls on her head. She looked like a Zoe. He cradled her as she smiled, this time in her dream.

Somewhere in the night, the smell of formaldehyde got worse. His toes became ice and he knew M was there. Right there in the darkness, as he and Zoe lay. M was close, too close, because now his ears were ice. When the house talked, this time it was the swell of a roaring river cascading over a ledge. He unheeded it. Dozed, woke up thirsty. He put his feet on the floor—it was flooded.

He bundled Zoe into his arms. She was asleep.

He stepped out to the backyard into crisp air away from the morgue smell, from the pulse of the house's malevolent spirit. The night was shimmer-free, no stars. But it was windy. He sat under the penis tree. Cradled Zoe from the breeze that thawed the frost in his feet and ears. An unkindness of ravens jumped in soundless unison from a branch.

The sky in the horizon unlocked itself to a float of light scanning the universe. As the penis tree unfurled its gnarled phallus, as branches reached and reached, cocooning Calder and Zoe from the biting wind, a shooting star shimmered and twirled with satellites out yonder.

Calder immersed himself into the language of life. I'm a receiver, he thought as he closed his eyes. For the first time in a long time he fell into a deep sleep.

# A MAN FULL OF SHADOWS

Leaves crumble underfoot. Ralph Cooper steps into the mouth of woodlands awash with starlight. He carries night with him. Darkness chases his path. An owl leaps from a branch with a fearsome cry.

Ralph pushes his way inward. There is blood on his face, arms, bare legs and feet. No sound escapes his lips. Fear is nonexistent. He shreds through forest tight with black trees, gray leaves. Shadows. Claws and toes slash at undergrowth. Slash. Slash.

Lightning cracks overhead.

No rain. No pain.

Slash. Slash. Reason is diminished.

Ralph staggers out of the woods and breaks into a quiet place. Here, he takes one weary step forward. His spirit is willing; his body fails. He falls, drained. Bathed in blood at the jaw of a new world.

He opens his eyes to a face full of light. Green eyes. Cascading hair.

She smiles.

"How are you?" she says.

"Rent money is dead money."

"Are you in pain?"

"Elusive peace."

"Do you understand why you are here?"

He lifts his head off the ground. "The scallywag," he says in a dry rasp.

His head falls. He is unconscious.

✦✦✦

Something soft and warm drapes around his shoulders. He opens an eyelid to blinding light. A blanket rubs his chin. He shrugs it off. Tugs at his shadows to hold him. He cannot stop the shaking. His night fights the light of this world.

The room blinks with darkness and then brightness. Darkness. Brightness. The world resists. Darkness. Brightness. Finally, spent, Ralph stops fighting the light. His fog wraps around him like a wrap. His fingers shake oddly. His mind is a mosaic. A cascade of rocks.

✦ ✦ ✦

"You are in parallel reality," a voice says. "You have traveled between levels of consciousness. A portal of time."

He blinks. Green eyes, a cascade of red hair swathes her cheeks. She is bending over him. He watches her without thought or fear. His fingers uncurl. Slowly, he reaches out. Touches the silk of her hair. Spreads his fingers, slides them to the white of her coat. The corners of his lips pull down. Fingers trace upward to her face.

"Pretty," he says.

"And so are you." She strokes his face. "In a complex way."

He looks at her. She looks at him.

"I think I can help you," she says. "I want to."

He gazes one last time at her exuberant face before his eyes close.

✦ ✦ ✦

Cables. Sockets. Circuitry.

Peripherals clasp him. He lies horizontally in the belly of a capsule strewn with gadgets. Two chips grip either side of his head. One end of the capsule elevates. His feet lift upward. His head lowers into a square of glass that swallows him. Wires plug into him.

"It won't take long," a voice says in the distance.

"Dead money," he mutters.

Light. Darkness. Light. Stillness. Tremor.

*Scallywag*, he thinks. *Elusive.*

Beep. Beep. Beep.

His eyes are shut. He tries to move his limbs. They refuse instruction from his brain. He can't move. But he can see through the eyelids. He can see what she sees.

Information download. She surfs through his memories.

*Coo* . . . There is the child in him: fat legs. Moonface. Cobalt eyes. A tuft of honey hair stands in a natural Mohawk on his head.

Softness. Warmth. Music: his mother.

Now he is a toddler. Asleep. Swift breaths.

Older. Long hands, all knees.

Older. Small town: pub, general store, post office, petrol station. The last two are an extension of the pub.

There's Harriet. Lying by his side on a golden meadow mottled with violets. Legs entwined. Whispers. Giggles. Touch. He combs grass from ebony hair. Touch. Sun and chocolates on Harriet's lips. Flowers on her skin.

Beep. Beep. Beep.

His limbs jerk. The controller circuit network strains to hold him.

War. He sees war.

Marching. Running. Crawling. Swamp. Bog like black jelly. Pits. Caves. Field: abandoned. Dust: heat. Building: engulfed in fire. Tanker: rolling. People: screaming. Bullets: cracking past his head. Jungle. Jungle. Jungle. Explosion. Shouts. Bayonet: blood. Smoke: stench. Horizon: cloaked orange. Soldier: head blown off. Hospital: hysteria. Straitjacket: madness.

Beep. Beep. Beep.

He is roaming naked in the streets.

*Clank!* tins tied to his ankles.

A hoard of children yell behind him, tailing him as he mutters over and over: "Rent money is dead money. Elusive peace. The scallywag. Pretty."

Beep. Beep. Beep.

Keyboard. Command. A screen opens. Inoculation, it says. Memory buffer. New profile module. Installing permanent blocker, it says. War memory deleted. Insanity deleted. Monitoring information upload, it says.

Beep. Beep. Beep.

Cloud. Blackness. A burst of light. He is floating, floating, floating . . . He opens his eyes to a shaft of sun through the window.

Perfume. Purple magnolias, heart drops and white lilies stand in a vase half-filled with water. Sound fills the room. Two swallows sing on the ledge.

A stir on the left.

He turns his eyes.

Jade eyes. Cascading hair.

"How are you?" she says.

"Good. My head feels light. What happened?"

"Your fog of shadows has lifted."

"What fog?"

"Tell me about Harriet."

"Who are you?"

"Radiance," she says. Cool fingers touch his arm. "Tell me about the war."

"What war?"

"I think the treatment has worked. Tell me your name."

"Ralph. Cooper."

"Ralph. Don't close your eyes. Look at me. Ralph."

He looks at her.

"What are you thinking?"

"You are beautiful."

"As are you."

Ralph Cooper smiles.

"In a complex kind of way," he says. "Now get me out of here."

# PLAYBACK, JURY OF THE HEART

## 1

Up the hill, they come. Ancient lovers old as sunset, younger than dew. Nothing is weathered about them, everything is new. They walk close-knit, fingers clasped. They know the land as distinctly as they understand their love, and theirs is a love of an unusual kind. Away to the right, past the hills toward an emerald stream below, white cedars sway. Their leaves hum, a lowly grove song much filled with wonderment. The year is 5019.

At the apex of the climb, the lovers stand silent. They listen to the cedars and an otherworldly sound of wind, first a soft chuckle, then something merrier that rolls. Now, slowly, a resonant echo winds up the columns of the trees from the ground up until, by and by, it is tall enough to stir the hillcrest with fresh notes of a brand-new song.

And so, the lovers dance. Their dance is expression, direction, transition. Her foot slides to the left. His steps in to close the space, alternates and glides to the back. She flirts toward it. He grinds his hips to her pelvis and guides her dance. When her foot meets his, she lifts it, flexes her knee, until her leg wraps fully around him. Her back is supple, leaned in a downward bend away from him. She sways from side to side, arms afloat, and then a complete stillness claims her. It is the stillness of a timeless kind. Finally, gently, the flat of his palm at the nip of her waist carries her rise from the ground until she is tall once more, until their lips are near enough to brush.

She tastes of rain and sun and snow.

Her hands are soft and beautiful about him; his are firm and coarse, strong and tender in their claim of her waist. Liam Keen opens his eyes, thinks how striking the world beyond her head, how happy and wild the wind blows, how it draws closer, closer still, until its closeness widens curls from their cozy tightness on her head, until they blow left and away from her face in a single, white sheet.

Dancing with her is easy as one. He kisses her deeply into dawn.

## 2
## *Summer of 2013*

Sounds of singing cicadas filled the air. A red box chocolate selection (bite-size) lay scattered on the road. Heart-shapes soaked and melted in warm crimson as Liam Keen lifted off the ground. He looked from a distance at mangled remains of him—meat, blood and bone—wedged around tire, glass and metal. He felt no emotion seeing himself like that. But he knew at once that he was dead.

A blonde woman with a bleeding face, driver of the Roaditor Turbo, a four-wheel jumbo, was dead too. Tossed through the windshield, impaled on a stump growing by the wayside. Her powdered cheek gashed to white bone. Crimson-spattered wood protruded through a jagged gap in her back. Torn flesh and blood hung from the stub's spear. Sticky puddles spread from purple grass and crept along the road, as the malevolent spike of wood faced a lime sky. Streaks of cloud waded toward a golden sun in the horizon.

The world around and beyond Liam moved at normal pace. No crowd gathered, three-people thick to amaze at death. Two streets away, Hoochi Mama was baking fresh cinnamon bread. Cabbies leaned lazily by their yellow cars chewing gum as if it were cud. Forlorn cigarette butts stuck out of green, silver-capped rubbish bins. A curly-haired male carried shopping bags marked "Neutral Planet" in both hands. He gave the accident scene a passing glance and crossed the road.

Cyclists and cars diverted to unaffected streets. A woman with bouncy hair walked her dog as skimpily clad joggers ran this way and that past a revolving fountain sprinkling crystal water. Only naked mannequins stared, some in shocked silence, from the perspective of a shop window, others quietly amused at the magical indifference of the Metropolis.

## 3
## *Audrey*

Before that summer there was Audrey.

Tonight, dinner was molecular food. It reminded Liam of black caviar and rose champagne. But it was neither. His wife Audrey, a born cook, was a retired actress. What she had placed at the dining table in a sizzling plate on a linen placemat was soft on the tongue. Its texture was like the pulp of a summer fruit. Its chew finished with a hint of zucchini flowers.

Together, they cleared the table.

Audrey handwashed the dishes, Liam dried. They worked in silence, always like this.

And then: "There then." She pecked him on the cheek.

"Already?"

She smiled in a tolerating way. "It's been a long day."

"Alright then."

She climbed up the stairs to her room whose walls were sprigged with heart-shaped bouquets. His had 3D rendering, cubes, fires and dark.

He tried to read the news, swiped his handheld tablet. He flicked through articles and stories, restless. Same old: celebrity scandal, teen gang arrest, new gadget on the market.

He retired not long after to his own downstairs bedroom.

He dropped his day clothes, insurance guy smart casual. He took to the bathroom. A blast of heat as the shower ran. He polished each tooth one by one inside the hum of an automated toothbrush. The tiles on his floor sparkled around the shower mat. He used a spare towel to wipe the spray. He rubbed his hair as he walked out of the ensuite bathroom, and stopped short.

"Someone's been sleeping in my bed," he said lightly. "Someone's still sleeping in my bed."

Audrey lay neat inside his doona. He felt a flutter of excitement. This was unbelievable. He threw aside the doona. Inside it, on his bed, she lay posed for him. She was wearing a black, lacy number he had not seen before. It was far different from her nightgown that resembled in shape, color and feel what a medic on call might wear. The lace Audrey wore was nothing like the medic's cloth: this one showed everything.

Liam blinked. She was still there: Audrey. In his bed. Not in her own aurora bed, four-poster, in her room at the top of the stairs. She was here, laying on her back, posed and ready for him. And it wasn't his birthday.

That's right: he got lucky on birthdays and special occasions.

Liam threw off his pajamas and climbed in his jocks beside her. "What's this?" He touched the straps of her lacy number.

"For the love of—".

"Have I forgotten something?"

A flitting in her eye. "What do you mean?"

"Special something?"

"Nope."

He couldn't remember the last time . . . No, he remembered. Every detail. Her cream ankles.

Who knew what snatched couples apart, why after a starry-eyed start they wound up living, perhaps quibbling, like siblings? But Audrey didn't fight. How did you pick a fight with someone unruffled?

He slid the straps off her shoulders. His lips tailed his hand as he moved the clothing.

"Please," she said.

Mesh covered her velvet skin. He traced the lines of her tiny undergarment, a black silhouette, vivid against her skin.

"What are you doing?" she said.

"I don't want to rush this."

"It's not rushing—we need to sleep."

He pressed against her. She gave him an uncertain smile, one that said he was too close. He kissed her fully on the lips. Her lips were soft, but she did not kiss him back. Audrey didn't, couldn't, kiss anyone back.

"Really, Liam. Stop mucking around. Please."

She lay immaculate, quiet. Then she pushed his weight, slid from him.

"Night darling." Her peck on his forehead. Her graceful glide out the door, away from him, away from the disquiet of his room, toward the safety and normality of her own room.

+++

Before the dinner, with Audrey, always with Audrey, Liam reminisced about his homeworld: Bathox. No Roaditor Turbos there, four-wheeled jumbos: just gruntless gliders, flexi vessels that shape-shifted into any trajectory. In Bathox, travel was another realm. Everywhere was possible.

Nero was one of the first of this world that Liam saw the day he poured out of an acorn. There was a freshness about the air. Liam sat naked, gliderless, arms wrapped about himself, before he unfurled. People stared as he walked. Someone shrugged off a coat and hugged it around him. It was Nero. Later, Liam understood why people stared. Not so much for his nakedness, but for the magnificence of the body he inhabited.

In those early days, Audrey said he was perfect. And Audrey was not a black mirror. The reflection was true. In those days, the two of them spoke, truly spoke. They communed with easiness, easy words, easy eyes of friends, of lovers. Audrey asked no questions. His past was just that: history. From the moment of his arrival to this world, Liam understood that now was now. Immediate. But not a day went past without hauling his mind to Bathox, to the ones he left behind.

In the early days of Audrey, Liam's heart was still a wasteland. He was bruised, disheveled, whisked inside out. Reeling at the aftermaths of an intergalactic war that brought him to this world. He was ready to neck himself. But Audrey fixed him. The moment their eyes met, they had a real moment right there. Be choosy, his heart said. Females are moths, they flitter from light to light. But Audrey stayed.

+ + +

Might have been easier if they'd fought. If Audrey were tight-faced and screaming, shrew-like and abusing, spitting out words that not only goaded but stuck. Abuse that returned to haunt in little bursts: in the stillness of the bath, between pages of a novel, in the heart of a dream.

Liam might have understood if there had been a wrestle, if—as he held her by the hair to subdue her and she punched girly fists into his ribs—she had said it. Or if she had flung something at him and it bounced off his cheek, cracked on the floor and, as he touched his flaming skin, she had said it. Or if he'd beat her up so bad and, as cops pressed him to the back of a car, she had said it.

But there was no precedent. Even if she had said it that normal way, fought him, lashed horrible words at him, then spat intentions of leaving, it would have been hard, so very hard, to let her go.

+ + +

It was middle of spring. Audrey sat delicious and serene across the dinner table. She listened with slanted head to the flavor of a buttered parsnip on her tongue. She smiled at *Ride of the Valkyries* playing in the background. She held her fork with nails faultlessly shaped; chewed delicately and moved lips immaculately painted; dabbed at those lips with a napkin flawlessly white. She sat there clad in cat-walk material: baby-soft, catchy enough to intrigue, toned enough to not encroach.

When the serenity of Bach touched their world, there was no disdain in Audrey's look at Liam. No wonderment at a fool with the table manners of a possum, as he fingered corn on the cob, greased cutlery with messy hands, and pushed aside parsley with a thumb.

That type of derision was not in those temptation eyes that lifted from her plate, not in those lips that smiled a tender smile, and said, "His name is Flint."

The music stopped. Perhaps the classical selection had come to a natural end. Audrey's smile, directed at something between Liam's nose and his forehead in that long stretch of silence, rendered him useless. He looked at Audrey and said nothing. Not "Why?" or "How?" or "When?" Perhaps she would have understood if he had spoken, would have perfectly understood with that efficient air of hers. But he gave nothing.

Now was no longer now. No longer immediate. Who was this Audrey?

She forked a sliver of beef, placed it in her little mouth, toyed with the flavor as she ate it. She even nibbled and swallowed a second parsnip, began to pierce a capsicum but thought better of it.

He waited, fork and knife poised in space. Stared in silence at the woman who was everything to him, and more: his firework—the sparkler on the wick; his candle—the orange on the flame; his flower—the velvet on the petal. Audrey was his stream, his river, his moon. And now she, she . . . He said nothing.

Liam remembered the bright stars and triple moons by day back home in Bathox, gazebos overlooking natural air-loft gardens that shimmered like ruby and emerald chandeliers, cratered beaches full of water birds . . . He remembered how back home in Bathox mating was for life.

Audrey laid down her fork, dubbed at soft lips, folded the napkin and laid it on the calm table. She sipped a baby nip of burgundy wine, left no stain of lipstick on its rim. She stood up, hedged the table, paused. Even lifted hair from her face with immaculate fingers, smoothed it and pushed it to unruffled waves. Only when she turned away did he grip the edge of the table as if to rise, as if to follow her with those questions: "How?" "Where?" "When?"

He began to rise but his knees gave. So, he sat with a tomb in his heart. A dark, uninvited tomb that deepened, filled emptiness with more empty, blackened darkness with more black. When anxiety began to rise, then confusion, pain, and finally rage so wild it was silent, his mouth tasted of cardboard.

Audrey moved away from the table. When the door shut quietly behind her, Liam watched the wood, as though his wife were embossed on it.

Suddenly, he felt fear. Fear of loneliness real as touch. Beyond that moment, that night, that revelation, what else? He hugged his fork, listened to her heels *clip! clip! clip!* toward the door, as they had done, even though she was no longer in the room. *His name is Flint . . . Flint . . . Flint . . .* The ghost clippity clip did nothing to soothe those words said calmly, yard-long words from the weight of them, words that had slipped with ease from such beautiful lips. Refusing to settle, the words filled Liam's air with resonance: *Flint . . . Flint . . . Flint . . .*

He sat with his knife and fork. Before he had time to grasp it, bank it, judge it, confront it, scorn the value of it, define it, comprehend it even—so deep was the astonishment, it rendered him powerless—she was gone.

Audrey took with her that wildflower smell associated with home. She also took her tennis racket, a rosy negligee, two suitcases, four yoga video tapes, a bunch of books, her classical collection, and Liam's heart.

+ + +

That night, he wiped clean the bottle of burgundy wine she had nipped with baby sips. Before long, such was his state, he had summoned moroseness. Together they pulled several cans from the fridge, sat on the floor, killed a pint of lager and then two. Beer raced down Liam's throat. When it pressed down on his bladder, he sorted it.

Then he took the advice of moroseness and reclined on a cushion on the floor, Audrey's velvet cushion soft as a cat. There, he sank to acres of drinking solace. When eyelids finally closed, he succumbed to a maudlin sleep where he once more became a little boy with freckles large as pebbles.

But that little boy snored like a swine and an amoeba of drool spread from one side of his lip down his chin.

+ + +

The corn was still on the cob on a dirty plate three days later. So were parsley and sleek cucumber slices, thin enough for a royal garden party, interspersed with cold beef julienne.

All Liam felt was . . . misplaced. He missed Bathox. He missed Audrey.

And somewhere out there Audrey was in bed tucked in the arms of a man named Flint.

On the fourth morning of drinking to a stupefied sleep, he woke with a blooming headache and bloodshot eyes. Soon as his headache waned, soon as he trusted his stomach, Liam ran. *Rock-a-tee. Rock-a-tee.* Past an abandoned pond lined with trees. Green trees, yellow trees, red trees, brown trees, leafless trees . . . A morning shadow raced with him below pale blue sky interspersed with silver gray clouds. A rising sun glided in and out of the clouds. Liam's feet pounded footpaths, cyclists swerved around him, some shouted profanities, but he kept moving miles, miles out.

*Rock-a-tee. Rock-a-tee. Rock-a-tee-tee-rock-a-tee.*

He stopped running.

A warm sheet of sweat poured down his back and his temples. Leaning forward, he caught his breath under the silvered sky, on nutty gravel alongside grass moist with dew. Hands on his knees, he studied mad goose pimples stealing off his skin. His sweatshirt prickled from cling. Wet cotton shorts gripped his thighs.

He jogged back home to an apartment tight with absence. Strewn with dirty socks and plates, empty beer cans and scattered bottles of Claret, Shiraz, even cleanskins. Treasures Audrey overlooked when she left. He phoned the office to call in sick. A tight-arsed receptionist, broomstick up her whatsit, put him through—finally!—to Wolfe, squad boss at the dastardly insurance company.

Wolfe was not having a barrel of it. "You're fired," he said.

# 4

Nero knocked the door down—nearly.

He was a ballistics expert. Married to Vivienne Frontczak, a hybrid of Plutian and terrestrial descent; a model, legs to her chest. It was Vivienne who introduced Liam to Audrey Rivers, a movie actress with ivory-white skin and delicious eyes.

Now Nero looked about Liam's forlorn house and said: "Place smells like rotten socks. It smells like something burning."

"My brain," muttered Liam. He was a dirty, disheveled mess on the bed.

Nero whistled. "Who let you out of the cage?"

"Audrey, she left me."

"Oh man."

That was before Liam told him about the phone chat with Wolfe.

"Man!"

And then he said: "Dude up, mate. Run, swim, do what you must. And you need a job. Two choices, matey. Moon over Audrey. Or consider a serious career in the martial force. Inside information—we're recruiting."

Serious career in the force, chose maudlin Liam.

Nero ended up filling the application tablet himself. Same day he put it in for initial screening and processing, Liam took his abandoned Streetwagon, wrapped a seatbelt around him and hit the road. He ran a red on Napoleon Street and got booked for drunk driving.

Nero bailed him out. Even drove him home.

"That's one quick way to get martial attention," he said to Liam. "Thirty-five kilometers per hour over the speed limit. Blood alcohol over 2.2. Way over. You're not a P-plater, Liam. Are you mad?"

Liam regarded him with riot eyes. "Go home now," he slobbered. "I'm good, Nero."

"I am *not* leaving you, matey," he said.

"I'm right as rain. Go home."

"Not a spotting chance." Nero dragged Liam to the bathroom. "Look at the mirror. Go on. Look at yourself."

Liam lifted his head enough to brush a swift glance. Sunken cheeks, a grim pallor and drooping jaws looked back at him. Liam did not know that man in the mirror.

"Go to the gym," Nero said. "Anything. Mooning doesn't bring her back. Sober up, matey. Audrey's gone."

He tucked Liam in bed, brought him kick-arse coffee from Star Frek, or Star Wars, followed by a whopper burger and a chilled can of soda.

"God bless soda," garbled Liam. "Lazarus in a can." He began to sob. Thick, manly sobs, awful and loud.

Nero snapped. "Pull yourself together, grief! An ability to splash your boots does not distinguish you."

He stormed out, leaving Liam with a hangover face streaked like a badly peeled orange. Next morning, Nero showed at Liam's door. Refused to come in and stood by the step. Quietly, he stretched out a small tablet with a phone code on it.

Liam took it. "Thanks buddy," he said. Pale cheeks and a lethargic smile.

"No worries."

It took nine days. Nine whole days for Liam to summon enough interest at the number. He was sure Nero had given him a hotline to a loony bin or some nut-cracking shrink. All Liam needed was a kick up the arse, and he could get that for free; why when he was job free would he want a shrink who charged a spleen? He fiddled listlessly with the tablet and put it down.

✦ ✦ ✦

For the first time in weeks, Liam took himself to an aqua center. It was deserted, nearly closing. An attendant with russet hair and vexed eyes made the rounds.

Liam stripped to his jocks. He stepped into the cool waters. He tucked on the wall, hips away from his feet, threw his arms out and his body arched into the peak of his dive. He aligned his body to the water. He timed the rotation of his trunk to the movement of his arm. He finished the stroke with a deep sweep that completed the cycle.

He swam like it was life. And death.

When he jumped out of the pool and into the shower, revigorated, he knew what he needed to do. He smiled at the attendant with an abundance of charm he had not felt in a while. That night, inside the hum of the automated tooth-brush, as he polished each tooth one by one, he gazed at the muddiness of the floor tiles, and observed that they needed a clean.

He picked up the tablet and finally dialed the code. It was no psychiatric hospital.

"I'm no six-figure case," a woman said after his introductory mutterings. "My fee is easy. I specialize in all conversions."

# 5
## *Sugar Sweetman*

Without reason or conviction, Liam accepted an appointment for which he promptly showed. Bunched blocks looked like little fists in Saville Row. Cab drivers idled and gossiped by the sidewalk. Given opportunity for something else, they watched Liam with lazy eyes.

He stepped out of the battered Streetwagon, rifled through his pockets for the address in a fit of panic, and found it:

*Level 3, 517 Saville Row.*

Hoochi Mama stood at 513, a bakery. Two doors away, Liam stepped through a doubtful, unnumbered doorway. It was tall between alternate numbers, which made it likely to be 517. A ground-floor reception with wall-to-wall carpeting (threadbare) stood unmanned. Hedging bets on the address and still having no clue as to what his appointment was about, he took a dawdling lift to Level Three.

A woman with cherry lips, cotton-white hair and black candy-eyes that went deep, deep, deep, answered the first door he knocked.

"Yes?" She smoothed her baby doll top.

No roots in that snow hair indicated altered color: auburn, blonde, brunette or flame. White-as-white brows matching the white-as-white hair suggested natural color. Honey skin, a bust firmed with youth, she was younger and far prettier than her voice. Fingers rubbing her chin, she cast a glance at Liam's bowed shoulders. His eyes touched the ground, uncertainty in them.

"No change, darling," she said. "Come along later. We'll find something. Maybe food too. Those bones need meat."

For his haggard, disheveled look, he realized, she had mistaken him for a tramp. He opened his lips to speak, to ask directions to one Sugar Sweetman. But the woman had already turned toward the inner room and was waving him inside.

"You look crook," she said. "Belushi, can of baked beans. Come in. I'll feed you, all right. This once. Come."

He followed.

"I'm no bargain store, chappy," she tossed over her shoulder. "But something's going down for you to look that crook." She nodded at a visitor's lounge. "We'll fix us up good."

"I'm—" He couldn't bring himself to say it was a case of mistaken identity. He wasn't a tramp.

"Yes?"

"Sugar. Sweetman. If you could just show me where she—"

"Who are you?"

"My . . . my name . . . Liam—"

"Keen?" Her gaze incredulous.

He brightened. "Are you Sugar Sweetman?"

"None other twenty miles round."

"On the phone . . ." he said. "We—"

She threw back her head and laughed. "You're worse than Nero said. Belushi, can of baked beans. Worse." Loud, rolling laughter spread free as a sneeze.

When Sugar's laughter subsided, she lifted a menu-like tablet from a chrome shelf unit. Wordlessly, she passed it over to him and left him to it in the visitor's lounge. He looked at the list spread out before him, the graphics and explanations of each, and flushed.

She returned dressed in a daffodil-yellow kimono of slinky silk. Lemon drops sprigged with crimson baby spade-leaves. They danced on the cloth. A topaz necklace swayed above smooth honey-colored breasts. A heady scent, clover and wild, wrapped around her as she moved.

She pressed a small shot glass into his hand. "Malt Rum," she said. Her hands were rough as a farmer's, the nails on them clean and trimmed. But her touch on his fingers was like a spinal tap. It shook him all over.

"Drink," she said. He hesitated. "You'll need it."

He took a gulp.

"You look comfortable," he managed through a tight throat, wary of what was on offer.

"Comfortable?"

She threw her head back and laughed, that loud-as-a-sneeze laughter, perhaps louder. It spread, it tinkled. One couldn't ignore it. He couldn't.

"Comfortable," she said again. "I'm comfy, darling. More than." Candy-eyes appraised him. "Now *you* need to be."

She led him by hand to an inside chamber, a room that smelled of lavender, primulas and cyclamens. It, in fact, had those very flowers in colorful array in a vase.

Liam noted a leather head on a Rustler king bed of solid timber in the Pharaoh suite.

Sugar sensed his severe mental baggage. She treated him like one on the critical list.

He exclaimed, closed his eyes and faded into a calm sleep.

# 6

He stirred to her coaxing, fingers and then hands, finally her mouth, rousing him.

He was lying on his back, but she pulled him so that he sat, entwined in her arms. She nurtured him in her caress. "Think of Audrey."

They soared to a cosmic dimension.

"I'm a body artist," she whispered, as he wept.

The weather was wild when he stepped outside the building. He hunched against a whooshing wind. Cold air touched his nostrils, inside a heady scent of warm cinnamon bread from Hoochi Mama. His jacket flapped about until he clutched the ends.

Hoochi Mama was impossible to resist.

"How you doing?" said a heavy mono-eyed woman with a bust ten melons wide.

"You're lucky to be inside."

She followed his eyes out the flapping shutters.

"Does that to people, the bread," she said with a twinkling eye. "How many bread you want?"

He settled for one loaf.

She peered into the oven. "Ready in a minute." Her *R* dragged. "Drink-a coffee? How you take it?" Gave him marks with index and thumb joined in a circle with the word "Good". It was a compliment. "Too much sugar no good. Look-a me!"

He joined her honest-as-music laughter. The coffee when it came was something else. One sip tightened his nipples.

"Have-a some apple cinnamon," she said. Wouldn't take no for an answer. The bun was crispy and golden outside, perfectly baked inside. It fell apart like snow in his mouth. He closed his eyes to linger the taste.

"You drink-a more coffee?" He couldn't. But she tossed a puffed bun anyhow into the brown paper bag with his crusty cinnamon bread.

"Don't insult-a me," when he tried to pay for the coffee.

In the car on the way back, he wondered about Sugar, how she fit in his picture of healing. Why exactly had Nero directed Liam to her?

When confronted, Nero mounted a very scientific argument. "You needed a score, baby. Been running on reserve, man. Seeping to subzero."

"But why?" Liam demanded.

"Why were you on reserve? *You* tell me!"

"Why did you give me Sugar's number?"

"Your existence was dominated by a woman who tossed you out like a bin. Now you've got momentum to find purpose beyond Audrey, you ask me why?"

"I thought the number was for a shrink," Liam said.

"You wanted a shrink?"

"No-o."

"Listen, matey," Nero put a hand on Liam's shoulder. "I did a bust once. Explosives. I was green, knew jack. And there were explosives. Know what the officer-in-charge did? He said: 'If you hear a big boom, lurch out the nearest exit, hop into a car and drive.' That's what our officer said. 'Drive like mad. Don't try and be a hero.'" He removed his hand. "You are in a boom, mate. One hell of a plonker. Drive."

"Yes. Well. Fine one to say. But—" he had to know. "How did you ... surely ... What in heaven will Viv think—?"

"Leave my wife out of this."

Liam finally squeezed it out of him: "First time I met Sugar, she was a tarot card reader."

And—yes—Nero did know about the menu in Sugar's no-red-carpet apartment.

# 7

Sugar paced him. She ran him through her menu, one that left no boaty burp. Sure, sometimes she cooked. But whatever it was on that menu, it had little to do with food.

Despite all that, Liam was dismayed to find Audrey hung on in his head, refusing to dislodge. He left lengthy messages on her mobile. She never answered, never called back. But he was possessed by the woman. She spread, filling every brain cell of him, growing more and more beautiful each dream. He soon succumbed to the realization he was a well-adjusted slob: Audrey had left an indelible scent of herself in his head; an imprint like a bloodstain that constantly reminded him of death.

Through it all, Sugar was a gun. A bit more each time.

One day, sensing his deep helplessness, his neediness as he sobbed in her arms with no self-preservation, she set him straight. "I give no absolutes," she said. White-as-white hair flicked. "Falling in love is a no-no." She squeezed him gently. "That's one potential danger slot." Sweet saucer eyes regarded him. Black candy-eyes that went deep and deep.

And though his heart raced tall and fast, he understood her words. They were simple. He could take what she offered. Use it, need it, but he could never, could never ever control it.

He accepted that space: no complications.

And it was just as well. He was home and hosed when it came to no complications. Liam could hold his own now. Love was black-eyed venom.

# 8

At the aqua center there was another swimmer in the water. She left the wall, arms first. Her head and shoulders came out of the water. Kick, she lunged forward.

On his way home, he saw her again, across the car park. She dropped something—her goggles.

"Thanks," her voice syrupy. Their fingers touched past the goggles.

He noticed her frumpy look: a jean shirt above a striped frock; a black jacket thrown over the shirt; soiled shoes and the most ridiculous rucksack. He also noticed her hair: sloppily contained with a single clip, but how lustrous! It was chestnut with highlights. It twinkled under a blonde moon, a single moon, unlike the triple moons of Bathox.

Bathox: memories of it ambushed him when he least expected.

He made his way through the dusk, stopped by a traffic light. The night was full of innocence, no angry clouds in the horizon. Down the road, the wink of a garbage van's lights. A chill in the air blew his way. The wind smelled lightly of smog, or smoke, or a whiff of reeds. Out yonder, a line of birds climbed on a silent migration to someplace.

Liam looked about him in the night. He spotted the odd folk loitering about: a man with a short crop, but half his face covered in a mustache, walking past a pharmacy. A girl with crystal eyes and a boyish figure. She clapped down the street in knee-high boots, past a fleet of shops: a closed fish and chips, a pawn shop, a shoe repair shop. She cut into a corner. A gent with a furrowed brow and receding hair. He walked in Liam's direction.

Liam wondered about them. Singly, he studied anyone he saw. Were there other visitors to this world like him? Hard to tell—how easily visitors blended. How they cleaved through people. Like him, arrivals didn't come with a beak on their face or bark in their skin. They looked like everyday folk. They played laidback and they fit. Like Audrey, who belonged to this world. She fit. Yes, he still remembered Audrey. Wisps of her catapulted in chambers of his mind: the kitchenette, the lounge, the bedroom. Memories of her lunged at him with the intensity of a longing that was also a nightmare.

At this moment, he thought, a man named Flint was in bed, dragging Audrey under his breath. Did she wear black lace that showed everything, sprawled on his bed and willing?

He remembered how he and Audrey that final night had sat together yet alone, how she smiled a tender smile, and said words that shot out like grenades. "His name is Flint." He remembered how the music stopped.

# 9

It took twelve full lunar cycles of Sugar and of Hoochi Mama's hot cinnamon bread before Liam's application to the force was screened and processed. Before he knew it, he was a recruit. Then he was a cop. His life was getting back on track. It had taken a while getting his faculties together, but he was no longer morose and maladjusted. Sure, he still wept at Sugar's. But the rest of him kicked to a new dimension. Sugar had repaired him to good nick. Keen career prospects were looking his way. The rate he was going, Nero was hinting at ballistics.

✦ ✦ ✦

One day, Sugar upped the ante.

"New item on the menu," she said. "*Obsessavaganza*."

She tossed her white-as-white hair. He ran his fingers through it, and agreed. *Obsessavaganza*.

First, she ran him a warm bath.

Liam soaked in the fat tub, legs wrapped around the faucet as water rushed against his body. He thought about the water, its hydrogen and oxygen molecules combined, reacted together, a chemical equation not dissimilar from person-to-person chemistry. In one combination, it formed water—purging, sustaining. In another: hydrogen peroxide—burning, toxic. Time slipped by. He sat and sat in that bathtub scented with tropical pineapple salt.

He remembered how he arrived in a glider. How it needed something compact and small to shoot into, else the energy scatter arising from velocity and impact would cause a blast. He wondered how many visitors to this world reached safe passage. Acorns made good landing. Or okra. Coconuts were too big.

He remembered Audrey's profoundly beautiful eyes teeming with something more, her smile genuine and big soon as she set eyes on him. He remembered their first bath together, how she scrubbed the parts of his back he couldn't reach, how the pleasure was near impossible to take.

What went wrong?

Now Sugar delivered him to the bedroom. She produced a towel, plush in its thickness, ripe in its yellow color. Toweled, dried, he lay on her Rustler king bed. He allowed himself to relax to the hum of ornamented music: it threw up slurs and bends and slides and wails. It rose and fell, jigged and reeled as music notes bent, cut and rolled before they softened to quiet.

Sugar caressed him all over. She explored with her fingers. First, she guided him through eye circles: look at the ceiling. Breathe. Move your eyes only. Look as far left as you can. Now as far right. Now toward your feet. Your eyes only moving, not your head.

Then she massaged his jaw. Breathe. Make a sound. Any sound. What sound? Be silly.

She held his jaw with her hands, wiggled it. She pressed her fingers into his lips, reached into his cheeks, massaged his teeth, his gums. She worked his head, lolled it from side to side. She touched his belly, kneaded gently with her hands and then fists. She squeezed and released until he felt loosened, and then tense as the pressure of her hands shifted to a new dance on his skin.

It was an awakening.

He strained for her touch, willed her hands to reach every part of him. Energy rushed through his body like steam. He felt new and hot all at once, breathed faster and faster unable to contain himself. As more and more energy engulfed him, the intensity pushed tears to his eyes. It felt like any moment he would fly. He took a breath. He thought about the water, its hydrogen and oxygen molecules. Just then, Sugar moved her touch. His breath fell.

The sensation . . . It was ecstasy, a dance drug, a spa. Firepower. Release. Pressure. Release. Heightened senses pulsated in every inch of him. Liam's life stood still, then he was flying into a bright light. He swallowed his cry—only just. Something snapped and exploded. His body whistled in all parts.

*Obsessavaganza.*

It stamped Audrey right off his head, a complete whitewash. First, fragments of her sprinkled away like shards of glass, and then blew away like fairy dust. Liam nearly danced outright. He started a victory dance with his hand, but Sugar restrained him.

"You have matriculated with honors," she said.

"Therapy," his voice full of wonderment.

To celebrate, Sugar cooked for him. She tossed a live, squirming lobster into an angry frying pan spitting oil. Stirred it with a wooden spoon until the shell snapped. Inside, the meat was white and tender.

They ate from one bowl with their hands, spat shells into another. Liam's fumbles with the lobster, pinching its legs with thumb and index fingers, snapping clumsily to arrive at moist meat inside, amused Sugar.

Tender, juicy, fresh—that lobster eaten so primitively was far different from Audrey's thread-thin bream, ribboned bell pepper arranged on a plate in a bouquet of purple, green and orange around baby strips of beef. No classical music, Valkyries and the like. Just Sugar's fat laughter that tinkled, prickled and spread bigger than a sneeze.

Sugar was vintage. And she was addictive. With a girl-next-door demeanor, candy soft eyes and big white-as-white hair, she was no spread for a magazine cover. But she mastered a fine art few women could boast. After *Obsessavaganza*, Liam never thought of Audrey. Not once. In fact, she receded to a very thin memory that did not meaningfully upset him.

No sterner measures were necessary for healing at this point.

Yet to oblige Sugar—or perhaps to expand his horizon—Liam tried, in a pivotal moment, *Erase*. Sugar dropped a gloop of oil on his body, and greased him up. She lunged at him in tackles, one knock and down he went on flexed knee clutching at his ribs.

She swung a hook in an unprecedented back flip that had plenty on it. She swooped him, kneed him, punched him, kicked him. Threw him, choked him, tonged him, cuffed him, chained him, concussed him. Left purple bruises bigger than grapefruit on his skin. He caved, driven half-mad with pain and pleasure.

He knew that when he left Sugar's to stop at Hoochi Mama's, she might ask, "You run-a red light? You bang-a into a wall?" He could well have slid under a freight train, the way he looked. Winded, he amazed at Sugar's strength.

*Belushi, can of baked beans!* he thought on a whopper flyer. *Celestial. Pigs might fly.*

# 10

They lay side by side on a fuchsia carpet, feet touching. A lime sky streaked with smoky cloud out the far window. Tall glasses sizzled with bubbly between them. It was the first time, he realized, she'd got a sparkly for them.

"What did she do to you?" Sugar asked.

"Who?" he asked, tongue lazy with vintage fizz. Distinct apricots, acid and a blend of something biscuity toyed on his lips.

She raised on her elbows. "Audrey."

"What do you mean?" he hedged.

"Why did her leaving make you like you were? Break you?"

Light from a white, shifting sun caught the mahogany wood of a chiffonier. He was silent for a moment, not sure where this question had come from. Bothered him where it was headed.

"I don't know," he said quietly at last. "I really don't know."

A distant craft soared across the streaked sky. Liam followed it with his eyes until it vanished beyond the window. Even then, he still thought and wondered about why "His name is Flint" had left him so off the rails. Broken him enough to need fixing.

Sugar rose from the floor and stood there in a Fanta-orange kimono by the chiffonier. Layers of age formed unique contours on the wood. She gazed at him.

Slowly, his words began to form. He let them spill out in bits and fits as they came. "She was the works." There was no texture in his voice. "Audrey was. A prime cut."

Sugar nodded lightly. "A fine, fine lady she must have been."

"She wasn't."

"Then life insurance. Was she? Life insurance to you, Liam?"

"Hell no." Texture came back to his voice. "Never."

Sugar laughed. A tickling, prickling whooper laugh that spread enough to make him smile.

"Then she was a fine cigar," she said when she stopped laughing. "Or beautiful music you couldn't dance to."

"Or a cab," he said. "I thought she would drive me someplace in this world. Didn't know where. Didn't care how. I just wanted her there with me."

"How about that heartfelt! Never spoke more candid."

Tinkling laughter again, merry as a clarinet.

"Come here," he said. He reached to pull her down to the floor, but she dodged his fingers, until they were both helpless with mirth. He smiled into her eyes.

And then it was too cozy. The simplicity of it brought with it a complication that first surprised him and then confounded him. He felt under pressure. Pressure rising from his toes. What the . . . He lost his heartbeat. Something hauled him to his feet. Suddenly the carpet on the floor with its salmon color sprigged with magentas didn't look right. The moment . . . He didn't like it. He wanted to be forty-light-years away, traveling faster than light.

In the silence that followed, he reached for words to fill the awkwardness. Tiny talk, thoughts, distractions . . . They eluded him in the bracket of that moment, perhaps because the candy-eyes were serious. They sucked him in with something finer, something that frightened him. Warm stars in her eyes told him something. They were eyes saturated with fondness. He realized with dismay she had broken her rule. The agreement was simple: no absolutes. But she had fallen in love. Sugar was in love with him. He couldn't herald it, allow her to express it. Had he guessed of this turn at the start of their liaison, there would have been more trepidation in his bite. He didn't know how to improvise. Or be adventurous. Was Sugar for life? He simply couldn't *love*.

He wondered how something this perfect could go so wrong. He pondered the rot that had fouled him and Audrey—how by the time he noticed, it was all too putrid to salvage. Putrid as the war of ages that nearly destroyed Bathox, but didn't. Enemies that fanned out with flashers and gliders from all over the galaxy. But now gliders were no more machines of war. They were vessels of peace, of interspace travel that landed into acorns.

He blinked once. Twice. Huge silence. A raging headache drummed a beat in his head. A flutter in his heart, and Sugar dropped her gaze. A great deal of hesitancy and sadness lingered in her smile.

"Get up," she said. "You look like a medically induced coma. Get out of here before the night lets out."

She understood. Though her candy-eyes now looked like tired woman eyes, flat eyes like Saturday after Good Friday, she understood. Liam's headache dissolved. And for the first time since he started seeing her, he took her in his arms and made love to her with the intensity of a man about to go away on a journey to Waggu Waggu, Woy Woy or Woop Woop—the end of the world.

Nestled in his arms, Sugar wept.

"If you start at a hundred," she said, "then you've got no more place to go." Her eyes were no longer flat. They were deep, almost calm. Her voice was sad as an oboe.

"Don't be a stranger, hey champ," she said at the door, clinging to his chest.

Inside the nearly deserted aqua center with its vexed attendant, Liam stripped to his jocks. He climbed on the block. He bent down and forward from the hips, knees bent, head low. He raised his head quickly, pushed away hands stretched and threw himself forward. He speared clean into the cool waters and glided back and forth, breathing every fifth stroke, until the peering of the attendant into his line of vision nudged him out of the crystal blue pool.

# 11
## *Meredith*

He found her in the mauve pages of the services directory under "G": Gentleman's escort.

"It's called displacement," said Nero.

Meredith lived in a beachcomber in Affleck Boulevard. She took only pre-bookings. She accepted bite-size chocolates and vintage bubbly. She asked no questions and demanded that none be asked of her. All was well if Liam did not succumb to a terrible impulse to reminisce, to talk about or prompt personal history. When he took her, she lay unruffled and wore a cool face of iridescent beauty.

He never guided Meredith into the positions he desired. He never angled her into poses he had achieved with Sugar: the rider—him on his back as she straddled and rode him. The spooner—both on their sides, rocking to orgasm. The chainer—reverse missionary, legs entwined. The cowgirl—her atop him, facing his feet. Oh, the visual stimulation of watching her buttocks. The tactile stimulation of stroking Sugar's neck, back, breasts . . . The erotic stoking of her hands on his body, her easy access to all important parts of him . . . The acute artistry of her hands. Fully aroused in this position, his holdback—the one he had practiced and practiced so many times with Sugar—dissolved. Liam barely lasted minutes before the whorl. A prolonged epiphany that left his entire body singing. The flair of his orgasms, it came complete with a rain of crisp white octagonal starlets floating in his vision.

Being with Sugar was nothing like the fumbled bum lifter—the one he tried with Audrey the last time they had sex. This recollection of Audrey was not an effort. It was flitting, a distant thought. A comparison: with Sugar he was etched with magic, and she delivered him to a sweet, impossible place. It was a place that was fantasy compared to moments with Audrey, or Meredith.

Unlike Sugar to whom it was nurture, to Meredith sex was . . . a burden? She held her hand delicately to the small of his back, as though they were dancing to a waltz at a Queen's ball. Once or twice a fair-feathered bird perched on the ledge, cocked its head and stared at them through the window.

Meredith glanced at her watch when time was up or nearly up. She calmly said, "Three more minutes."

Sometimes, when she said it, Liam was too close to the edge to be distracted. Sometimes his desire ebbed, and he coiled.

Later, if Liam floated naked in her marble bathtub or laid hands at the back of his head on a braided mattress, brooding into space, she let him. She only glanced at her watch when extra time was up or nearly up. Liam soon learned to pre-empt the clock: *There goes the hootie,* he would think, moments before her eyes sought the dial.

She wore sleek black skirts and fluffed windswept hair around a powdered face; always looked like she was going to the Oscars. The villa had a fire crackling hearth, natural light, a granite kitchen, marble bench tops . . . An ivory carpet, dovetail drawers, Holland blinds, English brass handles, jade ornaments, Dutch masters wall replicas in seamless spacing, swathed drapery. Class and finery.

One day, it dawned upon him: he had thumbed the mauve pages and found a whore who looked like Audrey. Who dressed like Audrey. Who moved like Audrey. Who had genetically harvested timber Venetians. Who spoke in a china-cup fragile way. Who fucked like a Queen's waltz.

Meredith was so like Audrey, and that made her safe—unlike Sugar who had dared love him. Liam paused with that thought, holding a red box chocolate selection (bite-size) in his hands. Turmoil and yearning filled every space of him, right there, in the middle of Meredith's open living room that spilled into a deep terrace with a curling swimming pool. A kind of realization opened in him. He was in love with Sugar. Madly, madly in love. And though it frightened him no longer, he tried distracting himself from it. Glanced at a famous portrait (Meredith said) of a medieval sprite named *Aquila, Degilla* or *Godilla.* He couldn't tell, from the way she said it in her china-cup fragile way, what was correct.

"That you, darling?" she said from somewhere upstairs.

He heard her climbing delicately down the spiraling staircase, pictured her autumn eyes and velvet skin, replayed her engineered ten-carat smile. Before hint of her wildflower scent reached him, before her trophy smile—poised for effect, bestowed as reward, held perfectly on a five-star face with movie caliber immortality—before all that could infect him, he was gone.

## 12

The water at the aqua center felt crisp to his skin. He built speed on his approach to the wall, faster and faster and tucked his nose to the knees, heels to the hips. He kicked off the wall and, with swift dolphin kicks, he fluttered away, away.

The attendant was waiting for him when he climbed out.

"Clear the head?" she said.

"Full of dunes," he said. "But they are singing."

# 13
## *The Dying*

He died five minutes from Automat Station on the way to Sugar. The blonde woman in a jumbo Roaditor yapped on her mobile as he crossed the road with the ribboned chocolate box selection. Last thing he remembered before lifting off the ground a bit dazed was a splash of rainbow, his blood leaving a flowering pattern that closely resembled a Persian carpet filled with red.

Past noon now, fat blue-black flies soaked, almost drowned, in dead body fluids in the purple grass by the roadside. Heat lazed. It charred foreheads and split callused hands. Those who napped in their houses, Liam thought, would feel sickened waking up two hours later in that heat. Those without a nap in their eyelids would slog, trying to find middle ground in and out of the heat. Perhaps fans or small leafed trees offered a little solace. Even butterflies dropped. Given the absence of cool winds to calm their feelers, they struggled anxiously, flickering one second or two, and then they simply collapsed. Drowsy bees fluttered around the heady scent of sun, wind, blood, and a little pollen caught between spring and summer.

A siren rose from the distance. It drew nearer.

Liam looked ahead, at the blocks bunched like little fists two streets away. A sign on one wall said: *We Have Moved*. Gray smoke curled skyward from Hoochi Mama's chimney where waves of oven fire made crisp cinnamon bread. He blinked. The sun's weight in his eyes was becoming unbearable. A bird cried in the sky, a glassy, wilderness sound.

"Loof!" said a cheerful dog struggling on his leash. The owner pulled him away, distracting him from the rusty smell of clotting blood on the road.

Something drew Liam's gaze past a yellow and black billboard announcing a fledgling singer with knockout booty. His eye settled on Level Three, Block 517, where he and Sugar had lain side by side with touching toes on a fuchsia carpet.

White-as-white hair flew wild in warm winds at the window. Charcoal candy-eyes beckoned him, gazing at him with such wonder. She was waving at someone behind him. As he turned and saw no one there, Nero's words flashed in his head: "She was a tarot card reader."

Tarot . . . tarot card reader . . .

Sudden elation gripped him. Sugar could see him. Not his body—meat, bone, blood—splattered under glass and metal. She could see him. Liam smiled. He waved. Sugar waved back. He started running toward her. *Rock-a-tee. Rock-a-tee.*

He crossed the road to busy Satsuma Road. Wheels of a tram groaned like a grinder's stone. They squealed. A door gleaming like a sword in the sun burst open. Liam didn't look back. He steered clear of the road, away from ticking traffic lights, away from rolling cars, grunting cars, purring cars, buses, bicycles, trams. His feet silently moved past Hoochi Mama's toward soft beckoning eyes filled with wonderment, toward a love older than sunset, younger than dew.

*Rock-a-tee. Rock-a-tee-tee-rock-a-tee.*

✝ ✝ ✝

A twilight cloud forms in the topaz sky, a wispy cloud which, if you look closely, you could begin to make out the ghost of its face: two eyes, the space of a nose, a set of smiling lips and sometimes, if your eye is kind and steady, you just might see some hands and feet. As the moonlit sky glimmers with morning stars that have eaten a lot of silver, pearls or diamonds, Sugar Sweetman speaks.

"You are together now," she says to Liam, perfectly reading his silence.

"Now, more than ever," he agrees. "I was some bit of a hazard back then."

"The heart is a complex thing, sometimes improbable to comprehend."

"But you are a maverick, the juror of my heart."

"Guilty," she whispers happily, "guilty as charged."

"And Nero?"

"In time you will connect. I will help you."

They savor the wind-kissed crest where they stand arm in arm, where they can see all, share all, be all one more time, before they would take their great happy feet down the hill to poinsettias and azaleas and huckleberry petals in full bloom; to baby breath, fairy tickle and a home sweet home aroma of Hoochi Mama's cinnamon cookies as they turn golden; to a wide-open place full of grace.

A place called home.

It no longer matters it is not Bathox.

# ACKNOWLEDGMENTS

To Toni Morrison—you're inside my head whispering language that is curious, playful, provocative. Poetic.

To Seb Doubinsky whose insightful foreword is like a sweet-tempered dream into myself.

To publisher Tricia Reeks of Meerkat Press for seeing more in my stories—complex, unsettling, distorted in their fulness. You were the first publisher to take me seriously. Truly, madly, savagely. Seriously.

# ABOUT THE AUTHOR

Eugen Bacon is African Australian, a computer scientist mentally re-engineered into creative writing. She's the author of *Claiming T-Mo* by Meerkat Press and *Writing Speculative Fiction* by Red Globe Press, Macmillan. Eugen's work has won, been shortlisted, longlisted or commended in national and international awards, including the Bridport Prize, Copyright Agency Prize, Australian Shadows Awards, Ditmar Awards and Nommo Award for Speculative Fiction by Africans. Website: www.eugenbacon.com Twitter: @EugenBacon

## Did you enjoy this book?

If so, word-of-mouth recommendations and online reviews are critical to the success of any book, so we hope you'll tell your friends about it and consider leaving a review at your favorite bookseller's or library's website.

Visit us at www.meerkatpress.com for our full catalog.

Meerkat Press
Atlanta

CPSIA information can be obtained
at www.ICGtesting.com
Printed in the USA
LVHW092351161120
671835LV00011B/2235